The Opposite of Fiction

by

M. Jane Early

Copyright © 2021 M. Jane Early.

www.mjaneearly.com

To the women who stepped up
when I needed them.
Julia, Debora, Jodi...
thank you.

Chapter One

Norah

"Every girl in this room would rather be horizontally face-to-face with a gorgeous man than be in this bar right now."

"You're ridiculous," I retorted and laughed.

"Whatever. *You* are one of those women." Janet grabbed her drink and crossed her arm over her torso, letting her other dainty hand dangle.

"No, I'm not," I answered defiantly.

Her expression was one of disbelief. She knew me too well.

I sat back on the sofa chair in the middle of Stage 19, a bar in the heart of downtown Manhattan, taking a sip of my martini.

"I mean." I rolled my eyes. "Would I be opposed to it? No."

She arched her eyebrow.

"Shut up," I said, looking around the bar.

She laughed. "You need a good one-night stand to

get over this drought." Her smile brought out the rose undertones in her skin.

"I'm not in a drought."

She stared at me. "Oh really, Norah? When's the last time you had—and I mean, hit your head on the headboard until stars are flying out of your ass—good sex?"

I took a breath to speak, then hesitated. Furrowing my brow, I darted my eyes around the room. Jesus, when *was* the last time?

"That's what I thought." She moved her long, straight, jet-black hair to one shoulder and adjusted her sapphire dress over her slender body. Her thin, deep brown eyes scanned the room. She wouldn't admit it so soon after her divorce, but she was hunting too.

She nodded to her right. "What about him?"

I followed her gaze to a gentleman in the corner and tilted my head. "Left hand, ring finger."

She tightened her eyes. "Shit." She looked over her left shoulder for a moment, then turned to me again. "Third stool on the right. Black sweater."

The guy she referred to wore an expensive watch that reflected the dim lighting behind the bar. After he set down his cocktail, he swiped the corner of his mouth with his finger and studied something on his phone. He was handsome and put together perfectly in his slim black slacks and complementary shoes.

"He's cute," I answered.

I kept watching until an even cuter guy came up behind him and kissed him below his ear.

"And gay." I looked away, taking another sip.

She glanced at him again, then shrugged. "Maybe he's bi or pansexual." The hope in her voice made me laugh.

"Stop it. I don't need to be set up. I've already had my monthly meeting with my friend with benefits. I'm set."

"Parker?" She twisted her face in abhorrence.

"You're not the one sleeping with him."

"Thank god," she responded with her glass by her mouth.

"He's nice, and the sex is…adequate."

"Adequate? Norah, listen," she leaned forward, "Parker doesn't make your toes curl. He's safe and convenient and not nearly good enough for you."

I chuckled. "I'm not looking to marry him. We have dinner, he gets me off, then I go home—I'm good with that."

"You know he wants more." She eyed me.

"I told him what this is. That's not my fault." I drank the rest of my martini.

"Yeah, but I've never heard you even breathe a word about a man you actually like." She sat back and waited for me to argue.

I didn't answer.

"Marriage, kids? None of that seems to interest you."

I shrugged. "It's not a priority."

"Why not?" she pushed.

I hesitated. "You just changed your last name back and finalized your divorce. I didn't think you'd be an advocate for getting married."

"Hey, just because my ex is an asshole doesn't mean I don't believe in the institution."

"Using the word 'institution' does not make the idea sound tempting. At all." I raised my eyebrows.

"I've known you for almost ten years. You've never even mentioned anyone you were interested in, let alone seen regularly." She tipped her empty wineglass from side to side and watched me.

I sighed loudly, not wanting to go down this road tonight. The truth was my heart hadn't been broken into pieces by anyone. I wasn't afraid of love or sex. I was sure all the popular girls in my hometown of Lubbock, Texas, had the life Janet was referring to. A life with two-point-three kids, a husband who perused dating sites while the wifey and kids were asleep. None of that interested me. I had grown up in a house that didn't encourage me to want a family of my own. That was it.

I picked up my wallet and stood. "Want another one?" I pointed at her glass.

"Yeah, why not? It's Friday. Not like I have a husband to go home to anymore."

"What am I, chopped liver?" I smiled. "I should make you get these, you're the one who works here," I retorted, walking away.

I met Janet when I'd first came to New York. A few months after I moved, I went to a party of a new friend of a friend, where I had hoped to make a few connections. Janet and I ended up bored and standing against the same wall, commenting on people and their attire. We became quick friends in our mean-girl moment.

Watching what Janet went through with Micah just solidified what little interest I had in marriage. She had moved in with me right after she left him. He told her to stay in their home, but she didn't want him to show up unannounced whenever he felt like it. Plus, she wanted to give the façade that he didn't devastate her by serving her papers. By moving out against his wishes, she felt

4

it would let him know she couldn't care less, which I knew she did. Janet was nothing if she wasn't brutal to those who had wronged her. On the other hand, she loved harder than anyone I knew and was devastated when her marriage was over.

Janet had gotten a job bartending here a few months ago and constantly tried to pay part of my rent, but I wouldn't hear of it. She needed my help, and I was more than willing to give it to her. I hadn't had a roommate since leaving Texas. It was nice having someone around again. We stayed out of each other's way and came together for gossip, TV, and a lot of wine. It was turning out to be a great matchup.

I walked through the hordes of people in the building. Friday nights in a Manhattan bar always made for some interesting exposure. I'd either get hit on by Wall Street brokers with a wife and kids at home or the off-Broadway actor who would promise he could introduce me to Lin-Manuel Miranda.

The liquor on the back wall behind the bar glowed from the yellow LED lights. The tall and slender bartender leaned towards me to get my order. He had bright blue eyes and a three-day-old beard.

"Grey Goose martini and a merlot, please," I said, setting my wallet on the bar.

"You got it," he responded in a thick Middle Eastern accent.

I smiled and sat.

"You don't come here often, do you?" a voice asked.

Turning to my left, I nearly bumped into a guy already uncomfortably invading my personal space. He had to be at least ten years older than me, and his cologne mixed with cigarette smoke made it hard to breathe.

I tilted away. "I'm here from time to time."

"No, I'd remember a pretty face like yours." The wrinkles near his eyes creased as he gave me a creepy smile, and his stained yellow teeth gleamed.

I exhaled and rotated towards the bar again, wondering how I could get the bartender to hurry with my order. I would literally flash him just to get away from this guy. Sadly, the oblivious bartender didn't notice my urgency to remove myself from being hit on in the most unattractive way possible.

"I'm Isaac." The older man reached his hand out to me.

I stayed still and stared straight ahead, mad I had left my phone at the table, so I couldn't give this guy the ultimate sign I was not interested by scrolling through Twitter.

He removed his dejected hand. "I own a laundromat on 34th. I feel like I've seen you there before." He cracked his knuckles.

"Nope."

"Somewhere." He leaned back.

"I work at a strip club on West 37th Street," I said and looked at him, then smirked.

He snapped his fingers. "Vivid! That's it! Vanessa, right?"

I closed my eyes and hung my head while laughing, then peered at him. "No, sorry."

"Oh, you were kidding?" he realized and laughed too. "You got me."

I faked a chuckle. "Yeah."

"What do you really do?" He slanted towards me again.

I angled towards him. "Isaac, I don't want to be

rude, but—"

"Hey, I found you," I heard behind me.

I turned from Isaac, then met the most brilliant, teal eyes I'd ever seen and attached to someone who didn't belong in a bar in Manhattan. He belonged in a museum with priceless, stunning works of art surrounding him.

"Sorry I'm late," he said as his loose, dark blond curls fell forward slightly. "Traffic was awful."

I continued to stare at the masterpiece standing in front of me, speechless. The top half of his six-foot frame leaned past me with his hand outstretched. "Hi, I'm Wil."

I glanced at the laundromat owner, who looked just as confused as I was. "Isaac," was all he said.

"Hey, Isaac," Wil responded, then bent down and kissed me on the cheek. A bolt of electricity shot from my face to my feet in an instant.

This gorgeous stranger tilted back slightly and gazed into my eyes. "Am I in trouble, or can we have that drink I promised?" The heat of his breath washed over my face. The aroma of beer melded with his fragrance. Not cologne, but his natural scent. It was divine.

My heart rate sped up as he remained in my bubble. "Sure," I whispered.

Wil's eyes flickered to the man behind me. "It was nice to meet you, Isaac." His dismissive tone made Isaac sigh and rise off the barstool.

Wil locked on me again. Slowly, a smile crossed his handsome face and took my breath away.

"I hope that was okay. You looked uncomfortable," he said, easing back, then landed on the stool next to me.

I inhaled and nodded, trying to find my bearings again. "Yeah, no, thank you for that."

He raised a finger to the bartender, then peeked at me. "No problem."

I bit my lip as I ran my eyes down the rest of Wil's body while he ordered. His gray sweater and black slacks hugged his athletic body, causing my imagination to run wild, wondering what was beneath. He glanced at me, and I looked away, embarrassed by my ogling.

Two drinks appeared in front of me as he motioned towards them and asked, "Who's the other one for?"

I paused. "I'm here with my roommate."

He smiled and nodded. "Sorry about the kiss on the cheek."

I tilted my head. "Are you though?" I teased.

He caught my eye. "Not particularly, no."

I laughed nervously.

He stared at me for a moment. "So, you know my name…"

"Norah Matthews."

"Hi, Norah." His voice dropped an octave, giving me the urge to fan myself.

I moved my focus back to the glowing liquor behind the bar. If looked at him for too long, I would turn into a puddle of sweat at his feet. The heat on my cheeks was already giving me away.

"My friends and I have a table over there," he said and gestured behind him with his hand. "If you and your roommate wanted to join us…"

I looked past him at two men who were just as good-looking and immaculately dressed as Wil. My mind made a quick calculation of exactly how much trouble I would allow myself to get into tonight.

"Um, no, thanks. I'd better get back." I stood and grabbed the two drinks.

He paused and nodded.

I leaned towards him, lowering my voice. "Nice to meet you, Wil." I took a few steps before stopping and turning back to him, then running my eyes up his body. "Oh, and thanks for the save…and the kiss," I said and smirked.

The corner of his mouth raised, and I made my way back to Janet, proud I still knew how to flirt.

She took her wine from me. "What happened? Do some guy in the bathroom?"

"You're disgusting." I set my drink and wallet on the table. "I got hit on by a guy I swear I saw on *How to Catch a Predator*." I faked a shiver and sat. "Then some other guy came and rescued me from him."

She put down her glass. "What guy?"

I peered over my right shoulder at the bar. Wil looked right at me as if I had called his name.

I turned back to Janet and said, "Eight o'clock."

She performed a search for him with zero stealth. "Holy shit," she whispered.

I shrugged. "He's alright," I lied. He was as close to my type as I had ever seen.

"Alright? You need your eyes checked."

"He's a womanizer or has a girlfriend." *And he's literally a god put on Earth, so there's no way I'd have a fighting chance.*

"Who cares?" she drawled.

"Janet. He is the epitome of hit it and quit it."

"Well then, he's right up your alley, isn't he?" She smirked at me, then looked over at him again. "I'll bet he's a serial monogamist."

I snorted.

"What? He's probably sweet and sensitive and

9

doesn't like models at all. They're too high maintenance. And—"

"If you say he doesn't watch porn, I'm leaving."

"I'll bet he doesn't," she mumbled.

I rolled my eyes and shook my head. "Well, I guess we'll never know, will we?"

She paused for a moment, staring at me, then quickly narrowed her eyes. She stood, grabbing her purse.

"What are you doing?" I asked, panicked.

I watched Janet in horror as she moved towards Wil and his friends. She turned and stopped between our tables, glaring at me with an expression that dared me to stay in my seat. My heart rate increased, and my forehead held a slight layer of moisture. If I didn't get up, Janet would make some sort of scene, or worse, convince Wil to come get me. Sighing, I stood and anxiously dragged my hair behind my ear. I joined Janet, and we walked towards their table.

Leaning into her, I whispered, "I'm going to murder you."

"Before or after the headboard is smacking against your skull?" she asked, dismissing me.

When we reached their table, I peeked at the other two men he was with, hoping they would be less impressive. Why did they always travel in packs?

"Hi," Janet greeted Wil with no fear or hesitancy. "I'm Janet Ogawa. You know Norah." She reached out her hand, and Wil took it.

"Hi, Janet," Wil answered. "I'm Wil. This is Chase and Byron."

Chase was shorter and bulkier than Wil. His black hair and beard complemented his hazel eyes and tawny hue. A silver band rested on his left hand. Whoever had

10

snatched him up was one lucky person.

A ringless Byron watched Janet with interest glinting in his onyx eyes. The closer she came, the wider his heart-stopping smile grew, shining his teeth against his walnut complexion. His relaxed demeanor was sure to draw Janet to him. She had a thing for guys who acted as though nothing bothered them.

After we all shook hands, Wil offered me the chair next to him while Janet slid next to Byron on the couch on the other side of the table.

I looked at Wil. "Hi again."

"Hi." He smiled, and I struggled to catch my breath.

"Sorry to intrude." I leaned in and inhaled his natural fragrance again. It really was intoxicating.

"Don't be. I invited you." His crystal blue eyes bore into mine, making the small hairs on my arms stand involuntarily.

Maybe I *did* need someone to replace Parker for my adult sleepovers. Despite what Janet thought, Wil probably wasn't the commitment type, and I wasn't looking for that anyway. I had a hunch by the way he carried himself in that amazing body, the physical side of him would be well worth it. Fuck it. Only one way to find out.

Chapter Two

Wil

I'd been watching her since she approached the bar, trying to figure out how to talk to her. When that dumbass with his cheap suit and corny lines leaned closer, I hung back to see how she'd handle herself. When she dropped the stripper joke, I laughed with her from a distance. She had a sexiness about her I couldn't pin down. A confidence I hadn't come across in some time.

Beautiful wasn't a fair description and didn't do her justice. She was breathtaking—I couldn't take my eyes off her. She interacted with everyone at our table without hesitation and was sweet, clever, and humorous. It was a relief to see she and Janet knew how to hold their own around these two jerkoffs.

This was the first time Chase, Byron, and I had hung out in months. We were roommates both on and off campus for our four years of undergrad. Once we graduated,

Chase and I moved from New York to California for jobs, while B remained on the island to build his own empire. But the miles didn't matter. Our friendship was bigger than distance or time—we were brothers for life. One phone call and we'd drop everything to be there for each other.

I tapped Norah's bare arm with my finger. Her wavy, highlighted blonde hair ran along her bare neck as she turned. "Did you want another one?" I motioned to her drink.

She smirked and arched her brow. "Are you trying to get me drunk so you can have your way with me later?"

"Not at all. Just trying to be courteous."

She ran her navy eyes down my torso while poking out her full pink bottom lip. When her gaze returned to mine, a hint of purple shined through her irises. "Bummer," she said with a sexy smirk.

She was flirting.

I took a chance and put my lips next to her ear. "In that case, yes, I am."

Her sun-kissed cheeks deepened and turned rosy. She hesitated and watched me, then slid her empty glass over. "Martini."

I stood and smiled.

So far, the signals were favorable. She didn't seem uncomfortable with my forward suggestions, which made me want to throw more out. When she touched my arm or knee with her hands, I took it as a sign that she was interested too.

I returned with our drinks just as Norah handed Chase back his phone. "She's adorable," she said. "How old is she?"

"Six months," Chase answered. "She's a handful."

13

"Chase was the lucky one to find his wife right out of college," I interjected and sat next to Norah again.

"You dated her first, dickhead. Don't blame me because she knew I was the better man." Chase laughed.

"You dated his wife?" Norah asked me, surprised.

"I only took her out twice, but she never called me after the second date. Turns out she was using me to get to him." I pointed at Chase.

Norah looked at him, her mouth wide.

Chase shrugged. "She has good taste, what can I say?"

"What are y'all talkin' about?" Byron came out of his conversation with Janet.

Norah spoke up, "How Chase's wife…" She stopped and looked at Chase with her eyebrows raised.

"Pamela," he answered.

"Pamela used Wil to get to Chase." She laughed.

"Ah, yep. We all knew it. Except for Wil, apparently." Byron smiled and took a drink.

I threw him my middle finger. "Why do you assholes bring this up when I'm trying to impress someone?" I motioned to Norah.

"She should know what she's getting into, second choice," Chase said, then answered his phone. "Hey, baby." He winked at me, then walked away from the table.

Norah turned to me, laughing. The melodic tone caused my smile to grow.

I had yet to experience the city's dating scene since I had moved. I was still hesitant, having left Elise and all her bullshit back in California. I wasn't ready to jump headfirst into another relationship yet, but I was open to spending the night with someone just to take the edge off.

Janet pulled Norah to her and whispered something into her ear while I raised my brows at Byron. He nodded. Seemed Byron was about to make his move with Janet, hopefully giving me the opportunity to be alone with Norah.

When the conversation between Norah and Janet leaked in volume, Janet looked at me. "Will you excuse us for a moment?" She grabbed Norah and dragged her towards the bathrooms before I could answer. B and I chuckled.

He took a sip. "What do you think?"

I shook my head and sighed, playing with my empty glass. "They're…"

"Sexy as hell," he responded for me.

"Yeah." I paused. "What are you going to do?"

"Just waiting for the go-ahead." He smiled.

"Are we getting too old for one-night stands?" I asked.

"Yes," Chase answered as he came back to the table. He picked up the last of his beer and drained it.

"Shut up," I said, laughing. "This conversation is for the single men who haven't found their soulmates yet."

"And you won't by having one-night stands. We're not in college anymore. You're not supposed to be trying to sleep with as many women as possible because you don't know when it'll ever happen again. We're adults." Chase was always the stern, moral father figure of the group.

B and I laughed.

"The last thing I need right now is another woman turning out like Elise. I moved across the country to get away from her. I'm not in a hurry to dive headfirst into that again," I said, unable to remove the anger from my tone.

"So, you're just gonna sleep with every woman in New York to get Elise out of your system?" Chase sat.

"That's a shitload of women, Chase," I answered.

"Wil, you like relationships. You're not fooling anyone with this player act." He looked down at his phone, probably texting Pam, even though they had just hung up with each other.

I looked at Byron for backup. He paused. "Can't help you, Dub. He's right."

"Thank you," I said sarcastically.

"Man, I don't know why you're even entertaining sleeping with this one." Byron pointed in the direction the women had disappeared to. "You're gonna end up fallin' in love with her if you take her home."

"Fuck both of you," I replied, and they snickered at me in unison.

I wasn't disputing my monogamist label. I could never handle juggling two, three, or four women at once. I tried it; it was exhausting. Sleeping with more than one woman proved nothing to my manhood—it was demeaning. Spending one night with someone was different. Elise and I had done nothing but fought until the very end of our relationship. She wasn't trying to have sex with me, and I couldn't get over her betrayal. Physical contact had never been our problem until I found out she was having an affair with a co-worker. She said I had become emotionally unavailable. Bullshit. She just wanted to fuck a guy who gave her gifts and attention. The things I sacrificed for her shot me in the foot. As much as I enjoyed being with someone, I refused to make that mistake again.

Norah and Janet returned to the table. Janet immediately landed in Byron's lap and whispered in his ear. Norah sat next to me and gave me an exacerbated smile.

I leaned next to her, touching her arm with my chest. "You okay?"

"Yeah," she said with frustration behind her stunning grin.

Byron smiled as Janet got off his lap. "Alright, y'all." He leaned over the table and gave me a handshake, then Chase. "I'll catch up."

Norah silently laughed and shook her head. Byron took Janet's hand and led her out of the bar.

Norah turned to me. "Is that going to be okay?" She nodded towards our friends.

"I'm sure he'll be a gentleman."

"I'm not worried about her."

I laughed. "They'll probably end up married then."

"She just got out of a marriage. I don't know how excited she'd be about that." She took a drink, staring straight ahead.

"That's it for me too," Chase announced and stood. "I've gotta pack. My flight's at ten tomorrow morning."

I stood too. "I'll drive you back to the hotel."

Chase's eyes flickered to Norah. "Nah, I'm good." He leaned past me and reached out his hand. "Nice to meet you."

"You too," she answered. "Congratulations again."

"Thanks." He smiled, then eyed me.

When he straightened, I gave him a hug, then pulled back. "Thanks for helping me move. I appreciate it. I know that was a long couple of days."

He shook his head. "Nothing to thank me for. Just

17

remember you're an uncle now. Don't be a stranger."

"First chance I get, I'll come out. Don't forget, poker night next month." I backed away from him.

"Yeah, I'll be here," he said and put on his jacket.

"Kiss the misses for me. And not a peck, I mean tongue and everything." I slapped his arm.

"You're a neanderthal." He laughed and turned to leave.

I sat again, peering at Norah.

"He's not staying with you?" she asked, her eyes brighter than before.

"There's nothing but boxes in my spare room. My couch isn't a pullout, he would've been miserable at my place."

She played with the napkin in front of her. "Where do you live?"

"Brooklyn."

She turned to me. "Where?"

"Williamsburg."

She smiled. "Greenpoint."

"No kidding."

She nodded.

"How did you get here?" I asked.

"Subway."

I smiled. "I still haven't adapted to the New York lifestyle yet. I'm the idiot who still drives everywhere." I crept into her space. "You're not taking the subway home, are you?"

She shook her head. "No, I was going to get a cab."

I hesitated. "I don't know if I'd be comfortable with that," I said and watched her carefully.

She faced me. "With what?"

"You leaving by yourself."

18

She twisted her tempting mouth in amusement. "Do you think someone's gonna kidnap me?"

I shrugged. "Possibly. I would."

Her eyes fell to my mouth, and her lips parted. "Did you have another idea?"

I didn't know this woman in front of me, but I wanted to take her home. I wanted to see what was under that black dress. Feel her soft curves and kiss her everywhere she'd let me. One-night stands weren't common for me, but tonight, I wanted to pretend this woman was the one.

"I could take you home." I gauged her reaction, hoping I didn't overstep her boundaries.

Her hesitation and expression made me rethink my confidence, and I began to chicken out. Maybe I was reading her signals all wrong. I hadn't done this in a while and obviously needed more practice.

She interrupted my thoughts by taking my hand. Her warm skin wrapped around my fingers. "Your home," she whispered and moved closer.

I reached under her hair and pulled her to me, gently meeting her mouth with mine. The taste of gin on her tongue made her even more delicious than I could've imagined. She stood, not breaking our connection, and fit her frame between my legs. Her soft hands moved up my arms and into my hair as she caressed my tongue with hers repeatedly. Even against me, she was still too far away. I pulled her closer, not wanting to lose her touch for a moment.

When we stopped devouring each other, I pulled back and stared into her eyes. "You ready?"

"Most definitely," she whispered.

Chapter Three

Norah

I didn't let Wil get in a word when we walked through his door. There was no chance for him to move, let alone turn on the lights, before I pushed him against the wall and kissed him hard. His firm hands were everywhere. My ass, my breasts. His mouth moved to my neck, then back to my lips. We were a whirlwind of wanting, pulling each other closer as to not let either of us get away.

I allowed myself to be nervous in the car ride but promised that once his front door closed, I would push aside those nerves and enjoy myself. It was a one-night thing with a gorgeous stranger I prayed didn't have an STI.

I broke our kiss. "You have condoms, right?" I asked breathlessly.

He nodded frantically. "Of course, yeah."

I kissed him again, moving into his apartment. He

unzipped the back of my dress while I removed his belt. The whipping sound it made wasn't as loud as when the buckle crashed on the hardwood floor.

He led me down a hall, our mouths still on each other, then moved me to the wall, so we could consume one another more evenly. I removed his sweater with a quick motion, then brought his lips back to me. His hands were no longer rushed or everywhere. He slowed his kiss and his attention, giving me the chance to focus on his touch. My skin burned as his fingers traced the curves on my body. He kissed my neck, and my eyes involuntarily rolled into the back of my head.

Janet was right; Parker wasn't the one to do this with anymore. Wil and I hadn't even gotten to the good part yet, and he had Parker beat in the kissing and caressing department.

My dress slid down my legs, then I stepped out of it and pushed it aside with my heel. Thankfully, I had attempted to match my black lace bra and panties.

He pulled back, running his eyes down my body. The moonlight coming from the room at the end of the hall illuminated us. I ran my fingers over the ripples in his abs. He was a rock, but his skin was soft and warm. I wanted to nuzzle my nose against him and smell his scent. I'd never seen anyone like him before. Not in real life, and definitely not looking at me like he was.

He interlaced our fingers and held them against the wall by my head. He pulled his bottom lip through his teeth as he continued to observe me. "How are you single?" he whispered.

I chuckled. "How are *you*?"

His smile fell for a moment, and concern covered his face. "Are you sure you're good with this?"

My pride took a minor blow. "If you want to stop—"

"No, I just... I want to make sure you want this. Just this."

What was he asking me? If I wanted to stop because he thought I'd want more than sex with him? Or was he concerned *he* would want more with me? As tempting as he was, I didn't need any emotional attachments, and I hoped he wasn't looking for that either.

I removed my hands from his hold and brought him closer to kiss me again. I hoped this gave him his answer as I tried to get that connection between us to move back to the physical instead of mental. I wanted him for the night. That was as far as I wanted to think at that moment.

Wil picked me up and walked us to the room at the end of the hall. He sat on the bed, causing me to straddle him. He took off my heels, then unhooked my bra, slipping it down my arms. He stared at my bare chest, then smiled up at me. He leaned into the hollow part of my throat, then kissed south.

Every muscle locked when his tongue and teeth teased my nipple. I pulled in my abdomen so hard I couldn't breathe for a moment. While feeling the softness of his hair in my hands as he orally tortured me, I let a moan escape, signaling he had hit a spot that caused a pleasure like no other.

He smiled against my chest as his muscular arms moved around my back and gently laid me down.

He stood and removed his pants and underwear.

My body shook with anticipation, seeing what he had to offer. *My god.* There had to be something wrong with him. He was an asshole or devoid of feeling. He didn't communicate well, or he cheated. There was no other rational reason for him to be in bed with me right now and not married, or at least with a girlfriend.

I sat up and pulled him to me by his firm ass, then took his erection in my hand, caressing him and watching his abs harden with every stroke. I licked his tip, eliciting a sharp breath that made me giddy. When I took him completely in my mouth, his hands move into my hair, and his delicious moans grew.

I hadn't given a good blow job in years. I'd slept with Parker, but it was more for my benefit than his. I didn't want him to expect head every time since we were just fuck buddies. My purpose with Parker was to get off—nothing more. But I would never see Wil again. Leaving a lasting impression was something I couldn't help but *want* to do. I wanted him to want me again, even though tonight would be it.

I played with him for a minute or two until he stopped me. He found a condom in the drawer of his bedside table and put it on. He spread my legs apart and dove into me, fitting perfectly, as if he belonged there. He quickly replaced the sweet lovemaking scene he had tried to lull me into earlier with hard fucking, and I welcomed it. He knew what a woman needed to climax and wielded that talent mightily. He was close, but he concentrated on getting me there first.

What was his game? This wasn't how a one-night stand should go. The men were always selfish, not caring about getting women to finish first or at all. Wil's effort in making sure I had an orgasm, a spectacular one at that, caused ripples to flow through me. I couldn't believe I was about to come.

His face contorted, his breathing stuttered, and his eyes closed from his own ending. Once his movement slowed, then stopped altogether, he rested his body on mine. When he had collected himself, he eased his saturated body over me and set his elbows on the sides of my head, running his thumbs over my cheeks. The smell of beer still lingered on his breath, and his post-orgasmic eyes were brilliant.

"Stay the night with me," he whispered.

I paused. "I thought that wasn't what this was?" I replied and ran my fingers down his biceps.

His brow creased for a moment. "It doesn't have to be." He wouldn't meet my eyes. "I just…would like it if you stayed."

I exhaled sharply. Great, now he was being adorable. This wasn't what I wanted or needed. I didn't want to *want* to spend the night with him, and I didn't want to have to sneak out when he was asleep to make it less awkward in the morning. But fuck if he wasn't so enticing that he *made me* want to stay. I wanted to see what else he could do with those amazing lips, firm hands, and that long, hard dick.

I nodded. "Okay."

His ridiculously handsome smile spread across his face, and he brushed his lips against mine. It was sweet and sensual and lit up my insides again.

After I was thoroughly satisfied and equally exhausted, I waited for Wil's breathing to fall into a rhythmic pattern. His clock read 5:21 when I slipped out from under his warm arm, causing various muscles to signify they had been overworked.

Worth it. Completely and totally worth it.

I found my underwear and bra around the bed, but my dress was still in the hallway. Tiptoeing, I went to the edge of the wall as the sunlight peeked out over the Atlantic. I grabbed my clothes from the floor and looked into the spacious living room. Everything from the hardwood to the paint on the walls looked upgraded and new. Boxes were spread everywhere, some labeled, some not. Tall windows looked out over the East River, and I stared at the Manhattan skyline in the distance.

In that instance, it hit me. I didn't know what Wil did or where he was from. He said he had just moved from LA but was that his home, or was he from somewhere else? If I didn't leave my number or at least wake him up, how would he find me again? As I stood in the middle of his living room, surrounded by his life in boxes, the urge to get to know him better overtook me. It wasn't just the sex, as immaculate as that was. He was amazing and smart, funny and charismatic. Why *was* he single? And what made him move to New York? I broke the delusion I was in with one thought and shook my head.

That's not what this is.

This was one night. There was no way this would turn into anything more, because we had already started out wrong. There was no recovery from sleeping with someone on the first night of meeting them. I had already messed this up before it could've even begun. I'd been here before.

Ten minutes later, I came out of the bathroom and crept into his bedroom again. He had shifted his position and was now facing me, hugging his pillow.

I walked to the bed and kneeled in front of him, not too close, just enough to study his dark blond curls, his soft facial hair, his cute nose, and full lips. I sighed at his perfection.

I grabbed my shoes and stood, then hesitated at the door before giving him one final look. A twinge of hurt deepened in my chest. It wasn't huge, just enough to make me wince. I wondered what would've happened if this night had been different. If I had agreed to see him again, or if I had postponed jumping into bed with him and gotten to know him first. But it didn't matter now. With that thought, I quietly snuck out of Wil's apartment.

I WOKE UP six hours later and rolled out of bed. When I'd come home, Janet's door was open, which told me she wasn't in her room. I smiled, glad my friend was moving on, even if it was just a rebound lay. She deserved some fun.

I heard clanking in the kitchen and threw on some shorts and a tee, then wandered into the room. Janet's back was to me.

"Hello, slut!" I announced, opening the cabinet door to grab a mug.

She laughed. "Uh-huh. Just because I came in later than you doesn't make you any less of a harlot." She finished cooking her eggs and turned off the stove, then faced me. "So, how was it?"

"I beg your pardon. How do you know I was even with Wil?" I turned my back after I poured my coffee and sorted through the mail, hiding my heated face from thinking about him.

"Stop it. I know you were with him. Byron got a text from him before I left."

I turned around. "He did?"

"Oh, look who just got all serious. Yes, he did."

I moved to the kitchen table without looking at her. "What did he say?"

"He wanted your phone number."

I looked at her. "You didn't."

"No, I didn't." She rolled her eyes.

I exhaled. "Thank you."

"I don't get it. Why don't you want him to call you?"

"Because…" I hesitated. "It was one night, and I don't have time for all of that." I pulled my chair out and sat. "I'm going to be traveling a lot for work. I can't have an anchor right now."

"An anchor?" She laughed. "Did I miss something? Are you two moving in together? Did he propose?"

"No, but… Listen, he's a nice guy, and…my god, the things that man did to me." I shivered. "But it's nothing I want to pursue."

She came over with her plate and sat down next to me. "Great sex? Gee, why would you ever want to see him again?" Her sarcasm was thick.

"And it *was* great."

"How great?" She moved her black hair behind her ear.

"I'm pretty sure there were stars."

She slapped the table. "Headboard sex great?"

I laughed. "No. There are no knots on my head, but shit, I didn't need it."

She threw her hands in the air. "That's what I'm saying! At the very least, replace Parker with Wil."

"I don't think Wil's a friends with benefits kinda guy." I remembered the way he asked me to stay the night and smiled.

She scrunched her nose. "Byron said he's a serial monogamist."

I sighed. "See, it wasn't hard to tell." I made an irritated sound. "He's so sweet and giving." I widened my eyes. "And I mean, *giving*."

She stopped chewing. "You mean he…?"

"Twice."

"Really?"

"The man has a tongue like a tornado."

She nearly spat out her food, causing me to laugh.

"I don't know. Maybe one day I can hook up with him again, but for now, I have more important things to do." I needed to bury the part of me that wanted to see him again. Wil couldn't be a distraction; I had too many other things to focus on.

I shook my head, then looked at her. "Now, it's your turn. What vile and nasty things did you and Mr. Byron do?"

She blew out a breath. "Let's just say he had me cursing in Japanese."

I looked at her, surprised. "Oh my god. Your mom would be so proud."

We both laughed, and Janet laid her head on the table.

"So? What do you think about him?" I asked and sipped from my cup.

She shrugged one shoulder. "I don't know yet," she said and looked at the table instead of me. A smile crept on her face.

She told me Byron was a trainer, which was why Wil was in such good shape. Byron had his own gym in Manhattan and trained a few players from New York sports teams during their off-season. He trained famous actors—big names—and would fly around the world when they had roles where they had to be shirtless on camera.

Janet sat back in her chair. "I guess Daniel Hutchinson was one of his clients."

"Really? Maybe you'll get to meet him." I stood.

"Meh, he just got married," she answered and took her dish to the sink.

I stretched my arms above my head. "I'm gonna go for a run. Care to join me?"

"Are you kidding?" She turned to me. "I'm going to bed. See if I can get that ten-inch penis off my mind."

I stopped moving. "Wow, did you measure it?"

"With my mouth, yes," she said as she went into her room and closed the door.

"You're right, we're both sluts!" I called after her, laughing.

"I knew it!" her muffled voice responded.

Chapter Four

Norah

My home life had caused me to spend an exorbitant amount of time in the library. I went through encyclopedias and watched videos on the internet as an escape. I went to India, Beijing, London, Beirut, all from the comforts of the Lubbock Public Library. I wandered through magazines and newspapers to grasp how the rest of the world lived, wishing I could escape the small town of nobodies, where I, too, was a nobody.

After I graduated from high school, I left Lubbock the next day. I hopped on a Greyhound and headed for New York with the money I'd saved working in fast food since I turned fifteen. I didn't want to think about or plan it, I just wanted to do it. My sister, Myra, left two years before I did. Escaping to Arkansas to go to college. *I* didn't want college. I just wanted out.

I sat at my desk on the fourteenth floor of the

Chronicle's office in downtown Manhattan, working on a story about the forthcoming election.

Georgia's state senator, Tylesha Morris, was making her way up the ranks and thinking about throwing her hat into the US Senate's ring. She was Black, in her fifties, liberal, and part of the LGBTQ community. If successful, she'd be the first gay Black woman to win in her district. The uphill battle against the incumbent senator would be tough, but the support behind Senator Morris was growing. There were whispers she could even become a presidential nominee someday, and being on the ground floor of her rising stardom could provide exclusive personal pieces for me and the *Chronicle*.

"Right," I answered. "Yeah, I know she's busy, Marcus. I just need a half hour." I waited for his reply on the other end and scoffed. "I'm not some second-rate reporter from a shitty paper, Marcus, this is the *Chronicle*, and I want to do a three-page spread on your candidate in the fiftieth-anniversary issue." I laughed. "I know she hasn't announced anything yet, but you and I both know she's going to. This is the twenty-first century, you need more than Georgia donors to pull ahead, and this article will pull her into the mainstream, but I need some direct quotes, or it won't work."

I shut my eyes tight and crossed my fingers while the silence between us hung in the air. And then he answered. "Yes! Perfect. I'm available whenever she has time. Great. Yes, I'm putting her in my schedule now." I entered a calendar event into my phone. "Yep, I got it. You're a peach, Marcus. Thank you." I hung up and pumped my fist in the air. I beamed from ear to ear as I walked to my editor-in-chief's office.

I knocked on the glass, then opened the door, sticking

my head in. "You gotta sec?"

Jerry Palmer was leaning back in his black office chair, his feet on the desk, his glasses on the tip of his round nose, and his tie loosened. One hand rested on the side of his face while he held a stack of papers in the other.

His head turned to me slightly. "Yep," he said, maintaining focus on the pages in his hands.

Jerry started as a newspaper reporter in the eighties and became one of the top political writers at the *New York Times*. He moved to the *Chronicle* in his thirties when all the bullshit in Washington DC got tiring. He focused on editorials and earned a reputation for fair insight. When the previous editor-in-chief retired, Jerry became his successor and had been at the helm of the *Chronicle* for twenty-plus years.

Jerry's blue-and-white striped, button-down shirt covered his dad gut, and he had his sleeves rolled to his elbows. His brown dress slacks were wrinkled, and his worn brown leather shoes needed to be replaced sooner rather than later. I shook my head at how little he cared about any of that. The magazine was his life—his baby.

I plopped down on the chair in front of his desk and waited for his attention. I looked lovingly at the framed picture of Jerry and his wife on his desk before turning my attention to my phone. Several notifications had popped up since this morning that I'd ignored.

When he finished reading, he threw the pages on his desk. "Crap," he said, annoyed.

I kept scrolling. "What is?"

"This." He pointed at the warped pages. "It's crap."

"Whose is it?" I glanced at him.

"Jamie's," he answered. He ran his hand over his

thinning hair.

"You still got her working on book reviews?" I continued deleting emails.

He paused. "I let her do a profile on that author, the new guy."

I looked up at him.

"The one who's supposed to be the next Stephen King?"

"Ah," I said and returned to my phone.

He picked up the stack again. "She describes his apartment in *great* detail and compares it to his dark sense of humor, but that's about it." He sighed.

I chuckled and put down my phone. "You need to send her back to proofreading. She's not ready yet."

"I was hoping she could help with some of the more pressing stories this year."

"Give her an exclusive in the book section. That's how you usually handle things when you're about to crush someone's dreams," I said, chuckling.

He took his feet off the desk and sat upright, then pushed the article to the side. "What'd ya got?"

"I nailed down the interview with Morris next month," I said and grinned.

He looked at me. "I thought she wasn't doing interviews until she decided."

"I've been working on her assistant, Marcus, for a few weeks now. You wouldn't believe how much I've spent ordering donuts for their office." Jerry laughed, and I shrugged. "I guess I finally wore him down."

"That's what you're good at." He smirked and shook his head. "Good job, kiddo."

"But it has to be the anniversary issue," I said, pointing my finger at him.

He nodded. "You got it."

I set my back against the chair and looked at my nails. "So, since we're talking about what a fantastic journalist I am—"

"*You* were talking about it."

"Should we revisit making me managing editor again?"

Jerry moved papers around his desk. "What did I tell you?"

"You said I had to prove myself."

"Exactly."

I leaned forward. "You don't think I have?"

Jerry looked at me.

"Jerry, I literally came from the mailroom and worked my way up to reporter." My voice rose. "I've been here for ten years. I've done every and anything you've asked me to do."

Jerry's chair creaked as he relaxed and leaned back again. "Kiddo, you're a talented writer. Hell, you're a brilliant writer, but I told you, I don't know if you're there yet."

I sighed loudly.

"Your technical ability is amazing, it really is. But…"

"But?" I pushed.

"You lack heart."

I scoffed and shriveled back into the chair.

"There's a human element missing in your work. You're fantastic with facts, but you're not warm in your delivery. We're not a news outlet, Norah. We tell stories about human beings. What makes them do what they do. Why people love them."

This wasn't anything new. Jerry had been trying to

get my "human element" to emerge in my writing for a while. In my everyday life, I had empathy. Those Sara McLachlan ASPCA commercials punched me in the gut like the next person. When I tried it in my writing, it felt forced...fake. I never wanted to be unauthentic in my work. It was the only true thing I had.

"Listen." Jerry stood and walked over to me. "You're in the running, and I have to decide soon. This is our fiftieth year; it has to be stellar. And with the elections coming up—we have to be ready. We need all the help we can get, and I need someone to take some things off my plate."

I met his eyes. "Who else is in the running?"

"A few people here." He motioned his head over his shoulder, then hesitated while I watched him squirm. "Also," he walked away from me, "I hired that guy I told you about last week."

I made an irritated sound. "You said you were undecided."

"Well, I decided. Norah, he's one of the top award-winning reporters in the country. He's outstanding. I think you could learn a lot from him."

I side-eyed him. "What does that mean?"

He sighed and went back to sit down. "We have a ton of things to do this year. You know you're going to be traveling a lot." He lowered his voice. "He's going to come with you."

I raised mine. "You hired a babysitter for me?"

"No, not a babysitter. Just...someone to offer you advice. Write with you. Maybe steer you in a better direction with a story."

I rolled my eyes.

"Kiddo, listen." He waited until my little brat within

subsided and I could look at him. "I have a lot of faith in you. I believe you can do this job. I do. But I'm not just going to hand this position to you. You have to earn it, and I think he can help."

I loosened my shoulders and nodded. Then a realization hit me. "Wait, is he being considered for editor too?"

He raised one shoulder. "I'm not ruling him out."

My temper grew. "So, you're pitting me against a guy with 'awards' and probably a Harvard degree—"

"Cornell."

"While I don't even have an associate degree from a community college let alone a bachelor's from an Ivy League school?"

"That doesn't matter. It's the experience I care about, you know that."

I exhaled heavily. "Jerry, I've been busting my ass for a decade to get where I am at this magazine, and you're considering a guy you've known for a week I have absolutely no chance against?"

"That's not true. His writing is clear and concise, but it's not perfect. There are qualities you have he lacks and vice versa."

I hated it when he placated me.

Jerry paused when he saw the look on my face. "How bad do you want this, Norah?"

"Pretty fucking bad, Jerry."

He smirked. "Then show me."

His play on my competitive nature was warranted, but he knew he couldn't lay down the gauntlet and expect me to ignore it.

I stared him down for a moment, then got up. "When do I get to meet Mr. Wonderful?" I asked sarcastically.

"He'll be here tomorrow," he replied calmly.

"You know I hate you sometimes, right?" I said as I walked out the door.

"Yeah, I know," he responded from behind the glass.

My phone vibrated in my pocket as I walked to my desk. I looked at the screen and made an irritated noise. Parker. I'd been dodging his calls for the last two days.

"Hey," I answered, forcing enthusiasm.

"Hi," he greeted, surprised. "I didn't think you were going to answer since you've been avoiding me."

"I'm sorry. I've been working on a story." *The title is Wil Has a Beautiful Dick and Knows How to Use It by Norah Matthews.*

"Well, can you take a night off? I miss you." He tried to make his voice low and seductive, but it was nothing compared to Wil's.

"I can't. I'm sorry. I've got a lot of things going on at work." I went to my desk and sat.

"What if I brought you Blossom's? Would you see me then?" He tried again. It did nothing for me.

"You can't dangle my favorite ice cream, that's not fair."

"That should let you know how much I want to see you."

I exhaled. "Can you give me until next week? I have some things going on here I need to deal with. I promise, I'll call you soon."

"Cookie butter," he sang into the phone.

I chuckled. "Stop it. I'll talk to you later."

"Fine. Just know the next time I see you, I'm keeping all the Blossom's to myself."

I rolled my eyes. "Whatever. You know you'll share."

"You'll have to call me to see."

A part of me wanted to tell Parker what we were doing wasn't working anymore, that I had someone else I wanted to spend time with—but it wasn't true. I would never see Wil again. As much as I knew Parker wanted more, there would be times I'd just want the release. It would be hard now that I'd had better, but to throw Parker away because I had become infatuated with someone not in my orbit anymore was foolish. Parker had been there before Wil, he could be there after. I sighed at that reality and went back to work.

Chapter Five

Wil

"Pull it up, Wil. You got this." Byron stood over me while I pushed the barbell away from my chest. His hands shadowed the bar to make sure it didn't crush me. I was on my last two reps when my arms locked, and I couldn't get the last one up. Byron grabbed the bar for me and led it to rest on the pegs. Sweat dripped down my face as I sat up and grabbed a towel, my breath heavy.

I glanced at Byron. "I'm done, man."

He walked over and handed me my water bottle. "You alright? Your head doesn't seem to be in the game."

I nodded. "I'm alright." I wiped my face and my shoulders with a towel, then took a long drink of water.

"You're still thinkin' about that girl," he said and chuckled.

I laughed once and rose. I grabbed the disinfecting wipes and wiped the bench down. "Nah, I just…" I couldn't put the words together. I *had* been thinking about Norah and that night. But more, I wanted to know why she snuck out. Why she wouldn't let Janet give Byron her number. I thought our night was amazing, but maybe she didn't feel the same.

"Cinderella bounced on you and didn't even leave a glass slipper, and now you're sad." He stuck out his bottom lip in mock despair.

"Shut up." I laughed. "I don't know, man. I just… liked spending time with her."

"If she's anything like her girl, I understand."

We walked towards the entrance of his gym.

"It's more than just sex. However fucking amazing that was." I glanced at him. "There's something else there."

"You don't know this girl from Eve, but suddenly it's more?" He shook his head.

"I'm sorry, who's got the date with the same girl he hooked up with Friday? Is that you or your nonexistent twin?"

He locked the doors, laughing. "Hey, she's fun and cute, and she's gonna cook for me, alright? What man would turn that down? Plus, I'm not opposed to demolishing that one-night stand title."

"Really?" I asked as we walked towards the garage.

He blew out a hard breath. "Man, she's got skills."

I put my hand on his chest, stopping him. "See, so why are you giving me shit because I want to see Norah again?"

He stayed silent for a moment and tried to think of an answer. Then, he shrugged his shoulders quickly and walked towards my car. My laughter echoed through the garage.

"There's not much you can do if she won't give

you a number or an address. Just forget about her, Dub. You're in New York now. There are plenty of women here who will take your mind off Elise and what's-her-name," he said as he stood by my car and waited for me to unlock the door.

I couldn't wrap my head around forgetting about Norah. It was true, I knew nothing about her other than she had a killer body and a smile that took my world off its axis. But that sparkle in her eye, her soft laugh, her above-average intelligence, and her cute southern drawl she tried to hide were the little things I wanted to know more about. Maybe it was the writer in me, but I smelled a story there.

When we pulled up to Byron's brownstone in Harlem, Janet was sitting on the steps with grocery bags by her side and her phone in her hand.

I looked at Byron. "You've got company."

"Gotta love a woman on time," he said, looking in her direction. She came to the car and knocked on the window. He rolled his side down.

Janet leaned both arms on the door. "Hey," she said to B.

"Hey yourself. Sorry I'm late. Wil drives like he's ninety." He pointed his thumb at me.

She laughed. "That's alright. You can make it up to me later." She stared at him, and he nodded, then whispered something to her, making her giggle.

I purposely cleared my throat.

Janet peeked around Byron. "Oh, hey, Wil."

"Hi, Janet," I replied, and Byron got out of the car.

When he closed the door, she rested on the window again. "So, I heard you and Norah had a good time the other night."

41

"I thought so. But evidently, the beautiful woman who snuck out of my bed didn't."

She hesitated, and her eyes drifted. "Norah is… complicated, and I can't speak for her, but trust me, the feeling is reciprocated."

"Yeah, well, since she won't let me call her, I have no way of verifying, do I," I answered with an edge to my voice.

Janet stared at me with irritation. I started to apologize for sounding so annoyed when she interrupted me. "Hang on," she said as she took her phone out of her back pocket, then turned and leaned her back against my car. Her muffled voice carried as she spoke to someone. Actually, it sounded like she was pleading. Forcefully.

She twisted back around, pushing her head and phone through the window at me. I looked at her quizzically.

"Don't say I never did anything for you." She winked.

I took the phone, looking at the scrolling name. *Ra-Rah*. I looked at Janet again.

"Beautiful woman," she mouthed, then smirked.

I brought the phone up to my ear and said, "Hey," trying to play it cool.

"Hi," Norah started, then exhaled with irritation.

"I promise, I didn't make her do this."

"Oh, I know. Janet never needs to be coerced into anything."

I laughed. "Listen, if you don't want to talk to me—"

"It's not that," she blurted. "I just… I have a lot going on, and I didn't want to make commitments I couldn't keep. But I *am* sorry I left you that morning. I guess I didn't really know what else to do."

"Well, you could've let me make you breakfast, and

then we could have spent the day in bed together."

She paused. "Damn it, that would've been good."

I laughed again, then let a moment pass. I couldn't deny I wanted to see her as much as I probably shouldn't. It sounded like she wasn't in a place to be bothered with me or anyone else, but I wanted to try my luck. "We could always try again."

I heard her laugh softly on the other end. "I'll…get a hold of you soon, okay?"

"You sure? I'm available now," I offered.

The line went silent for longer than I expected, like she was contemplating something, or maybe she had gotten too distracted to hear me. I cleared my throat. "So, I guess—"

"Okay," she whispered.

I furrowed my brow for a moment. "I wasn't trying to pressure you—"

"No, I know. But if you're willing, I am too."

"You sure?" I answered, hushed.

"Meet you at your apartment at eight?"

"Yeah." I smiled. "Do you need my address?"

"I remember." She took another pause. "Eight o'clock."

The line went dead.

I took the phone away from my ear and stared at it. I felt eyes on me from the passenger window. Janet raised her eyebrows as I handed her the phone.

"Better get going, lover boy." She ducked her head out of the window and walked up the stoop to Byron's door.

Smirking, I shook my head and put my car in drive.

43

The Opposite of Fiction

MY APARTMENT WASN'T in too much disarray for company. I didn't have to stuff things in the oven or hall closet so Norah wouldn't see the clutter. I had unpacked most of my boxes, but I still had several stacks of books on the kitchen table. I was waiting for my bookcases to be delivered from Modani Furniture later in the week. I was pretty sure Norah wouldn't mind or even notice.

My gunmetal gray sectional couch still carried the plastic scent they'd delivered it in. I tried to cover it up by keeping the balcony door open, but the scent still lingered. The dark brown hardwood floors needed cleaning from when we moved all my things, but nothing too embarrassing. I wished I still had my TV to keep me occupied until Norah arrived. That was another purchase I'd have to look into soon. I sighed as I sat on the couch with my phone.

There was a soft knock on the door a few minutes later. Unlocking the deadbolt, I stretched my neck to relieve my nerves. I met her innocent, deep blue eyes first, then moved down to her full, naked lips and smiled.

"Hi," I whispered.

She didn't speak, just pushed open the door, and her lips immediately met mine. I reached behind her and shut the door, then pulled her entire body to me. She pushed me against the wall and undid the string to my sweatpants.

"I can't spend the night," she said urgently against my mouth. Fluid in her motions, she took off my shirt, then removed my pants, not giving me any time to react to her statement.

She broke away from me and walked towards the bedroom, still wearing her tan trench coat and heels. When I followed, she turned and said, "Wait," making me stop in my tracks. "I'll be right back." She raised the right corner of her mouth and continued into the room.

I watched after her, amused but puzzled. I didn't know what to do. She was the one in control, which was a turn-on for sure. I just felt like an idiot standing in the middle of my living room with nothing on but my underwear.

She returned with a square condom package in her hand. But after closer inspection, I noticed there were two. I smiled at her confidence that there would be at least two acts between us this evening, even if she wouldn't spend the night. She returned to me, kissing me like no time had passed. She moved me to the couch and sat me down.

She stepped back from me and undid the tie around the waist of her coat, revealing a light pink lace bra and matching panties. My mouth fell open and my dick went hard.

The gentle material was the only thing standing between me and her full breasts and thick thighs. Without thinking, I grabbed her by her hips and pulled her forward to straddle my lap. I reached my hand up behind her blonde hair to her neck and stared into her eyes, my breath thick with wanting. She smiled at me and placed her hands on my neck too, running her thumb over my stubble.

I caressed her soft face with the back of my fingers while she closed her eyes, giving me an audible sigh. I moved my hand down to her neck, then ran my fingertips along the tops of her breasts.

She watched me as I leaned forward and unhooked her bra, slipping her straps down her arms. Her hard pink nipples begged me to taste them, and I happily obliged.

Her hands went through my hair as her moans filled my apartment—I reveled in the sounds.

She pulled my face to her again, kissing me. I hugged her to me, then laid her on the couch and removed our underwear. She took a condom out of the package and waited for me to sit between her legs. I reached for it, but she shook her head and moved so she could perform the maneuver for me.

She guided me into her and gasped, then wrapped her legs around my back, pressing the material on her heels against my skin. I, then, understood the two condoms. This first time would be fast. We both knew it without a word spoken between us.

Moving inside her, I tried not to come too quickly but recognized it was out of my control. She felt too damn good and sent my senses into overdrive. Her nails on my back, her soft skin lingering on mine, the scent of coconut and freesia invading my nose, and the small noises that had turned into full-throated moans were too much. My thrusts became more forceful as her body tightened around me. I couldn't hold on anymore and let my release spread from my chest out to my appendages while her sweet sounds heightened as well. Her grasp on me loosened as our verbal cues gave way to pants. I gently rested my body on hers, regaining my composure.

I lifted myself and peered at her. Her skin glowed with moisture—she looked radiant. "You wanna go into the bedroom?" I asked softly.

She shook her head. "I told you, I can't spend the night."

I twisted my mouth, then nodded. I didn't know this woman. I didn't know her character or even where she lived. There was no reason for me to like her other than the fantastic sex. I wanted to spend time with her to justify this curious feeling.

She touched my face. "I'm sorry. Should I not have come?"

"Oh no, trust me, I'm glad you came. In fact, I need to make sure you come again before you leave." I lowered myself to kiss her while she chuckled.

I moved beside her, propped up on my elbow, and rested my head in my hand. We watched each other, and I contemplated this "relationship" and what it was about.

"What's with that look on your face?" she questioned, turning towards me and mimicking my pose.

"I don't know anything about you." I took her delicate fingers in my hand. "And I want to."

She smiled. "I guess that's the danger when sleeping with someone on the first night, huh?"

"Technically, this is the second night."

Her smile widened.

"Are you seeing somebody else?" I asked.

"Not seriously, no," she answered quietly. "Are you?"

I shook my head. "No. As a matter of fact, I moved to New York to get away from that somebody."

"Bad breakup?"

I looked away. "Yeah."

She was quiet for a moment. "There's a rumor you're a serial monogamist."

I chuckled. "Fucking Byron, can't keep his mouth shut."

She let her head fall against my chest as she laughed. I leaned down and closed my eyes as the clean scent of her hair, a mixture of floral and citrus, filled my nose.

She raised her head back to meet my eyes. "Is that

what you want?"

I raised my eyebrows at her as a question.

"A relationship?"

"No," I blurted.

She pulled back from me with a look of confusion.

"No, I-I didn't mean…" I took a breath. "We don't know each other enough for me to make that decision yet. To be honest, I'm in unfamiliar territory here. Not really sure about protocol."

She looked down with a relieved smile, but she kept her emotions close to her chest.

"From what I do know, I like," I continued, "and when you're ready," my voice fell to a whisper, "I'd like to spend more time with you."

A pink hue darkened her cheeks, and I touched it with the back of my fingers while she nodded.

"I'd liked that too," she answered in a hushed tone and met my eyes.

The deep blue in her eyes I was slowly becoming obsessed with sparkled and caused me to lean in to connect with her lips. It was only a matter of time before she left this couch and my apartment. Although sex wasn't a sign of anything real between two people, I wanted to feel her again. Taste her, enjoy every part of her. In case this time was our last time.

Norah

The apartment was pitch-black when I came home from Wil's. Janet texted me and said she was spending the night with Byron, so I prepared to be home alone for the rest of the evening. I opened the refrigerator door and searched for something quick to eat.

I inhaled and smelled Wil's body soap all over me, making me smile. I brought the hem of the T-shirt he let me borrow up to my nose and breathed deeper, closing my eyes. I'd finally given him my phone number but warned him I was horrible at getting back to people. He said he didn't care about that, he just didn't want me to disappear. My skin prickled remembering the way he tilted his head and watched me.

I shouldn't have gone to his place, but I couldn't say no. My need to see him again outweighed my rational side. Which, at its basic core, was simply a lack of fundamental information. We didn't know each other, and I had slept with him twice. It wasn't a good look giving away the milk for free, as the saying went.

But I liked him.

I liked the way he looked at me, the way he touched me so carefully even in the heat of the moment. Our conversations, while brief, indicated his intelligence and kindness. There would be time to dig into our backgrounds and pasts. I wasn't exactly in a hurry to divulge that information in the first place, but it was part of building a connection. He was a genuine sweetheart, and I wanted to give him a chance after all this bullshit at work stopped. Until then, I had to have my A game on point.

I grabbed ingredients to make a turkey sandwich, then I would head to bed. I needed to be ready to meet my Cornell nanny hired to monitor and "improve" my writing. I rolled my eyes at the thought of him. I pictured a frat boy, douchebag, condescending dick who thought he was better than me, because I wasn't Ivy League–educated like him. He likely knew about the managing editor position and was only placating Jerry with the promise to help me just so he could slip in and steal the job for himself.

Not on my watch.

I'd worked too damn hard for too long to relinquish this position. While he was getting his costly, pointless degree, I'd been busting my ass to make a name for myself and worked up the ranks. I didn't care if he was Carl Bernstein and Bob Woodward combined. He would not snake his way past me.

Getting ready for bed, I heard my phone vibrate on my nightstand. I grabbed it and looked at the lock screen.

Wil: Get home ok?

I smiled to myself.

Norah: I did, thank you.

Wil: I thought you were "horrible" at responding.

I chuckled.

Norah: You caught me at the right time.

Wil: So around midnight is a good time?

Norah: Occasionally.

Wil: Any chance I'll see you this week?

Norah: Don't push your luck. The fact that I broke the promise to myself and came to see you tonight was a gift.

Wil: A gift? You don't think much of yourself, do you, Matthews?

He remembered my last name? Cute.

Norah: Oh my god…

Wil: What?

Norah: I don't know your full name. I'm so easy, it's pathetic.

Wil: LOL! You won't hear me complaining. And it's Lockwood.

Norah: Nice to meet you, Wil Lockwood.

Wil: Nora Matthews, a pleasure.

Norah: Add an 'h' at the end of Nora.

Wil: Norah… I like that.

I liked the way I heard him say it in my head from our time on his couch. I shivered.

Norah: Goodnight, Wil.

Wil: Sweet dreams, Norah.

I PURPOSELY ARRIVED late to work the next morning. My new shadow would be met with every resistance I could think of. I dressed nicer than usual, determined to show what's-his-face I wasn't some young kid trying to make it in the big city. Fuck that. I was way beyond that. I was twenty-eight, ambitious, talented, and didn't need anyone to help me be a better writer. I would take everything this guy said with a grain of salt, then make sure I transferred the target on my back to his. I needed to not only produce stellar material in the next several months, but I would also insist this man was out of the picture. If he could move to New York for an editor's job, he could move somewhere else when he didn't get it.

Jerry called me into his office the moment I arrived at my desk. The cigar smell that had soaked into the walls and carpet from the previous editor-in-chief filled my nose when I crossed the threshold. I sat in the chair in front of Jerry's desk, crossing my legs and gently laying my hands on my lap.

"He'll be here in a minute. He just texted me from the lobby," Jerry said as he walked around his desk.

"Good for him," I answered. Jerry gave me a warning glare, and I tried to pull back my attitude.

"Norah, this is a good thing. Wilson is a top-notch journalist. I'm telling you, you two are going to mesh well." He sat in his chair.

"Not with a name like Wilson."

"Come on, kiddo." I could hear the irritation in his tone. "You gotta throw me a bone here. It's not a punishment. I'm doing this for you."

The door to Jerry's office swung open, causing a slight breeze to hit me. I moved nothing but my eyes in that direction, promising not to give this jerk the satisfaction of my attention until I had to.

"Hey," Jerry said as he stood and moved towards our guest to shake his hand. "Glad you're here."

"Me too. Thanks a lot," he answered.

The familiarity of his voice caused me to turn. When I met his ocean eyes, I froze with my mouth gaping open and my heart jumping out of my body and running out the door. Someone had removed the air out of my lungs, and my mind rapidly tried to find a rational answer for why he was here. When I landed on the most obvious, I closed my eyes.

Please, no. Not that.

I finally spoke when my lips and brain merged again. "What are you doing here?" My voice didn't sound normal.

Wil shook his head subtly, staring at me. "What am *I* doing here? What are *you* doing here?"

Jerry looked between us. "You two know each other?"

Wil didn't move his eyes away from me as shock grew in my chest. "Um… We met a few days ago," he answered.

I ripped my stare from him and tried to normalize my expression. "Yeah…just…" I exhaled, then looked at Wil again. "In Manhattan. It was quick." My jaw immediately clenched.

Wil gave a small nod but didn't look back at Jerry. My frustration stretched around us in the deafening silence.

Of course this is how our relationship would begin. Wil, or rather, *Wilson*, would be the guy who'd try to take my place. The guy I'd slept with…twice. The guy who had his mouth and hands all over my body and mine on his just the night before. I knew what he smelled like, what he tasted like. I knew the curves of his abdomen and how his strong arms felt around me. What his tongue felt like against mine. I was more familiar with Wil Lockwood than I ever should've been, especially now.

I thought something more would happen between us when I got work straightened out. When I told the person, who would supposedly make me a better writer, to piss off.

But now that possibility of us was over. All over.

"Well," Jerry said, walking back to his desk, interrupting my thoughts and disappointment. "I guess now that I don't have to make introductions, this part will be less awkward."

Not a chance in hell.

As Jerry talked, Wil continued to stand by the door while my muscles burned from the painful tension. I tried to keep my eyes locked on Jerry, even through the weight of Wil's stare.

Jerry continued, "I've briefed both of you on what's ahead. We have to finish this year out strong, and I'm going to need a right-hand man, or woman," he eyed me, "to help me out. Now, I don't mean to make this a competition between you two—"

Yes, you absolutely do. I couldn't stop my eyes from rolling.

"But I'm at an impasse. Norah, you've been here for a long time and have become one of the best writers I've got. On the other hand, Wil, your resume is impressive. I can't ignore how qualified you are coming out of the gate, but you're not an obvious choice. So, I want you two to work together on articles and the exposés I have planned over the next few months."

This was already complicated enough. Now Jerry

was going to send me on assignments with someone who'd just crossed the thin line between really like and hate.

I pulled air in through my nose, louder than I expected. "I need clarification," I said, trying to increase my volume to pretend this madness wasn't affecting me like it was. "Typically, when you have two opposing sides going for the same goal, I wouldn't think working together would be the go-to answer. Don't you want us to work separately, so we can give you our best work, then you can compare?"

"That's not how I work, Norah, you know this. You both have incredible strengths, and I want to see if working together will make you reach a new level with your writing... Both of you." Jerry was trying to help me save face in front of Wil, making it seem like there was some flaw in Wil's journalism I could help with.

I narrowed my eyes at Jerry. He turned towards his computer and typed. I glanced at Wil, catching his eye. His perfect lips parted, and his eyes read how sorry he was. I shut mine in irritation and turned away.

"There." Jerry looked between us. "I've just sent the last three articles both of you have worked on to your emails. Get a feel for each other's writing styles, and we'll meet back here tomorrow to discuss what you think. Sound good?"

The gleam in Jerry's eye and curve of his mouth always happened when he was excited about something. Usually, it made me excited too, but now, I was nauseated. Whether or not I wanted it to, this was going to happen.

Wil pushed himself off the door. "Sounds good, Jerry. Thank you."

I rolled my eyes at Wil's suck-up attitude.

Jerry turned to me. "Norah?" His tone was a warning about how I answered.

I took a breath and fixed my expression. "Fine," I said, upbeat but still through gritted teeth.

I stood and walked towards the exit, not wanting to look at Wil. He thrust the door open before I could reach it, making me stop moving. I peered at his worried expression and frowned at him. I glanced back at Jerry and tried to smile as genuinely as I could, then walked out the door.

This was going to be impossible.

I stalked forward, hoping Wil wouldn't follow me.

"Norah," he called.

His brown leather shoes made a muted sound against the carpeted floor as he got closer. I sped up. When I got around the corner, his hand wrapped around my arm, stopping me. I turned to him defensively and yanked myself from his reach.

"You're mad at me?" he asked, surprised.

I couldn't answer him. Reality was, I had no reason to be angry with Wil. It wasn't like he knew who I was or where I worked when we'd had sex. Still, it didn't stop my frustration towards him.

I looked away. "No, I'm mad at this whole situation."

He crossed his arms. "What situation?"

"You!" I looked around, hoping no one heard me. I leaned closer to him and whispered, "Look, you don't know me, and you have no idea what you're walking into, but…you literally just became enemy number one."

"Why?" he asked, baffled.

"Because you're here to take away the one thing I've been working my entire career for."

"Norah, I'm not here to take anything from you."

"Oh, really? So, if Jerry offers you the managing editor job, you'll turn it down?" I cocked my eyebrow at him.

"No."

I nodded once. "Enemy number one." I started to walk away, and he grabbed my arm again and turned me to him.

Anger had replaced his confusion. "I've known you for all of five minutes, Norah. Why would I sacrifice the reason I moved across the country for someone I spent a few nights with? We're not together." He stared at me with his brow furrowed. When he realized what he'd said, he let go of my arm and looked away. "I mean—"

"Oh, I know what you meant. And you're absolutely right, *Wilson*." My defenses had risen to mountain peaks. "You have no reason to give up something you want for me." I walked closer to him, our chests inches away from each other. "But if you think you're going to come in here and run me off with your big awards and Ivy League education, you'd better think again. Managing editor is mine. You're just a small road bump in my way." I turned on my heel and strutted away.

"I'm supposed to be here to help you," he called after me.

I turned my head over my shoulder. "I don't need your help," I said as I disappeared around the corner.

Wil

"Goddamn it," I whispered to myself as I watched that gorgeous, maddening creature walk away. The shock of seeing her here was still fresh, but my rational mind began to reemerge. None of this was our fault. I hadn't asked what she did, and she hadn't offered. Neither had I. I figured we'd have the opportunity to explore all of that in the future. Fate had a different timetable, apparently.

I walked to my desk, where I had initially thrown my belongings down. My brown leather satchel held a few extra things I wanted to store in and on my desk. A few photos of my family, some snacks, pens, and legal pads. Technology was great, but there was nothing like putting pen to paper with my thoughts. Seeing them in front of me helped me focus.

I pulled out my laptop and opened my email. Norah's articles Jerry had sent were sitting in my inbox, but I wasn't ready to read them. I didn't want to critique

Norah's work in the building. I kept looking over my shoulder for her every five minutes as it was.

I wanted to believe she wasn't mad but surprised by our circumstances, just as I was. I didn't mean what I'd said, or I didn't mean it the way it came out. I wasn't here to derail her career goals, but if Jerry offered me the position, I would take it. Just because Norah and I slept together shouldn't change that.

The *Chronicle* had been appealing even when I wasn't looking to get away from LA. Their editorials were the most recognized in the country. The pieces written about various public figures from Nixon to Beyoncé were unbiased. There weren't many people who wouldn't talk to the *Chronicle* because of their reputation, and I was tired of being hung up on when I said I was from the *LA Post*. While it had started as a typical newspaper, it had turned into a gossip rag not known for being honest or rational in its articles. This was my chance to get back to doing balanced stories and editorials without a lot of pushback.

I began to unpack my bag when my new, self-proclaimed nemesis caught my eye. She had a coffee mug in her hand and stopped in her tracks when she met my gaze. Her stare wasn't sexy or seductive like I was used to, she was distant and cold. She rolled her eyes, then moved to my right and out of my sight.

Four-foot partitions divided each desk. The gray pegboard walls were rough to the touch but held thumbtacks well. I heard her plop down in her chair next to me, and a long, drawn-out breath followed. I'd have recognized the sound of Norah releasing tension anywhere. I stood and set my forearms on top of our separation, and the metal cooled my bare skin instantly.

"Can I help you?" she quipped, punching the keys on her keyboard without looking at me.

God, even angry, she was completely captivating.

"Looks like we're roommates," I answered.

"No. We sit near each other. And this is not a room, it's an office space."

"It's a room. Four walls, floor, a ceiling," I retorted.

"If you say so." She continued to type on her computer.

"Wanna show me a good place for lunch later?" I asked, trying to put out an olive branch. We were working together, no need to be malicious towards each other. Plus, if I were being honest, I wanted to leave that physical window open between us. Working together complicated things, but we had initially agreed that we weren't looking for a committed relationship. No reason our physical relationship should stop.

Her typing ceased, and she twisted her mouth into something between anger and amusement. She pushed herself back from her desk and stood, picking up a ruler from her pencil holder. She violently jerked it under my arms, causing me to remove them quickly.

"Let's get something clear," she said in a low tone as she moved closer, pointing the ruler in my direction. "Whatever happened between us is over. Thank you for providing the multiple orgasms over those two nights, but that's done now. We work together, we sit close to each other, that's it. We're not friends, and there are no longer benefits. Got it?" The gravel in her voice was not only sensual, but it also created the opposite effect she'd intended. She wasn't scaring me away. I couldn't help but snicker at her.

"Something funny?" She put her hands on her hips.

I shook my head at her irritation. "Nope," I answered simply and with a smirk.

"Well then, if you'll excuse me, I have work to do." She turned away from me, shoved the ruler into the metal cup she'd removed it from, and sat, pulling her seat closer to her keyboard.

"So, that's a no for lunch then?" I asked.

She put in her earphones, still not looking at me and went back to typing, taking another audible breath.

I sat and chuckled to myself. So much for continuing our physical relationship. At this point, I'd take her just tolerating me, but the sound of the keyboard receiving the brunt of her anger over the gray wall told me otherwise.

My phone vibrated against my desk. I picked it up quickly when I saw the caller. "Mom? What's wrong?"

"Nothing," she answered and laughed. "Hello, son."

My tensed body relaxed. "Sorry. You never call me on a weekday. I thought it was Dad. Or Devin."

"Your father is fine, and Devin's at a meeting. I was calling because of Elise."

There was immediate tension in my body. "What about Elise?"

"She showed up here."

I sighed. "Mom, I'm sorry. What did she say?"

"She was a mess. She wouldn't stop crying, then when she did, she begged me to tell her where you were."

"What did you say?"

"I told her it was none of her business. Trust me, I know theatrics when I see them," she said flatly.

I loved my mom. "Thank you."

"No one cheats on my baby and then gets sympathy because that no one is an idiot."

I laughed. *Loved* her. "Did she say anything else?"

61

"She basically told me the same story you did, then said something about the guy she was with wasn't you and that she missed you, blah, blah, blah."

I fiddled with the pen on my desk. "The grass isn't always greener, is it?"

"It certainly isn't." She moved the phone away to say something to my dad, then returned to me. "Enough about the ex-girlfriend. Tell me about the magazine."

I raised my head to see if Norah was listening, finding she wasn't paying attention to me at all. Still, I got up and walked away.

"So far, so good. I'm working with another writer here who's competing for the job I told you about." *And she's someone I slept with who now hates me.*

"Interesting."

"You don't know the half of it."

She paused. "Uh-oh."

"What?"

"It's a woman, isn't it?"

"Why?"

"The tone of your voice went from my sweet boy to a frustrated Wilson Taylor Lockwood. Only a woman could do that. Do you like her?"

"Mom."

"What? It's a simple question," she pushed.

I exhaled. Even if I tried to lie to her, she'd call me on it. "Yeah, I like her."

"What's the problem?" I heard the smile in her voice immediately.

"It's complicated."

"Mm-hmm." The sarcasm in that sound was thick.

"Let it go. We work together and we're going after the same job. You can fill in the blanks," I answered, trying to hide my frustration.

"You know, I hated your father when I first met him."

"Yes, Mom, he was a cocky grad student who thought he was—"

"God's gift. Yes. Thirty-five years and three kids later, he's still the love of my life."

I rolled my eyes, glad she couldn't see. "This is different."

"So you say."

"I promise I'll let you know when we announce our engagement," I said sarcastically.

"Smart-ass."

I laughed.

"Alright. I'll let you get back to your frustration in the big city. Will you make it back for the Fourth of July?"

"It's only May, Mom."

"I plan, you know this. Everyone will be here. They need to see their big brother."

I was thirty-three, and she was still bossing me around. I smiled. "I'll let you know."

"Okay. I love you, Wilson."

"Love you too."

My mom was tough as nails but a hopeless romantic and probably heard how I felt about Norah from my tone. I would eventually tell her the entire story. There wasn't much I kept from her anyway.

I walked back to my desk and peered over at the focus of my thoughts. She looked up for a moment, then took a long, irritated breath as she looked away.

Screw it. She wasn't the only woman in New York, and now that we were working together, it would just complicate things. The two nights we spent together were incredible and could have led to something more, eventually. But I shared her sentiment; this was over.

NORAH DISAPPEARED BEFORE I left for lunch, still refusing to look at me. We were so different from less than twelve hours ago. We went from planning on seeing each other again to her being unable to stand the sight of me. I shook my head at the irony as I made my way down to the first floor to find something to eat. A small deli tucked in the corner behind the elevators would have to do. I didn't see a need to venture out into the city just yet. I'd eventually get accustomed to my surroundings again and find more interesting places to dine. Today, I just wanted a sandwich.

As soon as I spotted her, I smiled. She had her head buried in her computer, sitting at a table by the window, and absentmindedly threw a chip in her mouth. Never taking her eyes off the screen, she unscrewed the top of her bottle of water and brought it to those luscious lips I could still feel against my own. I'd never envied an inanimate object so much in my life.

I broke myself out of the brief fantasy of when I thought Norah would be something more and walked into the small eatery. As soon as I entered, she looked up at me, the irritation on her face immediately readable. She exhaled and returned to her screen, trying to find the place where she left off before I had interrupted her. I smirked and shook my head.

The cashier handed me my food when my order came up, and I turned and walked towards Norah. When I stood next to her, her eyes flashed to my shoes.

"Keep walking, Lockwood," she said defensively.

I took a deep breath. "Okay," I said as I sat in front of her. "We need to clear the air here."

A look of disbelief crossed her gorgeous face.

"There's absolutely no reason for us to hate each other."

She leaned towards me. "I can hate you all I want. And there's a big goddamn reason for me to do so," she snapped.

I mimicked her posture and lowered my voice. "Norah, I had no idea you were the person Jerry told me about. No matter what you've told yourself, I'm not here to torment you or steal anything. I heard the *Chronicle* was looking for a new journalist, and there was an opening for an editor, that's it. I didn't plan on sleeping with the woman I'm in direct competition with. This isn't a conspiracy against you."

Her eyes never left mine. "I never said it was a conspiracy against me, Wil, but I refuse to let you distract me. I've worked too hard for this to let you come in here and just take it, frat boy."

My anger at her stubbornness grew. "First, I was never in a fraternity."

She scoffed.

"Second, you think you're the only one who's worked hard to get to this point in your career? I built my status from a beat reporter at a trash paper to a top journalist in the business. I might not have been here the whole time, but I paid my dues. I've earned this just as much as you have. Actually, probably more."

"More?" she asked, indignant.

"Yes, more," I answered, just as annoyed. I didn't care how much I liked her before. She would not tell me how I didn't earn this chance as an editor, because she had some ridiculous delusion about being better. She was still a baby in this industry, and if Jerry didn't have the balls to tell her, I would.

She closed her laptop so loud I worried she might have damaged the inside. She leaned towards me again, the intensity in her eyes fierce and intimidating. "I'll make this as clear as I can. Just because you bought your way into an Ivy League education, slummed around LA for a few years, and got by doing half-assed work because you used your privilege to get ahead does not make you a good journalist. They give awards to anyone who pulls a tear or two out of a few readers. It's cute. But you will not gain applause from me because of it. You're in New York now—the clock starts over. As of today, you have zero experience being a writer in a city that actually counts, *Wilson*." She got up, almost knocking over her chair. She grabbed her laptop and the rest of her belongings in her rage and stormed out of the deli.

I kept my eyes forward and the smallest of smiles spread across my face. "Damn, was it something I said?" I asked, buried behind a laugh.

Norah wasn't playing or being coy. She was dead serious about being managing editor. As much as I wanted to dislike her after what she'd said, I couldn't. She had fire and was tenacious about what she wanted. This was going to be fun.

Chapter Eight

Norah

I came home and threw my stuff on the kitchen table. Janet was on the sofa on her phone and turned when she heard the random crashes. I pulled out the chair, sat, and laid my head on the table.

"How was your day, dear?" Janet mocked as she stood.

"You're never going to believe this," I said to the floor.

She stopped walking. "Are you pregnant?"

I lifted my head. "No! No." I put my arms under my chin.

Janet moved again, breathing a sigh of relief, then joined me at the table. "Then it can't be *that* bad. Come on, out with it." She tucked her foot under her thigh.

"Wil's the guy," I said, trying to keep the tears at bay.

"What guy?"

"The guy! At work, the guy Jerry hired."

Her voice rose. "What?"

"Yes! He's the Cornell graduate, award-winning journalist dickhead that's trying to swoop in for the managing editor job." I didn't like how small my voice had gotten.

Janet sat silently, and her mouth gaped open. "Holy shit."

I nodded.

"What… What are you going to do?"

I jumped out of my seat. "What am I supposed to do? We're not together. I spent two nights with him. There's no commitment. But…" I hesitated.

"But…?" She motioned with her hand.

I slumped against the refrigerator door. "I like him." I exhaled and played with my fingernails. "I know I don't know anything about him, and it was just sex. But why him? How many millions of people in New York, hell, in the United States, and Wil had to be the snake." My whiny voice was annoying even to me. I hated that I was this distraught about the situation.

Janet gave me a half-hearted smile. "I'm sorry."

I exhaled, walked back to the table, and sat down dramatically.

"You know you don't have to hate him," she hedged.

"What?" I responded, aggravated.

"I mean, I get it, but maybe this could be a good thing." She shrugged.

I looked at her like she had three heads. "You've got to be kidding me."

"No, seriously. Maybe you really will learn something, and maybe Wil will help you get the managing editing whatever it is."

I scoffed. "I don't think you understand the situation here. Janet, I've been at the magazine for ten years. The only thing I've wanted in those ten years was to be the managing editor. I don't want to run the magazine, and I have no desire to continue to be a beat journalist at Jerry's beck and call. I want to be the one to tell people where to go and who to talk to. I could literally help shape the direction of the magazine based on content. Good, quality content."

"Kinda sounds like a power trip," she teased.

I exhaled and sat back, taking a moment. "Maybe it is. I left Texas and came to New York to be somebody. Make a difference. Prove that I'm more than anyone ever thought I could be."

Janet's voice softened. "By anyone, you mean your mother."

I didn't answer as my jaw clenched. I scratched the back of my head with my fingernail and got up to look in the fridge. I wasn't hungry. I just needed to get away from that particular accusation.

I was under no delusion or denial. Yes, my mother telling me I wasn't shit my whole life was my motivation to be more. I wanted to prove to myself she was wrong. I had to be better than what she thought of me. I *had* to.

I grabbed a bottle of tea and turned back to Janet. "What am I gonna do about Wil?"

She rolled her eyes. "You've already made up your mind. He's your archenemy regardless of how sexy, handsome, kind, and lick-able he is."

There was no humor to my laugh.

"You have no choice but to make sure that position is yours. Work your ass off, do what Jerry tells you to do, and prove you're the better writer." She gave me a closemouthed, know-it-all smile.

I nodded and walked over to her. "Thank you," I said as I leaned down to hug her.

"You got it. Do you wanna watch something?" She patted my arm.

"No, thanks. I need to go run off this irritation," I replied, starting towards my bedroom.

"You mean sexual frustration," she said, standing too, then pushing in her chair.

I turned to her. "Ha, ha, slut. Don't you have a date with Byron?"

She walked to the couch. "Nope, he's working, I'm relaxing." She plopped down and grabbed her phone again. The giggle I heard when I closed the door to my bedroom implied she and Byron were already talking to each other. I shook my head as I got undressed.

I CAME INTO work the next morning full of determination. Wil was someone I'd thought could be something more, eventually. From what I knew about him, he checked off most of my boxes...but that didn't matter anymore. I would heed Janet's advice and see what he had to say. We were professionals, both with the same aspirations. I wouldn't fawn all over him, but I wouldn't cut him off either. My goal was to continue to show Jerry I deserved the editor position, more than Wil, and would do whatever I needed to accomplish that task. Even if I had to fake-grin my way through Wil's tutelage. Regardless of what I'd said the day before, he had to have done something right to win awards and get to where he was now—I just wanted to hit him below the belt.

When I walked around the corner, Wil was already at his desk, typing vigorously on his laptop. He had on rectangular, black-rimmed glasses and a white button-down shirt rolled up to his elbows. The sunlight behind him gave him a gold aura. All he was missing were wings and a harp.

This would be so much easier if he weren't so goddamned attractive. I closed my eyes and continued to walk around to my desk.

I set my computer bag and purse down gently. I wasn't ready to let Wil know I had arrived yet. I needed a few minutes to adjust my new attitude now that I'd seen him. I sat, then took my computer out of my bag. When I opened it, there was a loud sound from my email. I punched the volume key repeatedly, trying to lower it, and cursed in a whisper.

Wil stood to my left. "Good morning," he said, his raspy voice annoyingly sexy.

"Morning." I tried to smile, but it probably looked more pained than anything.

He leaned his muscular arms on the top of our partition and kept his voice low. "You didn't answer my texts last night."

I glanced at him. "I told you, I'm terrible at getting back to people."

"Norah," he said, then waited until I looked at him to continue. "I'm sorry about what I said in the deli. You're right. Just because I had a leg up in the business doesn't make me better, and it doesn't diminish your accomplishments. If you skipped half the steps I took and got to the same position I am, you're obviously good at what you do."

I paused. "Thank you," I responded, glancing away

from him. "And I'm…kind of sorry about what I said."

He smiled that brilliant smile I predicted no matter how angry I was with him, it would always melt me into a puddle.

"So, are you open for dinner?" he asked, hopeful.

"No." I met his perfect, clear blue eyes again. "Just because I apologized doesn't mean anything has changed." He straightened, and his shoulders slumped. "Everything I said may have been out of misplaced anger, but it doesn't make it any less true."

I swallowed, turning back to my computer, causing him to disappear out of my line of sight. The sound of his frustrated exhale collided with the creak of his chair as he sat. I clenched my jaw and tried to shoo away the self-created disappointment in my chest, reminding myself this separation between us was for the best.

Later that afternoon, Jerry called Wil and me into his office. I deliberately left a few minutes after Wil did so we could keep our distance. Still, his scent lingered on the pathway to Jerry's door, causing the immediate need to hold my breath.

When I sat, avoiding Wil's stare, Jerry folded his hands in front of him and leaned forward. "I assume you both read the articles I gave you."

"Yes," Wil and I answered in unison.

"Good. Do either of you have any notes?"

"Yes," we said again, then looked at each other. He smiled, and I turned away.

"Take it away." Jerry leaned back in his chair. "Whoever wants to go first."

Wil and I answered simultaneously. We both stopped and peered at each other. I spoke but got interrupted yet again.

I turned to Wil with annoyance. "Do you mind?"

He bit his lip and motioned with his hand to continue, then let it fall on his thigh. Seeing his irritation with this situation, too, comforted me.

"While I can see how the world has handed him accolades because of his ridiculously overpriced journalism degree," Wil looked in my direction, "it can't substitute for real-world writing experience. To be honest, I found his writing…a little soft."

"Soft?" Wil retorted.

I glanced at him. "Yes."

He leaned forward to invade my line of sight. "I'll let the comments about my education go for now. But I'd like to address the soft part. What about me is *soft*, Norah?"

Will made the word sound sensual, even though he didn't mean it that way. I looked at Jerry to see if he noticed. He sat still, watching me.

I cleared my throat. "You're all heart and no head." As soon as the words left my mouth, I cringed. Wil's lips curled into themselves to keep from laughing, and his eyebrows raised. I imagined he, too, flashed on a memory of either him or me giving that sexual act to one another. I continued anyway. "Telling facts about a subject isn't always a bad thing. You write like you're deliberately trying to make the reader cry."

"Yes, I write to create an emotional response." He shrugged. "What's wrong with that?"

"There's nothing wrong with it per se, but instead of using it to create a more complete story, you use it as a crutch."

"I beg your pardon," he said in surprise.

"You pull on heartstrings instead of delivering the

73

actual information."

"Ah, so I should be more like you," he said. The frustration in his tone was clear.

"What do you mean?"

"Your pieces deal with the person as if they're an inanimate object. You give no life to them, just a spreadsheet of facts with a few filler words. People aren't subjects, Norah. They're human beings with feelings. Feelings that I dig out to make them relatable. That's how I get the reader to care about what I write."

I clenched my jaw.

"Go on, Wil," Jerry said. "What did you think of Norah's writing?"

Wil glanced at me, then turned back to Jerry. "Frankly, I thought it was robotic."

"How?" Jerry asked calmly.

Wil leaned forward. "Her articles read like instructions. You could insert anyone in her pieces, and they would still read the same. The article about the governor of Oregon for example. She moved from prosecutor to mayor to governor. The data was there. I understood her history and how she got to where she was. But Abigail Sanders is the first woman governor elected in the state, and Norah glossed over it like it wasn't historic. There was minimal mention of her husband and four kids. How they lived their lives in the spotlight while doing what's best for the state. What kind of pressure that brings to her job or her family. There was no emotional connection to this woman whatsoever."

Wil looked at me and stopped talking for a moment. His eyes traveled down my face and back up. When he returned to my stare, his blue eyes went from warm ocean to ice. "She's got potential, but you're going to have to rip away that coldness to get to the emotional side of her." He leaned back in his chair. "Evidently."

A warmth rose from my feet to the top of my head. It wasn't anger—I was livid. He was going on the attack because I'd hurt his feelings? He had taken the work I was most proud of and tore it apart into little pieces, then threw it back in my face like confetti.

"And this is why I want the two of you to work together." Jerry raised his hands to the back of his head and leaned.

Wil and I turned to him.

His Cheshire Cat–like smile glowed. "You want to know what I think?" Jerry asked.

I answered, "Not really," while Wil said, "Of course."

"I think you two combined are the perfect writer. I agree Norah is mechanical—we've had several conversations about this."

I adjusted in my seat uncomfortably.

"And Wil, while I appreciate how you're invested in the emotional side, I think you lose sight of the whole story."

I couldn't help the smirk that inched on my face.

"This is a match made in Edward R. Murrow heaven. Work together, learn from each other. There's a happy balance here, and I'm confident the two of you will find it." Jerry leaned forward and set his hands on his desk. "Tomorrow, I'm sending you two to Memphis."

My palms broke out into a sweat.

"You're going to meet with Brad Wallace," Jerry said as he turned to his computer and typed.

"Who?" I asked.

"CEO of Roadmap," Wil answered.

"*Millionaire* CEO of Roadmap, Casinos Live, Friendly Followers, et cetera. Every popular app created within the last five years has been his. He's agreed to be featured in the tech section, and I want you both to do a profile on him." Jerry stood and came around the desk to the door, then casually rested against the knob. "Your tickets are in your emails. Be efficient, thorough, and do your research before you talk to him. Norah, go home and pack. Wil, hang out for a second."

I stood and exhaled, then walked to the door Jerry had opened. I stopped in front of Jerry and looked over my shoulder at Wil. His focus was on his phone.

"Hey," Jerry said in a hushed tone.

I pulled my eyes from Wil.

"Do your breathing exercises, take something if you need to—there's no shame in it," Jerry mumbled.

I nodded and swallowed hard.

"Call me when you land." Jerry's smile, blinding me with annoyance, returned.

I rolled my eyes and walked out the door towards my desk.

I wanted to focus on why Jerry wanted to talk to Wil and why he had kicked me out to do so.

But I couldn't.

The only thing I focused on was my panic and fear. It wasn't about meeting the millionaire CEO or doing this story with my adversary for the editor's job. It was my debilitating fear of flying.

Chapter Nine

Wil

I sat at the gate with my coffee, going through my news feed for the day. When I got through most of it, I put my phone away and people watched. The typical business crowd flowed through JFK. Families with excited children looked around as if there were nothing more interesting than the bright white halls of the terminal. I placed my ankle on my knee and sipped from my cardboard container. I scanned faces, waiting for the one who abhorred my company.

I had given up trying to talk to Norah about us. This was no longer about finding out if we were compatible. It was now about getting the woman to not seethe in my presence. The insults that flew from her in Jerry's office weren't warranted, and had she had basic knowledge concerning my background, she never would have concluded I was rich. I worked my ass off in high school to get a full ride to Cornell, because I never wanted my parents burdened with the cost of my education. Plus, I was one of three kids they had to feed. I learned fairly young that if I wanted something, I would have to get it myself.

Absentmindedly, I turned to my right and met her deep blue eyes as she stalked towards me, dragging a black roller suitcase and a computer bag resting on her shoulder. I couldn't help the smile that crossed my face when she came into full view. The woman was classic, even in light blue jeans and a white T-shirt. Her pouty, red lips didn't twitch when she saw me. They deepened in her scowl.

She exhaled as she put her things on the chair by me. "Good morning," she said. It wasn't low or monotone. She sounded normal, like she did the first night I met her.

"Mornin'," I answered.

She glanced at me, then went back to organizing her things on the seat. I couldn't tell for sure, but it looked like her hands were shaking. When she saw me observing, she squeezed them, then released. She took a long breath, but her face read she was trying hard to appear normal.

She pulled out her wallet. "I'll be right back." She walked away before I could respond.

I furrowed my brow as she dodged people to get to the airport bookstores. Something was off. Norah was usually confident and steady. Right then, she looked frazzled. It could have been having to be around me in a confined space for a few hours that annoyed her, but I couldn't tell for sure. I was interested in seeing what she brought back from the bookstore. If it were any kind of reading material, I would have my answer on whether we would converse during the flight.

I watched for her intently until she came into view. There was nothing in her hands but an opened bottle of water and her wallet.

Huh.

When she reached me again, she didn't talk or sit. She took a small sip and pulled out her phone, then slowly paced in front of me while scrolling. I continued to monitor her with interest.

"Did you see Congress voted on the Angel's Act?" I asked, hoping to get a conversation flowing.

"Mm-hmm." Her answer was quick.

"They're gonna have a hell of a time getting it passed in the Senate."

"Yep," she answered just as quickly.

I removed my ankle from my knee, then leaned forward, resting on my elbows. "The Yankees lost yesterday." I was trying my damnedest to find something that interested her. She didn't answer. Evidently baseball was off the table. "Are you a Knicks fan?" I smirked.

She exhaled forcefully. "No."

I was obviously getting on her nerves, but it was more than that. I could read it in her face. This wasn't about me.

"Are you alright?" I couldn't dance around whatever was happening anymore.

She stopped moving and looked at me. "Listen, I don't mean to be rude, but could you just stop talking for a while?" The anger I was used to getting from her had returned.

"Okay," I conceded, then rested back in my chair, still inspecting her face.

She nodded once and blinked a few times, taking another deep breath. She closed her eyes and paced again. The deep rise and fall of her chest told me she was trying to calm down. She was focusing on it, making it methodical. She was anxious.

The gate intercom came on overhead and made announcements about the flight. Norah's eyes snapped open, and she looked towards the counter. Every pigment of color drained from her face.

I stood and stepped in front of her, catching her eye. "You don't like to fly."

Her hand flew to her forehead. "Could you just not talk about it?" she asked, then walked around me.

It wasn't just that she didn't like to fly, she was deathly afraid of it.

I turned, then interrupted her stride again. "Hey, it's gonna be okay."

"Oh, gee, *you* think it's going to be okay? Yeah, thanks, that makes it better." She placed one hand on her hip and fanned herself with the other. "How long does it take for Xanax to kick in?" she said breathlessly, mostly to herself.

Although I had seen and experienced panic attacks in real time, I wasn't sure how to handle them with Norah. The process was different for everyone. While some people wanted interaction to help talk them down, others needed to be left alone. Norah seemed to be the latter.

When our rows were called, she stopped and closed her eyes again. She took a lengthy breath, then blew it all out. Pausing for a moment, she walked past me and picked up her things; the shaking of her hands had returned.

I stopped her by touching her hand and said, "I got it." I picked up her computer bag, purse, and carry-on, then grabbed my stuff. She merely nodded and walked towards the entrance to the jetway while I followed behind.

Norah immediately sat in her seat and stared out the window. I placed all of our luggage in the overhead bin, then sat, setting her purse and computer bag on the floor under the seats in front of us.

I stared at her profile while the other passengers boarded. She tried to regulate her breathing again as we backed away from the gate. I didn't like how uncomfortable she was and wanted to see if I could distract her somehow.

"You know," I began, "you don't have to come with me."

She looked at me, her eyes giving away her fear.

"I'm sure I'll be able to handle this all by myself."

She scoffed. "If you think I'm going to let you do this interview without me, you obviously haven't been paying attention." She watched out the window.

"I'm just saying, since you're not up to it—"

She turned to me again. "Excuse me?" she spat.

"I mean, hey, look, everyone has those irrational fears that they have to deal with—"

"Irrational?"

"And you're no different. It's okay."

The plane backed away from the jetway.

"Are you seriously being a condescending asshole right now?" The look on her face read annoyance instead of fear.

I smirked. "Not at all. But you know if we have to fly there, we have to fly back, and if you can't handle it…"

"Can't handle it? Listen, my teeny fear of flying has

not interfered with my job so far, and it's not about to start now."

The lights in the cabin went out as we approached the runway.

"There's no shame in admitting you can't go."

"I *can* go," she said belligerently.

"Okay, you were basically hyperventilating in the airport, but now you're under control?" I asked, drowning out the captain's announcement over the intercom as we prepared for takeoff.

"First, I was not hyperventilating, I was calming my breath, and there's a big damn difference. Second, you are already trying to literally screw me out of a job I earned. If you think I'm going to go running back into JFK because I get a little nervous about flying, you're ridiculous and need to get your money back from Cornell." Her voice was loud, but it was nothing over the engines.

Our backs deepened in the chair cushions as the force of our speed climbed.

"What do you have against Cornell?" I wanted to make sure this back-and-forth lasted until we were safely in the air.

"I have nothing against Cornell. I have something against the guy who thinks the degree entitles you to a job I've worked my ass off for."

"I earned that degree by working my ass off too. Who are you to say I'm not entitled to it?"

"Who are you to say that I'm not?" she retorted.

We stared at each other for a moment. Her color had returned to a warm tan, and her cheeks were rosy. Not from the anxiety but from our exchange. Her eyes were back to that brilliant shade of blue that first caught me off guard at the bar. My smile grew, and I raised my brows.

"What?" she spat.

I nodded towards the window. "Look."

She turned her head and gasped. She watched as the ground continued to fall below us. Her breathing was back to normal as the fasten seat belt light went off. We both looked up at the sign, no longer illuminated.

She stared at me. "Did you say all those things just to distract me?"

I shrugged. "Do you feel better?"

She continued to watch me, then barely nodded.

"Good, then it worked," I said as I reached under the seat to grab my bag. When I met her eyes again, I gave her a small smile and put on my glasses.

She removed her gaze from me and looked out the window again.

Eventually, Norah relaxed more and put in her earphones while working on her laptop. She glanced at me occasionally, and I gave her a supportive smile. Regardless of what she'd said, I cared about her enough to hate how afraid she was. If there was a way to remove that from her, even for just a moment, I would.

When we hit turbulence, her hand inadvertently landed on the armrest or my forearm. I'd take it in mine, feeling her soft fingers go rigid against my skin.

"Are we okay?" Her voice was soft but full of terror.

"We're fine. Just some quick air pockets," I assured her.

There was another bump, and she shut her eyes tight. "What did you and Jerry talk about in the office?" she asked as she squeezed my hand.

"He told me you were pigheaded, standoffish, and had a bad temper," I answered.

She looked at me with her eyebrows pulled together.

"And that you just happened to be one of the best self-taught journalists he's ever met. He's really proud of you."

She relaxed and tried to smile. "Was that it?"

"That was it," I responded.

That wasn't it. He'd also told me she had a tendency to fly off the hip in interviews. Sometimes it worked, sometimes it threw the whole piece off. If I saw she was veering a little too far left, he wanted me to rein her in to stay on track. Jerry thought Norah would have been better as an investigative journalist with the *Washington Post* or the *New York Times*. She, however, was determined to rise above her instincts and dedicate herself to the *Chronicle*.

Norah's reaction to landing was still tense but nothing compared to takeoff. When we were on the ground, she blew out a breath and shook out her arms to relieve the tightness. I stared at her.

"What?" she asked, her eyes bright from the adrenaline rush.

"Why are you afraid to fly?" I asked.

She gave a slight laugh. "I guess since I just squeezed all the blood out of your hand for the last four hours, I owe you an explanation why you might never write again."

I chuckled.

She leaned into me. "When I was ten, my sister and I went to see my grandparents in Oklahoma. It was the first time we'd ever been on a plane." She stopped talking and looked down. "One engine went out."

My eyes widened. "Holy shit."

"Yeah, everyone was pretty panicked. I just

remember looking at the flight attendants to tell us we were okay, but even they were nervous. We ended up having to land in Lawton. My grandpa had to drive an hour and a half to come get us. We were alone in a big airport with just each other. It was pretty terrifying."

I nodded. "Damn."

"I refused to get back on a plane when we had to go home to Texas. And I mean, I threw a huge tantrum in the middle of the airport."

"I don't blame you," I responded.

"Yeah, well, I'm sure there's a video on the internet somewhere. Feel free to use it as blackmail."

"Oh, I plan on it," I teased.

We laughed in unison.

She turned thoughtful for a moment. "It was just overall a very terrible experience." She looked away from me and collected her things.

I hated that she was terrified of anything but glad she gave me the chance to understand. I wanted to help take away her fear of flying. Her fear of anything.

After we grabbed our luggage and got a ride to the hotel, I asked if she wanted to get lunch, but she said she needed to lay down for a few hours. Because of her heightened anxiety, she was exhausted.

We were staying on the same floor, and our rooms were right across from each other. The noise in the hallway comprised of our footsteps and the wheels of our luggage against the carpet. When I glanced at her, she chewed her lip and kept her focus forward.

I stopped at my door without looking at her. She was still next to me when I put the keycard in. When I turned to her, her expression read she was having a hard time deciding something. I waited.

"What you did for me on the plane." She looked up at me. "Thank you," she whispered.

"You're welcome." I continued to watch her, wondering what she was thinking. Wondering if she wanted to kiss me as badly as I wanted to kiss her. I had no reason to think she felt differently than she had before we got on the plane. I was being absurd even having those thoughts.

I inserted the card again to open the door, dragging my bag with me.

"Wil?" she asked gently.

When I turned, she hadn't moved.

"Yeah?" I answered. Her full lips were parted, and her eyes had softened considerably.

She broke her gaze and shook her head. "Nothing." She turned and walked to her room, then slipped in the key and opened the door. Her movement stopped, and she looked at me.

For a moment, there was a silent communication between us as we peered at each other. Her hesitation to go in her room made me wonder if she was having issues with our distance too. I didn't comfort her on the plane to change her mind. I wanted to help. But if it made Norah rethink her hate for me, I would take it.

I lingered between the door and her until she went into her room. "Have a good nap," I called after her. She let the door close between us.

Chapter Ten

Norah

I stared at the ceiling as I lay on the hard mattress and freshly laundered white comforter. My anxiety from the flight was dissipating, and my nerves were no longer on edge, but thoughts of Wil had overcome my need to sleep.

His distraction on the plane was annoying, combative, and incredibly sweet. He could've let me deal with my nervousness on my own and looked at me like I was crazy or dramatic. But he didn't. Every bump I jumped at, he tried to comfort me. He held my hand in his, and I felt…better.

I rubbed my palm, trying to relieve a tingling sensation that had remained since then, as if my hand missed his touch and connection. I thought about those hands pulling me close to him on his couch in his living room. Touching every inch of my body, lighting me up with desire and wanting.

I sat up with irritation. That was not where we were anymore. Wil was my rival. The Cornell frat boy trying to steal my future. What he did before was kind, and I was appreciative, but we couldn't be anything more.

I decided a nap was a lost cause and pulled out my laptop. There were questions in my head for Brad Wallace I needed to get on paper before I forgot. This interview would need to be golden if I were going to get Jerry off my back and Wil away from me. I hoped I could convince Jerry my original idea was the correct one. If we could do a few pieces together and I played nice with Wil, Jerry could send us on separate assignments. I was in competition for a job with him. The last thing I needed was to be across the hall from him for months at a time.

A few hours later, there was a knock on my door. I got up and looked to see crystal blue eyes distorted through the peephole. I put my hand on the handle and opened it.

"Hi," Wil said, with his damn perfect teeth and delicious lips. "I was going to find someplace to eat for dinner. Did you wanna come?"

I hesitated. "I-I hadn't really thought about it."

He had just taken a shower. The soap's scent mingled with his natural fragrance. It gave me chills.

"It's just dinner, Norah." He smiled. "You gotta eat."

I continued to stare at him. His loose, dark blonde curls were still damp, giving him that purposely unfinished look. That, along with his unshaven face, which unintentionally made him even more handsome, was reason enough for me to forego dinner, but I couldn't deny how hungry I was.

"Okay," I answered. "Give me a second."

I turned, allowing the door to begin to close behind

me, when I heard him catch it and open it wider. "You're seriously not going to let me in?"

I whipped back around to him.

"You made it pretty clear what we are, Norah. I'm not going to throw myself at you." His sexy smirk made me wish he would.

I rolled my eyes. "Fine, come in."

His smile got wider as he stepped into the room. The heavy door latched loudly behind him. I went over to the bed and gathered my notes.

"How was your nap?" he asked.

I shuffled papers around, then looked at him. His black sweater clung to his muscular arms. I tried to ignore how enticing he was. "I couldn't sleep. I went over questions for Wallace tomorrow instead." I typed on my computer and saved my progress.

He stood on the other side of the bed in front of me. "Can I see?"

I stopped typing and met his eyes.

He crossed his arms over his chest when he saw my hesitation. "We're doing this interview together. Remember?"

I bit my bottom lip, still staring at him.

"C'mon. There's not much more of yours that I haven't seen." His mouth curled at one end while running his eyes down my body.

I swallowed. Not only was he flirting with me, but it was also working. I begrudgingly turned on my laptop and slid it across the comforter to him. He bent over the bed, and I watched his face as he read through my list of questions.

His eyebrows raised for a moment, then he nodded. "Hm," he said, surprised.

"What?"

He shook his head and looked at me. "Nothing. Those are...very important questions."

"But?" I pushed.

"I thought being more personal was the goal?"

I rolled my eyes. "Isn't that what you're here for? The personal shit?"

He smirked. "I'm here to help you be a better writer. That includes adding personal shit to *your* line of questioning. What do you know about his family?"

"He has two kids—"

"Adopted," he interrupted.

"Right."

"Why?"

I paused. "Why what?"

"Why did he adopt them?"

I shrugged. "I don't know."

"You should. What else?"

I narrowed my eyes at him. "His wife is a pediatric oncologist and works for St. Jude."

"Those are the things you can bring up," he said while briefly pointing at me. "Find out why he adopted those two girls. And why does his wife work at a pro bono hospital when she could make well into six figures at a private hospital?"

"Is that what you were going to ask?"

"That's part of it."

I put my hands on my hips and exhaled.

"Why does this make you so uncomfortable?" he asked.

I shifted my stance. "It doesn't make me uncomfortable." *The way you stare at me makes me uncomfortable.*

A moment passed while we watched each other. His eyes bore into mine. My heartbeat picked up the longer he stared, painfully aware there was a bed between us—I had to look away.

Wil took a breath. "We can talk about the rest over dinner." He walked towards the door.

I didn't realize my body was stiff until I watched him leave, suddenly disappointed he wanted to go anywhere.

"WHY DID YOU want to be a writer?" Wil asked, wiping his barbeque-soaked fingers on the paper napkin. He had inhaled half of a slab of ribs mere minutes after the server set them in front of him.

"Because I wanted to tell a story," I answered, then ate a small bit of potato salad.

"About what?"

I looked at him and laughed.

He flickered his eyes to his left. "What?"

I pointed my fork at him. "You have sauce on your nose."

He stopped chewing as his cheeks darkened with embarrassment. He smiled as he grabbed his napkin and wiped his nose.

I hated how cute he was.

"Well?" He put his napkin down and waited.

I sighed. "I wanted to write about life."

"Life that happens to other people?"

I scoffed. "I certainly didn't want to tell everyone about mine." I regretted the words as soon as they left me.

"What's the matter with your story?" His tone turned concerned.

The Opposite of Fiction

I moved the food on my plate around with my fork. "It's like everyone else's. I grew up poor and escaped my feeble surroundings to make it in the big city. It's the quintessential bad movie plot."

He leaned his elbows on the table and intertwined his fingers, watching me. "Tell me more."

"No." I shook my head.

He laughed once and shook his head too.

"*You* tell *me* more," I said. "Why did you want to be a writer?"

His stare was intense and smoldering. My lips parted, and I took in an unexpected breath, but I didn't give anything else away. I kept reminding myself that this, *us*, was over.

He took a deep breath. "I was the kid that made things up at eight years old, then told them to my younger siblings as bedtime stories. And at fourteen, I wrote my first coming-of-age novel."

I looked at him doubtfully. "You wrote a novel at fourteen?"

"It was more of a novella." He shrugged.

I chuckled. "What was it about?"

"Amanda Klein," he said, then sighed.

I smiled at the look on his face. "Who's Amanda Klein?"

"My first crush…first kiss…first under the shirt action." He winked at me, then took a sip of his beer.

"Oh my god," I said, laughing.

"It was a love story."

"Was there sex?" I raised my left eyebrow. He looked horrified. "What? It's not romance without sex."

His full smile spread. "No sex."

"Too bad." I leaned back in my chair.

"I didn't have any sexual experience at fourteen. What was I gonna say? His wee-wee went into her hoo-hoo?"

I leaned forward and laughed hard, covering my mouth with my napkin. Wil watched me, then looked away, smiling and shaking his head.

"Did they live happily ever after?" I asked, wiping a tear from my eye.

"In the book, yes." He ran his finger on the rim of his glass, tipping it back and forth slightly. "She broke up with me to date a football player. So, I guess you can call her my first heartbreak too." He looked down.

His face went from playful to serious for just a moment. Like he flashed back to that time when Amanda Klein had pummeled his heart in two. The pain from the thought, although momentary, was evident in his entire demeanor. I didn't like it.

He smiled to himself, then looked at me. "Your turn."

His stupid confession did something to me. It made me want to share too. "I started writing for my high school newspaper when I was a freshman and was the editor by my senior year."

He paused and leaned forward. "Tell me more."

"Like what?"

"How did it make you feel?" He leaned his stubbled face on his palm.

"Obviously good or I wouldn't have continued," I answered, not only defensively but sarcastically as well.

Wil gave me an expectant look.

I rolled my eyes. "It made me feel special. I wrote things people could relate to. Kids would stop me in the halls, popular kids, and talk about what I had written." I paused. "I started a column called 'Norah's Nuances of Being a Teenage Girl.'"

"Did you?" He smiled.

I nodded and smiled back. "I mean, it was just ramblings about stupid adolescent bullshit. Like, why girls feel like they need to wear makeup, and why talking about your period in front of guys makes them uncomfortable." I looked at my hands while I played with my fingernails. "But it was mine, and I was good at it."

"So, you *can* be personal?"

My face fell. My mind flashed back to the first time I showed my mom my column. "It was a long time ago."

I felt his stare from across the table. "What changed?" he asked.

I met his eyes. "What?"

"How did you go from being able to write about emotions and feelings to barely mentioning them?" The air between us had shifted. He'd read my face and matched it with his tone.

I vacillated on whether to tell him. "Someone once told me that kind of vulnerability was weak."

His face read his confusion. "Who?"

I shook my head. "Doesn't matter."

The night I'd shown her, she'd berated me about wasting my time with the paper. That my writing was garbage, that *I* was garbage.

I stared at the plate in front of me for longer than I expected, replaying the memories of the many times my mom said I wasn't good enough. As I got older, I learned the way she treated me wasn't about me at all—it was about her. She wasn't good enough, and she didn't want me to be either.

I glanced at Wil and took a deep breath. His eyebrows furrowed as he watched me closely. "Sorry," I said as I picked up my fork and moved my food around again.

"Don't be sorry." His voice was low and protective. It made me feel safe while revisiting a time where I felt anything but.

I needed to divert the conversation away from my mother and Texas life. I had moved on. I couldn't dwell in the past, there was too much to think about in the present.

Wil continued to stare at me with unasked questions he wanted answers to. I pleaded with my eyes to let go of whatever inquiries lingered on his beautiful face. He leaned back as a sign of retreat.

"Tell me more about why you moved from LA to New York," I said and took another bite of food.

Wil grimaced. "What did you want to know?"

I read his expression and hesitated. "If you don't want to talk about it—"

"No, it's fine," he said, chuckling with no amusement. But he didn't fool me. Obviously, this subject was his sensitive spot.

"What did she do?" I couldn't help but ask.

"Besides rip my heart out of my chest and grind it up like ground beef?" His smart-ass grin emerged.

I raised my eyebrows in surprise.

He laughed once through his nose. "She cheated on me."

"Someone cheated on you?" I asked in disbelief.

He smiled. "Elise, yeah."

Wil was gorgeous and intelligent. One of the last true gentlemen on the planet, and this woman, whoever she was, was dumb enough to cheat? I was flabbergasted.

"I'm really sorry," I offered, still amazed.

He shrugged it off, then paused. "Have you ever been cheated on?"

I sighed softly. "No. But I've also never had what you would consider a boyfriend to cheat on me with. So…"

"Never?" he asked, surprised.

"Nope."

"Why?"

I shrugged. "I've always been focused on the magazine."

Wil watched me for at least thirty seconds, wavering on something he wanted to ask. "You really want this job, don't you?"

"It's what I've been working towards my whole life." *It's all I have*, I thought. I couldn't meet his eyes with that amount of truth.

He nodded slowly and looked away, rubbing his hand against the back of his neck.

I leaned forward and pushed away what remained on my plate. "We should talk about tomorrow, with Wallace."

He nodded once. "Okay."

Chapter Eleven

Wil

Norah wrapped her sweater around her and crossed her arms over her chest as we walked back to the hotel. The chill coming off the Mississippi made the humid air colder, causing her to shiver. I wished I had a jacket to offer her. She was quiet as we walked and seemed to be deep in thought. She held the same look she had at dinner when I got a brief glimpse into her past.

"Can I ask you a question?" she asked, staring straight ahead.

I shrugged. "Sure."

"What's your family like?" Her voice was barely above a whisper.

I put my hands in my jeans pockets to warm them up and laughed. "How much time have you got?"

She smiled but didn't respond, keeping her eyes on the sidewalk in front of her.

"I'm the oldest of three." I eyed her when she

glanced at me. "Melanie is three years younger. Devin is two years behind her."

"Where are your parents?" she asked.

"Orange County."

She looked at me. "Where in Orange County?"

I chuckled. "Are you trying to ask me how close they live to Disneyland?"

She hesitated, then let her smile grow. "Yes."

I laughed. "Why? Do you want to go?"

"I mean, I've never been."

"Tell you what. Stop calling me a Cornell frat boy and I may take you."

She laughed again and walked ahead of me, her hair blowing in the breeze. A hint of whatever sweet scent she wore hit me and threw me back to the first night she came over. How her fragrance lingered on my sheets for days after she left.

"Are you close?" she asked, interrupting my thoughts of her underneath me.

I cleared my throat. "Yeah, pretty close."

"Does everyone still live in California?"

I caught up to her. "My sister and I left. Melanie's a lawyer in DC."

"Your brother?" she asked.

"Devin still lives at home, trying to get his life together." She looked at me, and I met her eyes. "He's recovering," I answered.

Her mouth hung. "Wow, I'm… I'm sorry."

"Don't be." I shrugged. "It's been rough, but he's better. Every day's a step."

She hesitated, then said, "Jerry's twelve years sober."

I looked at her profile. "Our boss?"

She nodded. "My uncle."

I stopped moving. "What?"

She turned to me and placed her hand in her hair, messing it against her scalp gently, then smoothing it out. "My father's brother. That's how I got in the door with the magazine."

I continued to watch her, shocked. "Why didn't you tell me?"

"I mean, it's not really a big deal." Her defenses came up. "But I started in the mailroom and worked my ass off to get to where I am."

I smirked. "I'm quite certain you did."

"I mean, I don't want you to think because we're related, he just handed me this job. As a matter of fact, Jerry was harder on me than anyone else on the floor."

I nodded. "I could see that."

"I might not have a degree in journalism, but the experience is really what matters." She sounded like she was convincing herself more than me.

I walked closer to her. Her deep blue eyes watched me carefully, but she didn't move.

"You're a talented writer, Norah," I said. "And I'm glad Jerry gave you the chance to prove it."

Her hair blew into her face, causing me to step forward, then run my finger across her forehead to collect it and tuck it behind her ear. Being this close to her made it impossible not to touch her. We held each other's gaze as I cupped her cool cheek with my hand. She leaned into it, taking a long blink and exhaling. I continued to keep this small connection until she inhaled sharply, suddenly realizing our proximity. Before moving back, she met my eyes with confusion. When she turned, my shoulders slumped as I watched her walk away.

We entered the hotel and wordlessly moved to the

elevators. I watched Norah and waited. I wanted some sort of sign from her telling me she knew there was no reason to hate each other. Yes, we had the same goal, but that didn't mean anything between us had changed. There was a pull there, something more than what happened for those two nights. I felt it, and I was sure she did too.

The long walk down the hallway was irritatingly silent. When we got between our doors, she turned away from me.

"Norah," I said breathlessly.

Her shoulders rose and fell. Then she slowly turned to me, and all traces of her hostility were gone. Her cheeks and the tip of her nose were pink from the cool air outside, and the waves in her hair were fading and a little disheveled. But she'd never looked more striking.

I couldn't resist her anymore. I walked towards her and stopped when our chests touched. My hand found the back of her neck, and her soft hair fell between my fingers. I needed to kiss her, feel her mouth against mine. It had been killing me for days, not touching or tasting her.

I leaned forward and continued to watch her for resistance. Something telling me to stop. The heat from her breath hit my face, and she closed her eyes, leaning forward. I smiled with relief, then collided with her.

The sweet taste of tea and lemon on her tongue caused me to deepen the kiss. Wrapping her arms around my neck, she hugged her body to me, and I could feel every curve through her T-shirt and jeans. My need for her grew by the second. But even while we were entrenched in each other, I could sense her hesitation as her lips slowed. I wouldn't force her into anything, but I needed to know if she would wake up with me in the morning.

She slowed and pulled back, watching me. The indecision in her eyes was apparent and heartbreaking. I wanted her. I'd never stopped wanting her, but her resolve wouldn't allow her to share that same feeling—I could read it on her face. This usually decisive and stubborn woman was lost with what to do.

With my breath heavy, I leaned my head against hers. "Go in your room, Norah," I whispered.

She leaned away, confused.

"Go in your room," I repeated, "or I'm going to pull you into mine."

The air left her lungs, and she searched for the words but didn't allow them to come out. She looked down and squeezed her eyes shut, trying to find the answer she wanted. When she decided, she locked eyes with me, then brought her hand to the back of my neck and drew me into a kiss. It turned voracious and wanting. Something I had prayed for since the last time we were together. She broke our kiss urgently and turned around, unlocking the door with speed. When the lock beeped, she turned to me again and dragged me into her room by my hand.

She threw everything on the floor and undressed me, and I her, while the room remained dark. We kissed between her shirt coming off and my pants falling to the floor. My hands and lips went everywhere on her. Her neck, her chest, wherever she'd let me go. When we were naked, she stopped touching me and moved backwards. The light from the streetlamps outside was the only thing allowing me to see her outline.

"This doesn't mean anything," she whispered. "And when this is over, promise you'll go back to your room."

The Opposite of Fiction

I couldn't read her expression or tell if she was joking or being serious. The breathlessness in her voice held no inflection. When I didn't answer, she came to me again, and our naked bodies touched. The heat emanating from her chest was like a warm flannel blanket during a December night in Alaska. She wrapped her arms around my neck and gently kissed me again.

I should have stopped her. Stopped us. I didn't want to leave after it was over. I wanted to stay the night with her, convince her that maybe there was still a chance for us. But feeling her against me, the smoothness of her skin, the curve of her beautiful body, wouldn't allow me to stop wanting her. My will caved, and I knew I would do anything she asked of me.

I picked her up, and she wrapped her legs around me. I started to walk to the bed when she pulled away.

"Get that chair from the desk," she commanded. I set her down and did as I was told.

I brought the heavy wooden chair near the bed, wondering what her plan was. She went to her bag and took something out that crinkled.

"Sit," she said from across the room. Again, I complied.

She sauntered to me, then stood against the light of the window. I couldn't see her face, only the shape of her stunning body. She leaned over me and met my mouth with hers. She reached down and took me in her hand, caressing me, making sure I was hard. It didn't take long.

She then broke our kiss and kneeled down, taking me into her mouth, I gasped, then moaned just as fast. One hand assisted her in her venture, the other was on my thigh holding a condom with the wrapper scratching against my skin, but I couldn't care less. It could have cut me into shreds as she took me in deeper, and I wouldn't have noticed.

While I loved she was so willing to do this, I didn't want our time wasted on just me. I needed to feel her against me and wanted her moans heard in the next room. I loved the sound of her orgasms and how she called my name, as if I were the only man in the world who could make her feel that way.

I stopped her as soon as that sound she produced returned to my memory. I had to have it. It had become my heroin hit, and I was long overdue.

I pulled her up and grabbed the condom from her hand, opening it with my teeth and rolling it on. I made sure she felt my fullness as soon as she sat on my lap. She inhaled sharply and met my mouth with hers. Her bare feet against the floor helped her movement while her hands clung to the back of the chair for leverage. I grabbed her ass and moved her back and forth to make sure I hit her clit in the right spot. The warmth we created together filled me completely, and I didn't want it to stop. Ever.

Norah gave me everything I wanted. Every groan told me this wasn't a mistake. Every time she met my eyes with her animalistic stare, I knew she felt something for me too. This was not casual or temporary. There was something more between us. Something stronger.

She flung her head back as the intensity climbed. She tightened around me, causing an ecstasy I couldn't hold back much longer. Her breasts shook, along with her legs, as the full-throated cries of her orgasm hit their peak. It was all I needed to climax with her.

I kept my rhythm going while she had temporary paralysis in her entire body. Watching her continue to come was fucking delicious. I wanted to savor it for as long as I could and continued to move her to prolong it for as long as she needed.

When her body was back under her control, she rolled forward against me, her aftershocks still pulsating. I wrapped my arms around her and hugged her close, kissing along her collarbone. Her breath was uneven as she inhaled fully. She leaned her head to the side, resting it against my shoulder. A tear fell onto my skin.

"Did I hurt you?" I whispered against her neck.

She sniffed and shook her head, then leaned back and looked at me. Her fingers traced my cheek, then my lips. We gazed at each other until I couldn't help but kiss her. Before our lips connected, she pushed back from me.

She sniffed again. "You should probably go."

I hesitated, making sure I heard what she said correctly. "What?"

"Wil, please," she breathed and laid her forehead against mine.

I exhaled, frustrated. "This isn't fair," I whispered. A hollowness in my chest expanded. I didn't want to leave her. As much as my body wanted Norah, I also wanted her to stop being afraid to enjoy this, to enjoy us. See what we could be together.

She closed her eyes and kissed me softly, then got up and went to the bathroom, closing the door behind her.

Chapter Twelve

Wil

I tossed most of the night, both from wanting the woman across the hall and preparing for the interview with Wallace. I tried to muster enough courage to knock on Norah's door to tell her this separation was bullshit, but fear and pride stopped me. I had to convince myself our encounter was just a moment of weakness on both our parts. While I was losing sleep about it, she probably thought it was nothing. She was the one who dismissed everything that happened between us. There was no reason for me to think sex would change anything.

When morning finally came, I wanted to take advantage of the continental breakfast on the first floor of the hotel. I stepped out of my room and stared at the door across the hall. I wanted to knock but decided against it. It was still early, and I didn't want to wake her. Or I didn't want to face her just yet, knowing we would have to talk about last night and the likelihood of being rejected again.

The smell of bacon, sausage, maple syrup, and coffee invaded my nose before I stepped out of the elevator. I turned the corner and scanned the area, stopping on the back of a head with platinum highlights. Her knee was pulled up next to her chest, and her laptop was open. She diligently typed away and ignored the plate of food next to her. I smiled. How naïve of me to think she wouldn't be up.

I walked towards the buffet, trying to think of what to say to the woman who equally excited and confused me. I kept peeking over my shoulder at her, seeing if she'd spotted me yet. She remained entrenched on the screen in front of her and leaned closer as she analyzed what she wrote, oblivious to everything else around her.

I stepped on the back of someone's heel in front of me, not watching where I was going.

"What the hell?" the woman shouted and turned around quickly.

I came face-to-face with a brunette in yoga pants and a cut-off T-shirt.

"I'm so sorry," I said to her.

She looked at me and smirked. "You're forgiven." She ran her emerald eyes down and back up my body curiously.

She was petite and athletic. Beautiful, really. The kind of woman I would typically give my full attention to. But the angry blonde sitting by herself at a table on the other side of the room was where my focus resided.

"I'm Morgan," she said and extended her hand.

"Wil," I answered and took it.

"Where are *you* from, Wil?" she purred.

"New York. You?" I didn't care, I was just being

polite.

"Tampa." She came closer, and I stepped back. Not only to grab a plate but also to escape her proximity.

When I returned to Morgan, a good twelve inches farther than I was before, I glanced over at Norah, who was watching my new acquaintance with interest. When I caught her attention, she looked at her screen again swiftly, taking a deep breath.

I turned back to Morgan and smiled. "It was nice to meet you. I'm gonna grab some breakfast."

She lingered by me. "Are you eating alone?"

I paused, unsure of what to do. "My…associate is over there." I pointed towards Norah. "I'll probably sit with her."

"Mind if I join you?" she asked.

"Uh, we have a big day ahead. It's going to be a lot of shop talk. I wouldn't want to bore you."

She moved closer and lowered her voice seductively. "I don't mind."

Subtlety was not working. "We're journalists, doing a big story about a local celebrity. Unfortunately, it's something we have to talk about privately." I kept my eyes on hers to make sure she understood this was the end of the conversation.

She opened her mouth to say something else, then closed it and smiled. "Alright. What about later?"

"Thanks, Morgan, but it's gonna be one of those days. I'm sorry."

"Well, I'm in room 424 if you change your mind. I'll be here for a few days. You should come visit." She eyed me and walked away without waiting for my response, to which I had none.

I focused my attention on Norah again. She typed

with the food beside her, still intact and probably cold by now. After I filled my plate, I walked over to her table, pulled out a chair, and sat.

"Mornin'," I said.

"Good morning." She didn't look up.

"You know you're wasting food."

She met my eyes and glanced at the plate.

I smirked at her. "Do you want me to go reheat it?"

She started typing again. "No, thank you." She was back to being tense and distant.

I stared at her, trying to get her attention.

She took a deep breath.

"Everything okay?" I asked, twirling the fork in my hand.

"Yep." Her tone said otherwise.

I lowered my voice. "Do you want to talk about last night?"

She brought her eyes to mine, then softened. "I don't think there's much to talk about. Besides," she picked up her coffee, "I don't want to get in the middle of your fan club," she mumbled as she took a sip.

I jerked my head back. "What does that mean?"

She didn't answer as she set her mug down and leaned back in her chair.

"Are you talking about just now?" I pointed to where Morgan and I were standing.

Her tongue found the upper side of her teeth in irritation. She was mad about Morgan? I tried not to smile. Jealousy. Now we were getting somewhere.

"She wanted to join me—us—for breakfast," I defended.

"So why didn't you let her?"

I paused. "I didn't think it would be appropriate

108

given our situation."

She moved forward and focused on her screen again. "I don't care what you do."

My pride took some time to recover. "Is that right?" I asked flatly.

She shrugged and continued to type.

I scoffed and stood, grabbing my plate. I began to walk away but stopped next to her, staring down at the top of her head. "I almost believe you."

She looked up and watched me move past her.

Chapter Thirteen

Norah

I'm such a bitch.

I closed my eyes and exhaled. I was being exceedingly unfair, and I knew it. I told Wil we couldn't happen and that our nights together were over. But then I had a moment of weakness. A passing lapse in judgment I would never make again. He was just so close to me, with those hypnotic blue eyes and that masculine, clean scent that still lingered on my clothes this morning. I caved because, for a moment, I wanted to touch him and have him touch me. And when he did, it wasn't enough—I needed to be with him.

It was stupid and dangerous.

I was in so much disarray, I even left my room in the middle of the night to knock on his door. But I couldn't. I was being a hypocrite. I couldn't continue to lead him on. It wasn't right or fair to either of us.

But this morning, my internal temperature rose with every moment he stood in front of her. Watching him with another woman burned me, and every bat of her fake eyelashes fanned my irritation. I wanted to stake a claim, run over there and tell her she wasn't wanted nor invited to talk to Wil. Until reality struck me to my core. Wil wasn't mine. I had no right to interfere, and that bothered me more than anything.

I couldn't keep letting my guard down. Wanting to be with someone who might take the job I've always wanted from me was already soul-crushing enough—I couldn't add to it.

I stood and emptied my plate into the trash. We had only an hour and a half before the interview with Brad Wallace. I needed to apologize to Wil, then shower. We couldn't go into this angry with each other. As much as I hated to admit he was right, we needed to do well on this piece, so Jerry could see I could work with Wil, be a team player of sorts.

I got in the elevator, pressed four on the panel, and leaned against the back of the car. I thought about what I would say to Wil in my head. I had to be honest and sincere. Wil had only been in my life a short time, but he could smell bullshit a mile away. Vulnerability wasn't usually my thing, but with him, it had to be. Whether or not I liked it, we had to work together.

When the elevator doors opened. I heard a high shrill of laughter coming from the hall. I walked out, turned the corner, and stopped moving.

Wil and the girl from downstairs were standing in front of each other. She had her hand on his chest while he leaned his back against his door, smiling. I thought about turning around and going back downstairs, but I couldn't get my feet to move. I needed the shock to wear off quicker so I could push aside this frustration to be the bigger person. The anger that echoed through my body was pointless.

Grow up, Norah. He's not yours.

I closed my eyes for a moment, gathering the strength I needed to get through this, then walked forward. I met Wil's stare the closer I got to him and his devotee. He straightened, watching me, and she turned in my direction, following his stare. I reached where they stood and stopped, trying to fake a smile properly.

"Hi," I said to the dark brunette with fake boobs and short, stubby legs.

Be nice.

I reached out my hand. "I'm Norah. I work with Wil."

"Morgan," she replied and laid her petite fingers in my palm.

I stuffed my hands in my hoodie's pocket and met Wil's confused stare. I gave him a half-hearted smile. "Um, I'm gonna take a shower." I pointed at the door behind me. "I'll meet you downstairs in an hour?" I kept my voice even. I couldn't invoke cheerfulness, but at least I didn't sound pissed.

Wil gaped at me with his brows furrowed, then nodded. "Okay."

I nodded back and turned to Morgan. "It was nice meeting you," I lied, then turned and went into my room.

Before the door closed, I locked eyes with Wil for a moment, then severed the connection with the sound of the catching latch.

I WAS DOWNSTAIRS in the lobby an hour later. My laptop sat by my side in a purple computer bag Jerry had bought me for my birthday. It was old and tattered, but it was something I treasured. He repeatedly said he would buy me a new one, but I didn't want it. I wouldn't replace this one until it had a hole so big the computer would fall out, and not a moment sooner. It was the first thing Jerry ever gave me as a reporter, and I loved it.

I scrolled through my phone, waiting for Wil. My imagination had run wild since meeting his groupie. I wondered if he had spent time with her while getting ready. Would she walk down with him to say goodbye? Had they made a date for later? These torturous questions continued to play in my head as someone stood beside me.

"Hey," I heard above me.

I looked up at him and straightened in the love seat. "Hey," I answered, surprised.

The dark blue button-down shirt accentuated his bright eyes, and his black jeans molded against his body. He wore his glasses and a mouthwatering sandalwood cologne. He took his laptop bag off his shoulder and sat across from me on an identical couch. He leaned forward with his elbows on his knees and clasped his hands together.

He took a breath. "Listen. Morgan and I—"

"No," I interrupted and put up my hand. "Really… it's none of my business. You don't have to explain anything. And…I'm sorry for what I said this morning. I had no right."

He watched me and tilted his head. Those impeccable lips separated.

I exhaled. "Um, was there anything we needed to go over before we leave? Anything that you… Anything?"

He looked away. A gambit of emotions crossed his

face, as though I had thrown him a curveball he'd never seen before and didn't know how to swing at it.

After a few moments passed, he finally spoke, still not looking at me. "I think we covered everything. You have good questions, and we'll just feed off each other."

I nodded. "Okay."

He locked eyes with me again. "Norah…"

"Wil." I tried to smile. "It's okay."

I stood and grabbed the strap of my bag, picking it up. "I ordered a car. It should be outside by now."

He looked up at me, then twisted his mouth in defeat. He grabbed his bag, then stood. His six-foot frame was tense, but he nodded, placing his shoulder strap across his body.

I turned away and started towards the hotel entrance, feeling him a foot behind me the entire time.

WIL AND I walked into the office space that held Brad Wallace's empire. It wasn't extravagant or auspicious. Very humble and minimal, to say the least. The receptionist greeted us and got on the phone right away to announce our arrival.

Wil had said nothing during the car ride. He just watched downtown Memphis pass outside his window while I'd focused on the task at hand. I had added additional questions to ask Wallace after I showed them to Wil, and I tried to put them to memory during the drive.

A gentleman in a long-sleeved denim shirt, black jeans, and white Nike's came out of the glass doors. He was handsome, redheaded, bearded, and athletic.

"Wil, Norah." He reached out his hand. "Brad

114

Wallace. How are you?"

"Brad, pleasure," Wil answered.

"Hi," I said as I took his hand.

"Come on back." He held open the door for both of us to walk through, then sprinted ahead of us to lead us down the corridor.

The walls had black-and-white framed posters of Martin Luther King, Jr., Steve Jobs, Oprah Winfrey, Bill Gates, Barack Obama, and Malala Yousafzai.

"I call this the Game Changer Hall. It's a daily reminder of what we all should strive to be in this building and in life," Brad said as he reached another glass double door and pushed it open.

On the other side, the rumblings of an office were working. I scanned the area, finding every employee to be at least five years younger than Wil or even myself. There were dogs under desks on beds, sleeping peacefully while their parents worked away. Against the farthest wall were full-sized arcade games—*Pac-Man*, *Galaga*, and *Donkey Kong*. I looked around for a ping-pong table but was disappointed.

Brad led us into a conference room with floor-to-ceiling windows overlooking the Mississippi. The table was a strange, nonspecific shape. Not a rectangle or a circle, something in-between. The chairs were multicolored and lingered around the room. The wall on the side of us read words like *Productive*, *Be Kind*, *Ideas*, *Smart Risks* in huge, black-and-white print.

Brad grabbed three chairs and arranged them so that we sat in a circle. None of us at the head.

I pulled mine out and sat. Wil and Brad did the same.

"Pretty original space you got here," I mused.

Brad smiled. "What fun is it if you don't love what

you do *and* where you work?"

"It looks like everyone is out in the open, no offices?" Wil asked.

"Nope. I believe in equal footing. I'm the CEO, but I'm no better than any of my people. They're way more important than I am. Without them, I don't succeed," Brad stated.

Wil took out a notebook while I grabbed my laptop and opened it. "Mind if I record this?" I asked.

Brad shrugged. "Of course."

Once we were settled, Wil and I looked at each other. I nodded and pressed record on my computer.

"Thank you so much for meeting with us, Brad," Wil began.

"No problem. I've had a good relationship with Jerry for a few years now. I'm happy to be a part of the magazine's big year."

"We'll just jump in," Wil said and uncapped his pen. "We're focusing on innovators and people who have made a difference, either in politics, business, or their community. You've made quite a name for yourself in the gaming industry but more with some very personal moves." He looked down at his notes. "You've partnered with *Bridge* in Uganda and Kenya and have helped built public schools."

"There's no reason a child shouldn't be given a fair shot in life because of things that are out of their control. I grew up poor in Nebraska and was given a chance to do amazing things, because I had a mentor who paid for my college and made sure I had a path to success. I'm just paying that forward."

"Your wife seems to live by those rules too. She's a pediatric oncologist at St. Jude?" I asked.

He came forward in his chair and rested his arms on the table, his face full of adoration. "Sasha is very much invested in helping others. She's one of the most amazing women I've ever met. The work she does with St. Jude just blows me away."

I continued, "I heard she doesn't take much of a salary at the hospital, is that correct?"

"Yes, she has a very modest salary because she wants the money to go to kid's care. She does it because she loves it, not for the paycheck."

"Plus, it's not like you're struggling." I smirked at him playfully.

He smiled. "Right."

"I wonder how she feels about the lawsuit against your company at present," I pondered.

He sat back. "I beg your pardon?"

"Michelle Wheatly has filed a complaint against you and the company for paying women significantly less for doing the same work as men. She claims she brought this to your attention a while ago, and you refused to do anything about it."

Wil leaned towards me. "Norah."

I glanced at him. "Just a moment." I returned my attention to Brad. "I just wondered how your wife reacted to knowing your company is fine with unequal pay between the sexes."

Wil moved away from me. "Brad, I'm sorry. Would you excuse us for a moment?" Wil stood while glaring at me, then walked to the door and waited.

I turned back to Wallace. "Excuse me."

Brad's eyes were wide and stunned.

I got up and walked through the door that Wil held open for me. He eased me by my arm, out of Brad's sight.

"What the hell are you doing?" His tone was heated.

"An interview?" I questioned, annoyed.

He came closer. "Norah, he didn't vet that question."

"It's national news, Wil. I'm not springing anything on him."

He leaned closer so he wouldn't raise his voice. "This isn't a gotcha piece, it's a fluff story for the anniversary issue. We're not the *New York Times*. We're not trying to *get him*."

"This *is* part of his story, part of his company. Don't you think people should know about this?"

"Like you said, it's a national story, those who want to know already do."

"I'm just trying to get something on the record about the lawsuit. He doesn't have to answer it."

"If he doesn't, you'll say he *won't* answer it, which makes him look guilty."

My voice rose. "That's his choice." We both looked around to make sure no one heard us.

Wil stared at me, then exhaled. "Norah, you're going to go in there, apologize, and we're going to try to pick up the pieces so he doesn't throw us out."

"You know, you're not my boss," I said defensively.

He lingered over me. "No, but maybe we should call your boss and see if he approves of this line of questioning. Shall we?"

That was the last straw. "Oh, so you're going to tell Daddy on me now? Need I remind you, I've been working at the magazine for a decade. I take the lead on stories, not you. I'm the senior writer here." The venom in my voice was clear.

"Then fucking act like it," he spat back and walked towards the door to the conference room. He opened it without waiting for me.

I stood there for a moment with my mouth ajar and my anger ablaze. I followed Wil back into the room and glowered at the back of his head.

"Brad, I'm sorry about that," Wil said as he sat down. He was still vexed. "I hope you can forgive my colleague. She didn't mean to offend you." He watched me as a warning.

I sat and glared at Wil, then turned to Brad and cleared my throat. "Forgive me, Mr. Wallace. I didn't mean any harm."

"It's Brad. And your question is perfectly legitimate." There was amusement in his features, as if this interaction was actually funny to him.

Wil and I both stopped moving. "It is?" I asked.

"Yes. I'm afraid this next part has to be off the record."

I hit stop on the computer.

He took a breath. "Michelle and I were together before I met Sasha. When she realized we were over, she threw all kinds of claims my way just to hurt me. But amid the chaos, she found something that wasn't kosher, even to me. Women were being paid less compared to their male counterparts. Although I'm not thrilled about how the lawsuit was presented, I was glad she brought it to my attention." He tapped on the top of my computer. "You can go back on the record."

I hit record again.

He smiled. "I was going to announce this next week, but I have no problem giving you the exclusive. We're in the process of matching pay scales so that everyone is paid what they should be, according to their titles."

I stared at him with my mouth opened. "So, you

settled the lawsuit?"

"Yes. Just yesterday. I presented the plan to the judge and have agreed to pay Michelle back pay for her years here."

"That's...amazing," I replied.

"It's the least I can do." He scratched his beard. "I hope I can lead the way so that other CEOs will follow."

I smiled. "As a woman, thank you for doing so and for trusting me with the story."

He smiled back and nodded once. "Thank you for holding me accountable."

I took a deep breath in for nothing else than relief. "We'll obviously release this part online sooner than the anniversary issue. Probably tomorrow."

He shook his head slightly. "That's not a problem. I plan on telling my employees by the end of the day."

I smiled at Brad, then looked over at Wil with a death stare. The smirk on his face showed he had relaxed and accepted that I had beaten him, but I didn't smile back.

Few things in this world pissed me off more than being told I couldn't do something. My mother had said it for most of my young life, and I made it a point to prove her wrong. Wil stepping over that line made me wonder if he was really the good guy I thought him to be or just another hindrance to my growth.

I turned back to Brad and continued with my questions.

Chapter Fourteen

Wil

Norah wasn't mad. I'd seen her mad. This was more. She was pissed—enraged, even. The story that would break in the morning about the settling lawsuit was Norah's, and I wouldn't interfere. She was on the phone with Jerry the moment we got out of the conference room. More than to tell him she got the exclusive, but also to ignore me in the process.

The tension between us weighed heavily on the car ride back to the hotel. I could barely breathe with the disdain radiating off her. I wanted to apologize, to make her understand that pulling her back wasn't to demean her character or skills. I thought, incorrectly, she'd gone too far. What she *had* done was take a risk. A risk I typically wouldn't dare do. But instead of it backfiring, it worked. I was wrong for what I did, but I couldn't apologize while she was fuming. She wouldn't hear it.

When the car stopped, she got out and slammed

the door. The driver looked at me through the rearview with raised eyebrows. I nodded in acknowledgment and exhaled loudly.

"Good luck," he said as I got out of the car.

I placed my hands in my pockets and started towards the hotel. By the time I had reached the elevators, Norah was nowhere in sight. Instead of waiting, I climbed the stairs to the fourth floor. My phone vibrated in my pocket as I opened the door from the stairwell.

Morgan: *r u in ur room?*

Not only did I not want to see Morgan, but I also had a feeling she was already at my door. I turned the corner and sighed at my confirmed suspicion.

"Hey," she said with flirtatious enthusiasm. Her boy shorts showed the tops of her thighs, and her crop top sweatshirt barely covered her breasts. Her hardened nipples were visible. *Oh boy.*

"Hey, Morgan." I walked towards her cautiously.

"What's up with your friend?" She pointed her thumb towards Norah's door.

I looked in that direction and sighed. "Long story."

Her tongue hung on her top lip as she got closer, and her hand found my chest. "So, I was wondering if I could come in. Hang out for a while?" Her voice turned seductive.

I couldn't lie and say she wasn't tempting. Her curves didn't stop, and her scent was entrancing. I'm sure a night with her wouldn't disappoint. There'd be no attachment later. She lived in Florida, and I was in New York. It would be one night. Just like it was supposed to be with Norah.

Norah.

All questions of sleeping with Morgan went out the

window with just the thought of her name. I couldn't fool myself. There was no way I could think of Morgan, even in the most intimate way when the woman across the hall occupied my brain.

I stepped back from her. "Can I be honest?"

Bewilderment covered her face briefly, and then she recovered. "Yeah." Her voice got higher.

"There's someone else I…fucking can't get away from mentally." I laughed at both my admission and the ridiculousness of it all.

She stared at me with her full lips open. "Well, if you have a girl back home, that doesn't mean she has to know anything." She closed the gap between us.

I caught her hands before they touched me again. "She's not at home." I tried to tell her with my eyes, the woman was only a few feet away.

She looked at Norah's door and then back to me. "Oh." Her disappointment was evident.

I gave her a half smile. "I'm sorry."

She stepped back more, then shrugged. "It's okay." Her natural voice returned. She looked at Norah's door again. "Is that why she's mad? Because of me?"

"No. It's not you. She's…stubborn." I laughed and scratched my forehead with my fingernail.

"You'd better talk to her."

I looked at Norah's door. "I don't think right now is a good time." I shook my head.

She exhaled. "Well, I hope you two can work it out."

"Thanks," I said and laughed once.

Morgan continued to look at me, then stepped farther away. "You have my number. If things don't work out. Call me. I would be willing to move to New York for someone like you." She turned and headed down the hall.

My cheeks burned with embarrassment as I nodded and looked down, smiling.

I felt like an idiot as I took out the plastic key to unlock my door. Morgan would be nothing more than a one-night stand, and before Norah, I would have jumped at the chance. Especially after Elise and the heart stomping I'd endured. Had I not been spending time with the woman who hated my guts...again, Morgan would have been a pleasant distraction. I hated my former roommates at that moment. God dammit, I *was* a serial monogamist.

I sat in my room for a few hours, wondering if enough time had passed for Norah to get over her animosity and what had happened with Wallace. My ego wasn't so inflated that I couldn't admit I was wrong and would happily acknowledge it when she gave me the chance. It was just about her giving that chance.

"This is ridiculous," I said to myself as I got off the bed and walked to my door.

Without a second thought, I went across the hall and knocked on Norah's door. I put my hands on my hips, recognizing the nerves that flowed through me. This woman had a temper like a short-fused firework. There was no buildup, just an explosion of amazing colors and loud noises. I wasn't in a hurry to feel her wrath again, but I was hungry, and I was sure she was too. There was no reason we couldn't have a pleasant evening like we did the night before.

I continued to stand there. My eyes moved around the hall, waiting to hear a sound or movement from inside. Nothing. I leaned closer, trying to gauge if she was just hiding or not inside. I looked down at the bottom of the door and saw a shadow move across the lighted room.

I knocked again. "Norah, seriously. I know you're in there. Light travels, and when you walk in front of it—"

The door opened swiftly. "What do you want?" she blurted, irritated.

She was in white cotton shorts and a tank top. She'd wrapped her hair on top of her head in a loose bun. A perfect combination of sexy and annoyed.

"Dinner. I was gonna grab a hamburger at that place down the street," I said, trying to keep my eyes from traveling down her tempting body.

"No one is stopping you," she said with thick sarcasm.

"Come with me."

That took her down a notch. "No, thank you," she replied.

"C'mon, you gotta be hungry." I tried to lighten my mood a little and smiled at her.

"I'm not, and they have room service," she said as she began to close the door before I stopped it with my hand.

She looked between me and my sprawled-out fingers with her mouth wide, startled at my audacity and persistence about getting this hamburger with her.

I exhaled. "Okay, say you *were* hungry and didn't want room service. What would you want from the restaurant down the street?"

Her eyes blazed into mine. "I don't want anything from you, Wil. Now move your pretty, manicured hand from my door before I make sure you're unable to type with it any longer." Her voice was honeyed, sending a slight quiver through me.

I scoffed with a smile and removed my hand so she

could push the door closed in my face.

I turned away and said, "Fine," while walking down the hall to the elevators.

I ate at the restaurant by myself while people watching and scrolling through my phone. Norah's face kept flashing in my mind. The images toggled between the anger she held tonight and the irresistible way her features contorted while naked and on top of me. I shook my head and threw down my napkin. This relationship was impossible. One minute she and I were more than just co-workers. The next, she was spewing her venom, vowing she was better off without me anywhere near her.

I exhaled, wishing I didn't like her. Wishing we had never met at that bar. Then she would just be another obstacle in my career I had to get through to make it to the next step. Sure, I would have found her attractive in more ways than one, but I could've moved past that to get to the greater goal. But now, it was too late. She was in me, in my head, flowing around with my blood, moving in and out of my heart with force. For the first time in a long time, I didn't know what I was going to do.

I stood, about to leave the restaurant, when I stopped short and exhaled. Norah was hungry. She had to be. My shoulders slumped as I turned around and moved towards the counter to order again.

Our floor in the hotel was empty and quiet. I walked towards my room, listening to a voice coming from across the hall. She was on the phone with someone. Not loud enough where I could hear what she was saying but pleasant enough to know it was someone familiar.

The corner of my mouth raised, hearing her monotone conversation. I set the warm white paper bag on the ground with a bottle of water I had taken out of my pocket. She wouldn't answer if she knew it was me, so I didn't bother to knock. I went across the hall and unlocked my door, taking out my phone as I let it close.

Wil: *I'm not outside but open your door.*

I threw the phone down on the bed and took off my shoes. I fell backwards onto the mattress and let all the air out of my lungs. My phone's alert went off. I looked at the screen.

Norah: *You didn't have to do that but thank you.*

I smiled and set the phone down again, closing my eyes, hoping she took the fries as a peace offering.

Chapter Fifteen

Wil

Norah texted me the next day and said she would meet me at the airport. Our flight wasn't until three in the afternoon. I was hoping to apologize and move on, maybe tool around Memphis together before we had to leave. Instead, I worked out and watched random things on TV.

Norah sat on one of the black, plastic, connected seats at the gate, scrolling through her phone. She didn't notice me approaching her, but I could already see the nervousness in the bouncing of her leg. As I drew nearer, I tried to figure out a way to distract her during the flight again, so she wouldn't be so afraid. Even if she were still mad, I wouldn't let her go at this alone.

She looked up at me when I stood in front of her, and I could see her nerves were already shot. The fear in her face negated my caution at that moment. I let go of my bag and kneeled in front of her, between her legs.

"Hey. It's just like last time. Nothing happened then, nothing's gonna happen now. I got you, okay?" I rested my hands on her thighs.

She nodded frantically, causing a tear to fall from her gorgeous face. "I'm still mad at you," she whispered.

I smiled. "I'm okay with that."

She took a shaky breath. "I hope you have other tricks up your sleeve to get me through this one." She gave a half-hearted chuckle.

"We'll figure it out." I grabbed her hand, then placed the other one on the side of her face to wipe the tear away. She closed her eyes and leaned into it.

I stayed by her until they called our seats. She walked ahead of me, wringing her hands, then shaking them out to release the tension. I kept close to her, touching her body with mine when we were in line to board, just to let her know I was there.

When we got to our seats, I stowed away our luggage, then sat down next to her. She continued to look out the window as if she were saying goodbye to the ground.

"Hey," I said.

She glanced at me, and I found the smallest gesture of anger in her eyes. I drew her focus away from the window and towards me with my hand on her neck. I caressed her face with my thumb as I pulled her to me.

"I'm sorry for yesterday. I should have trusted your instincts. You made a ballsy move, something I wouldn't have been able to do. You were right, and I'm sorry," I whispered.

She closed her eyes for a moment. "I'm sorry too. About Wallace. I should have told you I was going to ask those questions." She shook her head. "I'm sorry about dinner, and about Morgan," she whispered.

129

I leaned closer to her.

She continued, "I was jealous and stupid. I have two emotions tearing me apart inside, and I really don't know how to handle them."

I ran my thumb over her soft cheek. "Tell me."

She paused, then spoke, "Wil, I need to hate you."

"Why?" I furrowed my brow.

"Because you have the potential to stomp my heart into pieces. Even if it's not deliberately." Another tear fell.

"I would never hurt you," I said with as much assuredness as I could give.

The plane pulled back, and the panic returned to her face. At that moment, I saw the little girl who overheard the plane's engine was out all those years ago. I lifted the armrest between us and pulled her into my shoulder and under my arm. I took one of her hands in mine and intertwined our fingers. Her other hand gripped my shirt as she laid her head in the crook of my neck. I kept my lips on her crown and inhaled the scent of her hair. She clung to me until we were in the air. When her grip loosened, it wasn't because her fear had dissolved, it was because she was fast asleep. I looked down at her face, so serene and gorgeous, and smiled.

Every inch of me yearned for Norah Matthews. With every fault in her arsenal that drove me nuts, there was someone brilliant and driven. She had aspirations, and nothing, not even me, was strong enough to stop them. I wanted to hear her story, her background and life growing up in Texas. I wanted her to trust me, to tell me about the good parts and the not-so-good parts.

I sighed and gently loosened her fingers from my hand. I was obviously not going to get any work done, but I didn't care. I had gotten a lot of my notes from the Wallace interview in my head down on paper, but I had to remind Norah to send me the recording from her computer to fill in the blanks. I laid my head back and closed my eyes.

The future between her and me regarding the magazine made me uncomfortable. Jerry would have to pick someone for this managing editing job, eventually. From what he told me, it would be Norah or me. To say I'd be thrilled if Norah got it wasn't true. I moved across the country to take a chance with the *Chronicle*, specifically for the managing editor position. To have it fall through wouldn't be optimal.

But what if I got it…

Norah would hate me. Fair or not, she had made it clear from the beginning, in her mind, this job was hers. For it to go any other way would crush her. And what would that do to us? If I told her I wanted her, I wanted to be with her, would the outcome be any different? I wished I could say yes, but it wasn't true.

I exhaled and looked down at the sleeping woman in my arms and cursed whatever benevolent force brought us together. I couldn't have this or her. There was too much up in the air between us. I wanted the managing editing job, and I promised myself I would never put a woman between me and what I wanted after Elise. I wouldn't do that with Norah either.

The jerk of the wheels hitting the ground woke both me and Norah. She pushed herself off me and looked out the window while I raised my arms over my head to stretch.

She turned to me. "I fell asleep?"

"You did," I replied and smiled at her.

She stared at me. "What kind of magician are you?"

I laughed.

She slowly twisted from side to side to crack her back. "Did you slip me something?"

"Not my thing, no."

She turned towards me again. "You're pretty comfortable."

"Had you stayed those three nights, this wouldn't be a shock to you." I chuckled and reached under the seat in front of me for my bag.

When I faced her again, something was different. She looked at me like she was contemplating her next move carefully. Her bottom lip raked between her teeth, and there was a seduction in her stare, a wanting I felt in my bones.

The plane pulled up to the jetway, and everyone gathered their things. I kept my eyes forward and waited for the aisle to clear. I couldn't meet those navy-blue pupils again, for fear I would change my mind about not getting involved.

When we walked to the carousel to get our luggage, she was still deep in thought and didn't say much. After I got our bags, she stood in front of me and took a breath.

"Wil, I… I have been exceedingly unfair to you," she said with the most sincerity I'd ever seen her give.

I swallowed.

"All you've been is nice to me, and I couldn't have been a bigger bitch." She quietly laughed and wrung her hands in front of her. "I'm really sorry." She let a moment pass before she continued. "I've been trying to talk myself out of feeling this way. But I can't." She lowered her voice to where I could barely hear her. "I really do like you."

A combination of elation and disappointment hit me at once. I exhaled, hating myself for what I would have to do.

She glanced down. "I was wondering if you would go to dinner with me?" She laughed again and made a sound. "That was so corny," she said as she closed her eyes, and her cheeks warmed.

My heart fell through my chest and landed hard on the floor. I looked away and joggled my head. My mouth felt like I had eaten a bag of cotton. I watched my feet move closer to her. I wanted to grab her hands but resisted. "Norah, I think, uh, I think we should keep this professional." I lifted my head to see the shock and hurt in her eyes.

She hesitated, then backed away from me when she understood. "Yeah, yeah, of course. Of course." She gave a feeble laugh and looked around. "You're right. It's stupid. I know there's been too much damage—"

"It's not that," I interrupted. "And it's not your fault."

She nodded and drew her lips into her mouth. Her eyes became misty as she turned away. And I hated myself.

"I just think…it might be better this way. With the decision about the managing editing job coming…" I was trying harder to convince myself than her.

"No, you're right," she repeated. "You are. I, uh, know it's important to both of us."

"I'm so sorry," I said, moving closer to her.

She backed up farther. "No, don't." She tried to laugh. "It's for the best." She nodded wildly, then focused on her bag below her, pulling up the handle. She looked at me again. "I should go. I'm exhausted."

I watched her rebuild the wall between us. As she carefully laid each stone between the slabs of concrete, one by one, I detested myself even more.

"Let me take you home," I uttered. I didn't want to leave her, regardless of what I had just said.

"No, I'm good." She smiled and continued to back away from me. "I'll send you the audio from the interview with Wallace over the weekend. We'll pull it all together Monday."

I nodded, still unable to take my eyes off her. "Okay," I whispered.

She gave a smile that didn't come close to her saddened eyes. "Have a good weekend," she said before she turned and put her head down, pulling her black suitcase with her. I watched until she went out the sliding glass doors, not giving me a backwards glance.

I put my hand on my waist, then raked the other one through my hair. The frustration in my chest was building, and all I could do to lessen it, was to yell a loud and quick, "Fuck!" in the middle of JFK.

Norah

By Sunday evening, my miserable feelings had not dissipated at all. While I understood Wil's rejection and more than likely had caused it, it didn't make it any better. If anything, it was worse. I was the idiot who told Wil there was nothing between us. This was all me. I didn't know how I would feel if Wil got the job I had wanted for years. If we were together, could I get past it? Would I be okay with him essentially being my boss? Was he being honest with himself? He moved from California for this job. If I got it, would he even stay at the magazine?

There were too many variables, too many questions that lingered. I hated how Wil and I couldn't be closer than this, but I couldn't deny the justification to remain strictly professional was valid.

I walked to my desk the next morning, pleasantly surprised to find I had beaten Wil to work. I wanted to get a head start on the article. We were going to have to work on it together, but I didn't want to be in his vicinity any longer than necessary. I was not only disheartened by him refusing me, but I was also embarrassed.

He came in a half hour later. I had worked on the piece and liked where it was going, but I was more excited to show Wil my progress. I expected to see his loose, curly, dark blonde hair above my cubicle when I heard him put his stuff down, but there was nothing. Of course, things would change between us immediately. He said he wanted to keep it professional. To hope he would still continue to flirt with me like he did was juvenile.

Exhaling my frustration out, I felt someone behind me. I turned around quickly and found his ocean blue eyes staring, holding two cups of coffee in his hands with some sort of pastry sitting on top of each. He was casual, in jeans and a long-sleeved, gray T-shirt. Still handsome but more relaxed.

"Morning," he said, leaning in and handing me a cup.

"Hi." I smiled while taking it. "You didn't have to buy me breakfast."

"Well, I figured we were going to be preoccupied with work. I didn't want you to starve." The side of his mouth curled upwards.

I laughed once. "Thank you." I turned around and set his gesture on my desk, then looked at him again.

He watched me, as if he wanted to say something but wouldn't, or couldn't.

I negated the tension for him. "I'll let you get settled, then we can get started." I glanced away, needing to break his gaze. It was unnecessary to talk about the airport or anything that happened before this moment. It was over. We both needed to go forward.

He bit his bottom lip, and I envied his teeth. "Okay." He nodded. "Ten minutes?"

"Take your time." I turned back around to my keyboard. My eyes found the breakfast sitting next to me, and I smiled at his kindness and cursed it at the same time.

We sat in the conference room for the better part of the day, going over our notes and the audio from the interview. We kept our distance, careful not to touch each other. I caught him watching me when it was quiet. When I turned to him, he'd look away.

"This feels awkward. Does this feel awkward?" he questioned, breaking the silence.

"It's only awkward if you talk about it," I answered, looking through my notes.

"Norah—"

"Wil, look." I turned to him and moved closer. "I get it. And you're right. This is complicated. I don't hate you, if that's what you're worried about. And regardless of what you say, it is my fault. I'm not strong enough to put aside my pride and ego to let this," I motioned between us, "happen. I like you, but I want this job more."

He furrowed his brow. "Okay. But where does that leave us?"

I shrugged. "Writers, co-workers… Friends?"

He looked down, twisting his mouth, and nodded.

I gauged his response. "We don't have to be."

He turned to me and smiled. "Honestly, Norah, if I have to make a choice between friends and nothing, I'll be the best friend you've ever had."

His alluring grin caused me to look away. I moved and faced my work again. "Okay. Friends then."

He went back to his computer. "I can't believe I've seen my best friend naked," he mumbled.

I laughed softly, feeling his eyes still on me.

With only a few hiccups about what we wanted to include or leave out, we decided the article was good enough to send to Jerry.

I stood to gather my things when I looked at Wil, who was still sitting in his chair, monitoring me.

"Where did you go?" he asked.

I stopped moving. "What?"

"The morning we came home. Where were you?" he asked curiously.

I glanced away. "Have you been thinking about this all weekend?" I said and chuckled.

He tilted his head to the side quickly. "Not *all* weekend."

I laughed louder. "My sister was in Memphis for a conference. We had brunch."

He paused for a moment. "You didn't want to introduce me?" There was a playfulness to his tone.

"I was mad at you, remember?"

"Right," he whispered. His focus went to the gray carpet. He shook his head slightly when he stood, then closed his laptop. "How long has it been since you've seen her?"

"A few years. We talk every once in a while. It's not like we're really close."

He walked to me with his computer bag on his shoulder. "Why not?"

I exhaled. "She and I never really bonded when we were younger. She was my babysitter when my mother didn't feel like being a parent, which was pretty often. I think Myra resented me for it." I kept my focus on the table in front of me.

"What does she do?" he asked.

"Veterinarian."

"Large or small animals." His odd tone made me laugh.

"Mostly large." I glanced at him. "Horses and such. She's getting married in a few months."

"Are you going to the wedding?"

I nodded, then stared in the distance again. "It'll be nice to see her happy."

A heaviness floated in the air between us. The questions he wanted to ask lingered. Wil was a journalist through and through. He craved as much detail as possible when he was curious about things he was interested in. I waited to see if he would try to delve further into my past.

He inhaled through his nose. "I'm glad you got to see her," he said sincerely as he walked past me.

I smiled to myself, appreciative of the space he was giving me. It did, however, just make me want to tell him more. Janet was the only person in my life who knew about my past and how I grew up. It wasn't something I advertised or used for sympathy. I kept it buried away, because I wanted to overcome it, not dwell on it.

I walked out of the conference room and saw Wil being summoned into Jerry's office. When Jerry noticed me, he motioned for me to join them.

Jerry had on his Monday tie. Blue with gold diamonds. A gift from his wife, my aunt Lydia. She had been gone eight years and was one of the sweetest women you'd ever meet. She insisted I stayed with them when I first moved from Texas. I had known them all of five minutes before she was making up a room for me in their three-bedroom brownstone. They never had kids, so it thrilled her to play mother to an eighteen-year-old kid who knew nothing about being a responsible adult. She took me shopping, taught me how to cook, and warned me about men. Lydia squeezed a decade's worth of lessons into the two years I knew her. I was devastated when she passed.

I sat next to Wil and glanced at him, giving him a small smile when I met his eyes.

"So, how'd it go?" Jerry put his interlaced fingers on his dad gut and waited.

"Good," I answered and glanced at Wil, who nodded.

"The article on the site about him committing to equal pay has gotten over a hundred thousand hits so far. The networks picked it up, and it trended on Twitter for a while. Good job, kiddo." Jerry nodded at me.

"Thanks," I said and smirked at him.

"How's the piece going?" He sat up in his chair.

"It's in your inbox," Wil said.

"Already?" Jerry put on his glasses and stared at the screen.

Wil put his ankle on his knee. "Obviously it needs some tweaks, but we got the first draft down. We wanted to see if you thought our combined writing styles meshed."

I met Wil's eyes. The pride in his smile made me smile too.

"The two of you thought that?" Jerry eyed me.

I laughed ironically. "I *can* be reasonable, you know."

"Since when?" Jerry asked and laughed too.

I rolled my eyes.

Jerry took off his glasses and looked between Wil

and me. "Since it seems you two have called a truce, can I assume you both can work together amicably?"

I crossed my arms over my chest and leaned back. "It was fine."

Wil chuckled. "Norah is a delight to work with."

I suppressed the stupid grin Wil continually caused.

"Terrific," Jerry answered. He moved his mouse around, clicking here and there, then turned back to us. "Your next few assignments are in your inboxes. Calendar invites have been sent as well."

Wil and I both pulled out our phones and inspected the notifications. There were three names on the list, then a subsection.

"What's 'Other'?" I asked.

"That's for the individual assignments I have for you. Like your interview with Tylesha Morris next month. Then a few other people I'm working on, but nothing is concrete yet."

I looked down the list farther, then stopped on a name. "Joshua Benton's on here?" I asked and looked up, surprised.

Jerry nodded.

Joshua Benton was the assumed Democratic presidential nominee. I immediately salivated at the possibility of sitting down with Benton. He was the front runner and the favorite to be the next POTUS. I scanned my phone again and noticed it wasn't in Wil's or my assignments.

"There's no name next to it. Is it confirmed?" I asked. I couldn't keep the eagerness out of my voice.

"It is. But I haven't decided who's going to take it." Jerry raised his eyebrows at me.

That look told me everything I needed to know. I

leaned back in my chair and had a silent conversation with Jerry. Whoever got that interview would be the managing editor. There was no way Jerry would let his second best speak with the next most powerful man in the country. I tried to exhale out my irritation, thinking it may not be me.

"You have your assignments, children. Go forth and change the world." Jerry dismissed us.

I stood, still thinking about the list and what it meant. Wil and I would work together at least three more times. Flying for two, and one was here in New York. I pushed aside my anxiety about flying again and focused on these pieces being the best I'd ever written. The bullseye was close. I just had to lock it down. Despite the tension that had settled into warmth between us, it had to be about my work, no matter how enticing Wil was.

Wil and I walked back to the annex together.

"Looks like we have some time until we have to fly again. That's good."

I nodded. "Yeah. Now I can let the dread build."

Wil chuckled, and his voice lowered. "I'll be there."

I exhaled. "I will eventually need to learn to do this without you." I looked at him.

"How did you fly before I was here to be your emotional support animal?"

I laughed. "A lot of drugs. My doctor and I have stopped my prescription. I didn't want to rely on it anymore. I have six pills left, then that's it."

"But if you need it…"

"It's all in my head. I just have to change my mind," I said resolutely.

I looked at Wil, and he furrowed his brows. My phone vibrated in my hand, and I picked it up without looking at it to get away from our conversation.

"Hello?"

"Hey, beautiful."

I glanced at Wil and panicked. I broke off from him and went to my left.

"Uh, hey, Parker." I looked over my shoulder. Wil stood at his desk, watching me. I moved around the corner and leaned against the wall.

"Sorry, I know you're at work, but I wanted to see if you wanted to get together this weekend."

I paused. "What did you have in mind?"

"Whatever you want to do. I just want to see you."

I smiled at the sincerity in his voice. I wished he gave me goose bumps and made my heart flutter like Wil did. But Parker was not Wil, and I couldn't expect him to be. I wasn't being fair to him. He deserved a fair shot.

"Sure. How's Friday?"

"Perfect," he blurted. "I'll pick you up at seven?"

"Sounds good."

I hung up and took a breath, letting my smile fade. Parker wasn't the one I wanted to take me out. He wasn't whose touch I craved or whose kiss I had missed. But I had to be realistic. Wil had turned me down. We were friends, and as much as I hated the title, I loved the space we were in. I had to admit my place in his life and move on. I knew Parker was a stepping-stone, something to do on the weekends like how it was before Wil. For now, I would enjoy my time with him while shedding the hope that Wil and I would be anything more.

Chapter Seventeen

Wil

A few weeks went by, and Jerry gave me a couple of independent assignments for the website while we waited on the next pieces for the fiftieth-anniversary special issue. They were quick over-the-phone interviews I could do in my sleep, but I was glad to have the distraction. Norah and I were on stable ground, but I still couldn't help the feeling of wanting something more with her. I'd hoped over time, thoughts of her would dissipate, but apparently, that wasn't in the cards.

My birthday was coming up, and just because I wasn't in California anymore didn't mean I would break tradition. My annual poker game *would* commence. I just needed to find new players. Byron and Janet were coming, and Chase was flying in for the weekend. I wanted two, maybe three more bodies to make it a game.

I stuck my head up over the partition between Norah

and me. "Hey," I said.

"I wasn't singing." She smiled at her computer.

I snickered. I had caught her belting out a Whitney Houston song when she thought I was away from my desk. I'd rolled my chair to the opening of her cube and watched her hit some very questionable notes until she saw me. The embarrassment that caused her cheeks to light up was cute as hell. I teased her for days.

"I told you, next time I'm getting a video and plastering it all over social media. You'll go viral in no time."

She lifted her middle finger. *I wish…*

I snorted. "That's not what the 'hey' was for. What are you doing Saturday?"

She stopped typing and looked at me. All traces of humor in her eyes disappeared. "Why?" Her voice was soft.

"I have a poker game every year for my birthday. I was wondering if you wanted to come," I said and smiled.

"When is your birthday?"

"Friday."

She furrowed her brow. "So, why not have the party *on* your birthday?"

"Chase won't be in until late Friday, and I would rather not rush home to clean before everyone gets there."

She smirked. "Your apartment's pretty clean, as I recall."

I stared at her. "You haven't been there in a while," I mumbled.

She smiled and looked down at her hands on her lap. There was a pregnant pause while she thought. She exhaled and met my eyes. "I have a date on Saturday," she said while contorting her face into what looked like an apology.

Of course she did. Even though I hadn't moved on, there was no reason to think *she* hadn't.

I kept my voice indifferent. "Bring him."

The look on her face told me my reaction threw her. "Are you sure?"

I shrugged. "We're friends, right?"

She nodded slowly. "Right."

I tapped the top of the partition with my fingers. "The game starts at eight but come whenever you want. I'll have food and drinks. Don't feel like you have to bring anything." I moved away, ready to sit again.

She watched me. "Okay."

"Okay," I said as I smiled.

That faded as soon as my ass hit the chair. Here I was trying to play it cool, not wanting to give away how much I hated our distance while someone else was with her. Someone was close to her, maybe even physical with her. The need to touch her when we were near each other was frustrating, because I couldn't act on it. What was happening between us wasn't what I wanted, not even close, but it was what I could have with her. I hated whoever this guy was.

BYRON AND CHASE had set up the table and chairs in my living room. I was busy in the kitchen, putting the food together and cooling the drinks in the fridge.

Chase came over to me. "Man, you okay?"

I looked at him. "Yeah, why?"

"You look…nervous." He took a swig of his beer. "Is it Norah?"

I exhaled and shook my head. "These women are going to be the death of me."

Chase laughed. "I thought you were friends now?"

"We are." I turned and took a pan out of the oven, then set it on the stove. "And I hate it."

"You're the one that cut it off."

"I'm aware, Chase," I said flatly.

"Listen, you said it yourself. This is what's good for the both of you. You're saving yourself a lot of agony in the future."

"No, I'm going through all of it now."

He put his bottle down and laid his hands on the counter, leaning forward. "Someone's gonna get that job, Wil. As much as you say you can handle it, and it's just her that would have the problem, I don't think you're being honest with yourself."

I threw down the oven mitt. "I wouldn't care if Norah got it."

"Bullshit. You left LA because of Elise, yes. But you moved to New York for this position. You might end up resenting Norah for taking away something you wanted just as much as she does."

I wanted to argue that I couldn't be mad at her. She worked her ass off for this, and she did it without a degree or any experience other than working at the *Chronicle*. But thinking of her with that title, after all the years working my way through the ranks of three publications, didn't sit right with me either. My expensive and well-earned degree should have given me a leg up. That was the whole reason I'd gotten it. Had Norah been any other person chosen over me for this job, I'd be disappointed, and I absolutely, one hundred percent, would *not* stay.

Shit.

A soft knock came from the hallway. I glanced at Chase as I walked to the door and opened it.

When I'd found out Norah was bringing a date, I'd reverted into a teenager and decided I needed a date too. I'd met a woman named Amber when I was getting my mail one afternoon. She had just moved into the building and lived on the second floor. I had been talking to her casually since Norah and I were no longer an option. I didn't see us going anywhere, but that wasn't the reason for the invite. We needed seven players, and I didn't want to be without someone when Norah would be accompanied by whoever this guy was. Inviting Amber to the game was a last-minute decision, one I was sure I would regret by the end of the evening.

Her long, wavy, platinum hair hung against her full chest, and the pink dress accentuated her hips and backside. Her eyes, complete with heavy black mascara and brown eye shadow, were a different color from when I saw her last. Contacts, probably. She was attractive but not my type.

"Hey!" she said joyfully.

"Hey, Amber. Come on in." I opened the door wider for her to enter. She stopped in front of me and reached up to kiss my cheek. She wore an overpowering floral fragrance. I cleared my throat, trying not to cough as she walked by me.

I moved to her side when she was spotted by my friends. "Amber, this is Chase and Byron."

Byron stared at her with interest but said nothing, just nodded. Chased waved with the bottle in his hand.

"Did you want something to drink?" I asked.

She turned to me. "Don't I get a tour?"

I laughed. "There's not much to see but sure."

I walked towards the hallway and passed B, who widened his eyes and tilted his head for a split second, giving me a look that told me he thought Amber was an interesting choice to bring to the party. I shook my head and continued forward.

I opened the door to my spare room, which was half guest room, half office. Chase had his stuff in there, so I didn't want to let her in.

I turned the light on in the bathroom and made a corny joke about how two people sharing one bathroom was the secret seventh circle of hell. Amber laughed like it was the funniest thing she'd ever heard and touched my chest to emphasize her point. I didn't mind ego strokes, but it wasn't something I thrived on. I had a feeling I would get quite a few tonight from her.

My bedroom door was open, but I stopped at the doorway to avoid inviting any misconceptions of my intentions. She wanted a tour, I was giving her a tour. I had no reason to lead her on.

She walked past me and inspected the room. She looked at family pictures on top of my dresser without asking who anyone was. She ran her finger along the wood while giving me a good showing of her ass. I can't deny I looked. Her head turned over her shoulder to make sure that was exactly what I was doing.

"Your apartment is nice, Wil. I'm kinda mad I'm just now seeing it." She moved to the edge of the bed and sat, running her hands over my comforter, looking at me with her doe eyes. "Why don't you come sit next to me?"

I hesitated, then heard fresh voices enter the apartment, and I pointed behind me with my thumb. "I gotta play host." I smiled at her, thanking whoever had just walked in for the escape.

I moved my body to the side as a nonverbal invitation for her to remove herself from my bed. She smiled and stood with a slight hint of disappointment beneath the surface. She squeezed past me as I followed her down the hallway.

Norah, her guest, and Janet had just come in the front door. I heard her voice before I saw her, and it made me smile instantly. I quickly sized up the guy Norah was with. He was short, or shorter than me. Dark brown hair, a face and wardrobe that read clean cut. His white-collar job was both boring and lucrative, and he seemed wound tight. Anyone who wore slacks and a button-down shirt to a poker party had to be stressed out a lot. There was no way she was serious about this guy.

Norah spotted me, then landed on the woman by my side. She glanced away and asked Janet for her jacket while taking off hers. She had on an oversized, ivory cable knit sweater and leggings that made her casually cute and fucking sexy all at the same time. I narrowed my eyes at the boring guy touching her lower back while talking to Chase.

Norah walked towards me with the jackets folded over her arms and a wrapped box in her hands.

"Hi," she said and smiled.

"Hey." I smiled back. "I'm glad you made it."

She looked down at the package in her hands, then pushed it towards me. "Happy birthday."

Stunned, I took the box covered in birthday wrapping paper with a red bow on top and looked at her. "You didn't have to—"

"Don't worry, it's…stupid." She laughed.

I shook it gently. The weight was light, and whatever was inside jostled. "What is it?"

"You're gonna have to wait until you open it," she replied and bit her lip.

I started to rip the paper.

She put her hand on mine, and I met those blue eyes I obsessed over. "Oh no, not now. I'll be embarrassed."

I stopped and smiled. "Thank you."

She nodded subtly.

Norah turned her attention to Amber. "Hi, I'm Norah."

"Amber." Amber's voice was unfamiliar and higher.

Norah turned back to me. "Is there somewhere I can put these?"

"Oh, here, I'll take them." I removed the clothes from her arms. While Amber's perfume masked everything else in my vicinity, I caught a hint of Norah's, and it reminded me of the couch just feet away from us. I caught her eye as I leaned into her, and our hands touched in the exchange, sending a surge of adrenaline through me.

As I walked to the bedroom, I heard Norah ask Amber how we knew each other, and I cringed. This wasn't how this was supposed to go. Everything felt awkward at once. Norah wasn't supposed to be talking to a woman I had no interest in, and she wasn't supposed to be here with a date. I dumped the jackets on the bed, then placed a hand on my hip. The other ran down my face to my chin.

When I came back down the hallway, Norah's date had joined her and Amber. "Hi," I said to him. "I'm Wil."

He reached out his hand. "Birthday boy. Nice to meet you. Parker."

I nodded at him and looked at Norah. She looked away uncomfortably, then landed on Amber. "I love this

151

dress." Norah pointed at Amber's body.

"Thank you." Amber ran her hand down her side.

"What do you do?" Norah asked.

"I'm an esthetician."

"Oh!" Norah's voice went up an octave.

"You have fabulous skin." Amber leaned forward and lifted Norah's hair away from her face.

"Oh, no. I'm a mess. I haven't had a facial in years."

"You should come to my salon. First one's on the house." Amber winked at her.

Norah chuckled. "Thank you." She eyed me. "I may do that."

"We both should," Parker interjected. "I'm long overdue for one as well."

I desperately wanted to roll my eyes.

"Absolutely. I'd be happy to do a couple's facial."

"That's a thing?" Norah asked, apprehensive.

"Of course. A couple that exfoliates together stays together." Amber giggled. "I made that up."

Norah's eyes went wide. "Okay. I'm gonna get something to drink. Anyone want anything?"

"A beer, please, babe," Parker answered.

Babe?

Amber shook her head, and I merely stared at Norah, envying the man who had his hand around her back. She turned away without a glance in my direction.

Norah

Janet was leaning on Byron, who was talking to Chase in the kitchen, when she saw me. I gave her an eye roll as I opened the refrigerator door. Janet tapped Byron on the chest with her fingers and moved away.

"Uh-oh. What'd he do?" She crossed her arms and leaned against the counter to my right.

"Which one?" I asked, annoyed.

"Start with Wil, then go to Parker," she answered, laughing.

"He's dating that woman." I nodded my head in Wil's direction.

She looked towards the three of them. When I straightened, I turned around and saw Amber had now wrapped her arm around Wil's.

"He knew you were bringing Parker, right?" Janet kept her eyes on them.

I nodded.

"She's here on purpose then. There's no way he was going to watch you and Mr. Boring while he had no one to snuggle his arm."

I exhaled and placed the cold beer on the counter in front of me, then asked Byron where the wineglasses were. He poured me a healthy amount and handed me the much-needed alcohol.

I turned my back on Wil, Amber, and Parker, then got close to Janet. "Parker called me *babe*."

Janet screwed up her face. "Ew."

I took a sip. "Mm-hmm."

She laughed and looked away. "Does Parker know?"

I lowered my voice. "About Wil and me? No. It's none of his business."

She nodded. "Don't be too surprised if he gets a little possessive tonight. The way Wil keeps glancing at you, a blind man can see there's something there." She raised her eyebrows at me.

I turned around and leaned against the counter next to her. Parker and Amber were speaking to each other. Amber was analyzing Parker's neck closely while he tilted his face towards the ceiling. Wil's eyes met mine for a second, then he glanced at the spectacle that was Amber and Parker. When he returned his gaze to me, he smirked. I tried to maintain my stoic face but couldn't. He made me laugh, which made him smile. *Goddamn that smile.* I didn't know who this woman with Wil was, but the burning sensation running through my body told me the large, green monster I'd heard so much about had bitten me. Fucking jealousy? Who *was* I?

After the pleasantries were over, Wil announced it was time to get the game going. Wil, Chase, and Byron turned from playful to serious in a matter of seconds.

154

While Janet, Parker, Amber, and I continued to make jokes, there was an eerie silence from the three former roommates. We had gone from present-day New York City to the Wild West.

I learned the basics of poker through a barrage of websites and YouTube videos after Wil had invited me. I didn't want to come to the table with no idea what I was doing.

We agreed on one-dollar bets to start with. No one was rich, and it was more for bragging rights than anything else. During the first few rounds, I folded my hand early, just to get a feel for what everyone else was doing. Byron had won two hands in a row, followed by an unmatched amount of smack talk which seemed to agitate Wil and Chase. Amber won a hand and squealed in delight. As wrong as she was for Wil, she was a sweetheart all the same.

After an hour of play, I finally got a decent hand. A queen of hearts, queen of clubs, jack of hearts, an eight of diamonds, and a two of clubs. Janet and Amber folded immediately. Byron raised the pot and then, like clockwork, Chase and Wil did as well. Parker and I called. I gave up the eight and the two and picked up the cards Wil dealt, then tried not to break my poker face.

Byron and Chase reluctantly folded, while Wil, Parker, and I remained in the game. Wil watched me closely as he decided on what to do with his turn. He narrowed his eyes, and I chuckled.

"What'd ya got?" he asked me in a low voice.

"Bet and find out," I challenged and nodded towards the pot.

He ran his tongue along the inside of his molars as he continued to stare. His eyes traveled down me for a moment, then returned to my face. I tightened my abs to keep the butterflies from fluttering. That look he gave me made my breath heavy and my insides blister. The tension between us was thick, and both of us knew better, but it appeared neither of us cared what anyone else thought. I squeezed my thighs as if that would do anything for the want that lingered. If no one had been around, I would have climbed over the table, undressed, and kissed him like I hadn't been able to in weeks. I raked my bottom lip through my teeth, and Wil exhaled.

I heard Parker clear his throat, bringing me out of my fantasy. Wil and I both looked at him.

"I'll raise you twenty," Parker said with irritation.

Fuck this, I was going to win this hand. "Call and raise you twenty-five," I said, looking only at Wil.

"Really?" Wil asked, surprised, and smiled. It nearly knocked me over.

I raised my eyebrows at him as a dare.

He gave me a sexy, throaty laugh and shook his head, picking up his chips. "Call." The only sound was the chips landing on the pot.

We both looked at Parker. He laid down three tens. "Three of a kind," he said, looking at me with no amusement.

I glanced at Wil and laid two jacks and three queens on the table. "Full house."

Byron whistled through his teeth and chuckled. "Damn, Dub. I hope you hid some aces somewhere."

The table laughed.

Wil played with the cards in his hands, his eyes never leaving mine, then threw them facedown. "I got nothin'."

The table collectively made an annoyed sound.

"I thought she was gonna fold!" Wil said, placing his hands high above his head, then wiping them over his face.

I laughed as I collected my chips from the center of the table. The rest of the group got up to go to the bathroom or stretch their legs.

Parker leaned into me. "Can I talk to you?" He didn't wait for an answer as he stood and headed to Wil's balcony. I stared at the table for a moment, knowing this conversation wasn't something I wanted to deal with here.

I pushed my chair back and followed Parker, then closed the sliding glass door behind me. Wil caught my eye from the other side of the room. Parker leaned his forearms against the railing, staring out into the city. I walked over and stood next to him, then leaned my back on the same railing.

"What's going on, Norah?" His voice was low, and he rubbed his palms together.

"What do you mean?" I looked down at my hands.

"Please don't play stupid with me." He glanced my way.

"Stupid," I repeated, vexed.

He straightened and turned towards me. "Yes, stupid. What the hell is going on with you and Wil?"

"Nothing is going on between us," I mumbled.

His voice got louder. "Bullshit."

I scoffed and walked away from him.

"You two have been flirting the entire night, and just a second ago? That was out of line. You disrespected both Amber and me with the way you looked at him. Like you would've fucked him on the middle of that table." His voice carried.

I turned around. "Parker, you and I aren't together. So I really couldn't give a shit if you like the way I look at him or not."

His chest rose as he stared at me. "You fucked him, didn't you?"

I looked away and took a deep breath. My silence gave him his answer.

"So, what is this? Why did you bring me here? To make him jealous?" He pointed at the sliding glass doors.

"Are you kidding me?" My anger grew. "I told you that my *friend* was having a birthday poker party. That's it. I didn't bring you here to make him jealous because there is nothing to be jealous of."

The hurt in Parker's eyes made me stop and lower my voice. "I didn't mean it like that."

He put his hands on his hips. "How *did* you mean it?"

I exhaled audibly. "There's nothing between Wil and me anymore. We ended it before it began." I hated the defeat in my tone. I wanted to be more confident in my denial of how I felt about Wil, but it wasn't coming through.

"I'm not an idiot, Norah," he said in a low tone and looked away. He inhaled through his nose and looked at me again. "Do you still like him?"

I stared at Parker, unable to speak. I could deny it all I wanted, but Parker would see right through me. I was never any good at hiding my genuine feelings.

I swallowed and looked down. After I knew what I had to do, I looked up at him again. "Yes."

His jaw locked and his face tensed. Looking past me, he shook his head with irritation and walked towards the glass doors. Then, without a word, threw them open and left.

I turned towards the Manhattan skyline and leaned against the railing again. I placed my hand on my forehead and blew out a long breath.

"Girl, what happened?" Janet came over to me.

"Did he leave?" I asked softly.

"More like stomped out the door." She widened her eyes at me.

I paused. "It's over."

"Oh shit," Janet whispered and leaned her back on the railing. "Wil?"

I nodded. "Yeah, he figured it out. Parker asked if I still liked him."

She said nothing, just exhaled loudly. We listened to the city below us for a heartbeat.

"Hey."

I turned towards Wil, inching his way onto the balcony. "Are you okay?" he asked with unease.

Janet looked at me, then went back inside.

"Yeah, I'm okay," I answered.

He walked over to me and stood by my side. "So, that's Parker."

I nodded. "That *was* Parker."

"Did you just break up with somebody on my stoop?" His tone was light and made me smile.

"We were never together. But I'm pretty sure we're through now."

His face fell instantaneously. "Can I ask why?"

I waited for a moment, remembering there was a woman inside waiting for him. "No. No, you can't."

The silence stretched between us. Whether or not I wanted to admit it, I'd brought Parker here for more than just a date night with him—I used him. I wanted Wil to see I wasn't waiting around, that I had moved on. But amid trying to prove it, I realized I was nowhere close to actually doing it. I was stuck in the middle of not wanting him and wanting him desperately. I had driven Parker away, made a fool of myself in front of Wil's friends, and I was still painfully aware I wasn't good for Wil.

I turned to him. "I hate for you to lose one more player, but I need to go home."

He pushed himself off the railing. "Let me take you."

"Wil, no. It's your party. I'll be fine." I started to walk out the door when he caught my arm. I looked up at him. A thousand little nerves rose because of his touch.

He released me and looked down. "Are you sure you're okay?"

I nodded and tried to smile. "Happy birthday, Wil."

I turned away and walked through the sliding glass door.

Wil

I was always watching Norah walk away from me. Whether at work, a hotel in Memphis, JFK, or in my own damn house. The heaviness in my chest told me I didn't want her to leave, but I couldn't ask her to stay. We were friends. Nothing more.

I turned toward the city and took a deep breath, watching the cars below. After a few minutes of internally kicking myself for not going after her, I went back inside. Janet and Byron were huddled together on my couch, Chase was cleaning up my kitchen, and Amber had disappeared.

I went to my island and laid my arms, then my head on the counter in defeat.

"You're pathetic, man," Chase said over me, chuckling.

"Did Amber leave too?" I said to the floor.

"No, she disappeared around the corner."

I lifted my head and looked towards the hallway. "Tell me she's in the bathroom." I turned back to Chase, panicked.

"I don't think so," he replied apologetically.

I sighed and stood, flopping my head back towards the ceiling. I knew what she was doing, and it was the last thing I wanted to deal with tonight. I lollygagged back to my bedroom, finding the door closed.

"Fuck," I whispered. I didn't want to hurt her feelings, but this wasn't happening.

I knocked on the door and heard her say, "Come in." I shut my eyes tight and turned the knob. Amber was lying on the bed on top of the covers. The front of her dress hung loosely, indicating the back was unzipped.

"Hi," she said seductively.

I tried to smile before walking in and closing the door behind me. I leaned against it with my hands in my pockets.

"You're so far away," she spoke softly. "I know you're not shy, Wil."

I hesitated, trying to decide how I wanted to say she was wasting her time without hurting her feelings.

"Oh, I see," she said while getting off the bed. "You're going to make me come to you."

She let her dress fall to the floor. I couldn't deny what was before me was beautiful and enticing, but I wasn't ready to start anything new with anyone. I opened my mouth to tell her to stop, but when she touched my chest and looked up at me with her hazel eyes—I couldn't.

She reached up and kissed me. It wasn't what I craved, and it wasn't who I craved it from, but it was comforting. Someone stood in front of me and wanted me with no complications. Nothing to worry about in the future, nothing to compete over. The more she continued to kiss my lips, my neck, my jaw, my want for her grew too.

I let go of my hesitation and took her in my arms, running my hands over her warm, voluptuous body. She wasn't Norah, but with the way things were, I wasn't sure I would ever get to be like this with Norah again.

I encouraged Amber back to the bed and tried to forget who Norah was, although I knew it was temporary. Tomorrow I would return to my misery, not being able to have the woman I wanted in my bed. Tonight, I would gladly take whatever Amber would give.

I WALKED INTO the *Chronicle* Monday morning, feeling hollow. I thought spending the night with Amber would be a pleasant distraction from my tumultuous relationship with Norah. It wasn't. It made me realize my feelings for Norah weren't something I could cure with sex with someone else, and now I had a bigger problem. That night with Amber was fine, but I'd hoped it didn't give her the wrong impression. I didn't want to be the asshole who not only used her to forget but broke her heart too.

Norah was already at her desk when I walked by. "Morning." She smiled as she looked up at me.

I couldn't meet her eyes. "Hey," I said, keeping my voice low. I sat at my desk and closed my eyes.

Norah popped up over our partition. "How was the rest of your party?" She was uncharacteristically chipper.

I glanced at her. "It was fine. After you left, it was pretty much over."

"I haven't even seen Janet yet. She's been with

Byron all weekend." She giggled and shook her head.

I didn't know when Janet and B left that night. It didn't appear they knew what had happened in my bedroom. I couldn't imagine Janet not letting Norah know I had been behind a closed door with another woman. Chase, however, heard Amber through the walls. She had made it known, loudly, that she had a good time. I cringed.

"Did you open your present?" Norah asked, taking me out of my shameful memory.

I shut my eyes for a moment. "Shit. No, I'm sorry. I haven't yet."

"It's alright," she said, then laughed. "I told you, it's corny. I hadn't gotten a text, so I just wondered—"

"No, I'll open it when I get home," I said dismissively.

She lingered and stared at me. "Are you okay?"

I glanced up at her. "Yeah. Yeah, I'm good." I tried to smile, but I couldn't get it to form.

"Okay." She was no longer chipper. "Um, Jerry wants to see us at nine in his office."

I glanced at her again and nodded. "Alright," I mumbled.

I felt her eyes on me for another moment, then her head disappeared behind our partition. I exhaled and tried to ward off the incoming headache by placing my thumb and forefinger on the bridge of my nose and squeezing.

Norah was in Jerry's office before I got there, talking and laughing about something I couldn't hear. When I walked in, I avoided Norah's gaze and sat, turning my focus to Jerry.

"Okay," Jerry started. "There's something that's come up that I want you two to drop everything for." I moved forward in my chair, given Jerry's intensity. "There's wind the billionaire theme park owner, John

Thornton, is going to throw his hat into politics. It's rumored he wants to be the Republican candidate for president."

"We're doing a piece on him?" Norah asked. I looked at her, confused by her disgusted tone, and she turned to me. "Most of New York hates him. He's that playboy, tough guy who thinks everyone should be his yes-man no matter how wrong he is," she answered my questioning stare.

Jerry came forward in his chair. "Exactly. Which is why I want you to find out why he has lawsuits against him."

"That's not public record?" I asked.

"Of course, he has the usual day-to-day court battles you have when you own any business, but there's something more. I have a source who thinks it has to do with female employees who work directly with him."

Norah paused. "Sexual assaults?"

"It may go even deeper," Jerry answered.

"Not that I don't love working with Wil," she glanced at me and smiled, "but why do you need both of us on this?"

"Because I have a connection to a lawyer in the Southern District here in New York," I answered. She looked at me, and I glanced at her. "He and my father were roommates in college."

Jerry tapped his nose with his finger. "And you can find dirt in a snowstorm, kiddo. This is perfect for the both of you."

Norah sat back in her chair. "You know this is going to take longer than a few days to figure out."

"Call it a pressing side project, but I want something before you leave for Chicago."

Norah's shoulders slumped, remembering our upcoming flight.

Jerry saw it too. "You'll be okay?"

Norah laughed without humor and stood. She walked behind me and laid her hand on my shoulder. "I have my support animal. I'll be fine."

I laughed once through my nose and smiled, shaking my head. She left out the door, and I watched her walk away from me again.

I put in a call to my father's former roommate. He hadn't sent me anything by the end of the day, so I called my dad to call him too, to see if he could move things along.

Norah was on the phone from the time we left Jerry's office until I was about to leave for the day. She had tried to connect with people who knew John Thornton personally. I marveled at her ability to pull things out of them. She was personable, even flirtatious sometimes, to get what she wanted. I smiled when I recognized her fake laugh. She gave whoever was on the other end of the line the impression she was interested in whatever they were bargaining with.

I snuck out later, glad she was entrenched in the investigation so I didn't have to give her an awkward goodbye. Amber had called me a few times during the day, but I didn't dare answer when Norah was around. The forthcoming conversation I needed to have with Amber made me wince. I was a weak idiot, about to be the jackass, who had to let her down easy.

I came back to an empty apartment. Chase had flown home earlier. He left something on my bed, wrapped in a bow with a folded card attached.

Happy Birthday, Dickhead.

It was a box of condoms and an STD test from the Dollar Store. I chuckled and threw it back on the bed. The wrapped box from Norah sat on top of my dresser and caught my eye. My first instinct was to ignore it—I'd open it when I felt better about life. But my curiosity got the best of me when I remembered she'd said it was corny.

I ripped off the paper and opened the box. A full-throated laugh grew in my chest as I looked inside. I pulled out the ugliest stuffed brown bear I'd ever seen. It wore a Cornell hat, a Cornell sweatshirt, and carried a small Cornell flag in its hand. I continued to laugh as I searched in the box for anything more. There was a handwritten note at the bottom.

Truce?

"Truce," I replied out loud and smiled.

I exhaled and placed the bear on my dresser among the framed photos of my family. I laughed again and shook my head at the present that meant more than I would have thought.

There was a forceful knock on my door an hour later. I was shoveling a bowl of boxed mac and cheese in my mouth when I cautiously looked at the door. I got up from the couch quietly, afraid Amber had come over for an unannounced visit. Tiptoeing around my apartment because I couldn't keep my dick in my pants for a night caused me to no longer hate myself. I had quickly descended into loathing.

The face in my peephole made me smile instantly. I turned the knob and opened the door wide.

"You're not going to believe this," Norah said, pushing past me, looking disheveled. She'd pulled her hair back, had on a TSU sweatshirt, matching pajama pants, and her computer bag hung over her shoulder. Beautiful.

"What?" I asked, standing behind her.

She set her bag down at the end of the island. "Thornton has seven, *seven* sexual harassment suits."

"Wait, what?" I asked as I closed the door.

"Yes! All around the same time, and all of them women who worked for him. Three of the women said they were pregnant with his children, and he *forced* them to have abortions. Threatening them, saying if they ever told anyone, he'd bury them. As in *kill* them." She widened her eyes.

I put my hands on my hips. "Holy shit."

Her voice rose. "I know!"

"How has this not been leaked yet?"

"He's a billionaire. There were probably so many NDAs flying around, the women couldn't breathe a word to anyone. But I found one of his former secretaries who quit because she couldn't stand to be around all of his chaos. She said she had seen everything. Even walked in on him having rough sex with a woman in his office. The prosecution is going to add her as a witness. We have to get this out there, and we have to do it now before we get scooped." I recognized the urgency in her tone.

"Did you call Jerry?"

She walked closer. "Yes. He wants us to get it done tonight to break it in the morning."

I smirked at her. "You up for it?"

"Do you have coffee?"

I looked at her as if she had just asked me what two plus two equaled.

"Then hell yes, let's do this." She went back to her bag and pulled out her battered laptop, then made her way to my couch. She slipped off her shoes and tucked her feet under her after she sat. I beamed, watching her make herself comfortable.

Just having her here alone in my apartment made me happier than I had been in days. I put on the coffee, poured two cups, and brought my laptop to the couch where she was already typing away to build the story.

We worked into the night and had Jerry on standby to approve the article when we were done. The adrenaline rush simmered down once we put in the final edits. We got three people on the record, including one of the seven women who was suing the mogul.

Norah was on the other side of the couch, concentrating. She continued to look at her computer but typed nothing else. "Is that it?" she questioned.

I nodded at my screen. "I think so."

"Okay," she released a long breath, "let's send it."

I heard the *swoosh* of the email leaving her out-box.

"I hope this doesn't end up an exclusive," she mumbled.

"I thought exclusives were good," I said, confused.

"Not with Jerry. You get an exclusive when he's about to deliver some bad news, like you're being moved to letters to the editor or something. He doesn't think anyone notices." She chuckled.

We both sat back and took a minute to revel in the work we'd just done. There was a calm between us. We had done something huge, and even if it wasn't huge for anyone else, we felt its importance.

"Can I ask you something?" Norah looked at me.

I nodded.

"It's personal." She widened her beautiful blue eyes.

I waited for her to say something else. When she

didn't, I responded, "Go ahead."

She hesitated, then shook her head, setting her computer on the floor. "Forget it. I shouldn't be asking you—"

"Ask anyway," I interrupted. The look of indecision on her face said whatever she wanted to know was important.

"Are you and Amber…?"

I looked down and exhaled softly.

When I didn't answer, she spoke in a rush. "It's just when Janet came home, she said something about you two not reemerging from your bedroom before they left." She looked away and paused. "You know what? Never mind. I don't think I want to kn—"

"She spent the night." I had to tell her. I didn't want to keep anything from Norah, even something that might hurt.

She nodded and pulled her legs closer to her body, wrapping her arms around them. "So, you're together?"

"No." I looked at her.

"Do you want to be?"

"No," I blurted.

A pain crossed her face.

"What?" I asked gently, laying my computer at my side, moving closer to her.

"I know I don't have the right. I mean, god, I even brought Parker over here." She stopped and made eye contact with me. "I hate that she was so close to you," she whispered and shook her head. "I'm sorry."

"What do you have to be sorry for?" I inched even closer.

"Friends don't get jealous of people they choose to sleep with." Her voice was small.

170

"Then we're not friends," I said. Her head snapped up to me. "Because I hated Parker before I even met him."

She watched me as her breath became noticeably labored, and I kept my focus on her, deciding what to do. I wanted to touch her, to make her understand Amber was just a stand-in, no one she would ever have to worry about.

She eased her legs down, her left foot touching the floor, and she scooted closer. That tether between us tightened, and the need to be in her space took over my logic. I laid my palm against the side of her neck to make her look at me. A layer of moisture had built in her blue eyes, and she covered my hand with hers.

We stared at each other while my heartbeat intensified. My attention was torn between her perfect eyes and those full, pink lips I needed to feel on mine. The seconds that ticked by felt like years.

"For the love of god," I whispered. "Please let me kiss you," I begged.

Not another second passed before she pushed me upright and straddled my lap, kissing me deeply. Both of her hands were on my neck, pulling me closer to her. She tasted like coffee and sugar. A perfect metaphor for our relationship—bitter and sweet, and I was addicted. I laid my hands on her back and moved them into her hair. The smell that lingered on her skin was clean, like fresh linen. Everything about Norah was comforting. Her touch was something I had longed for. Dreamt about. Even fooled myself into thinking I was feeling her instead of Amber on my birthday.

We melted into each other, slowing our kiss to lighthearted and playful. She smiled against my mouth, and I gradually pulled away to look at her. When we gazed at each other, her smile faded, and a shot of worry moved through me.

"What are we doing?" she asked in a hushed tone.

I shook my head. "I don't know. But I don't want to stop."

She looked down at the minimal space between us. "You said at the airport—"

"I didn't mean it."

She met my eyes.

"I never meant it," I confessed.

She studied me, her eyes searching for something in mine. "What do we do?"

I puffed out my cheeks, letting all the built-up sexual tension in my body out. "I know what I *want* to do." I tried to keep the lust out of my tone but failed.

She traced my face with her finger.

"But I won't," I breathed.

She straightened her head, her eyes full of confusion.

"I'm going to restrain myself tonight as bad as I want you."

She waited for me to say something, maybe even take it back. "I don't mean to sound like the slut that I obviously am, but… Why?"

I chuckled, then moved her hair away from her face. "I had sex with Amber forty-eight hours ago."

Her gazed dropped, and her forehead wrinkled.

"Yeah, that's not a good look. I haven't even changed the sheets," I said, disgusted with myself.

She moved off my lap slowly and sat beside me. "That definitely dampens the mood." She let out her own frustration in a lengthy breath.

I interlaced her fingers with mine. "Let's take our

time with this," I said, then watched her profile nod.

The silence in the air hung. I wanted her to be the one to decide on what to do next.

"I should probably go home then," she answered my thoughts.

I leaned my head down to catch her eye. "You don't have to." I smiled when she looked at me. "We could make out more."

She gave me a doubtful look. "I think we've had enough practice to know that's only gonna last so long before I'm stripping you naked." She stood and collected her computer.

I laughed, immediately regretting the decision not to take her into my bedroom, but it was the right thing to do. I wanted Norah more than anything, but I needed to do this right. We were already teetering on unsteady ground. We had to be smart about this.

I stood when she put her computer in her bag and threw the strap over her shoulder. She stopped moving and stared at nothing in front of her. The hesitation in her body made my concern skyrocket. I moved to her and snaked my arm around her back, then made her face me.

She looked at me wearily. "Am I really what you want?"

I scoffed and pulled her into a kiss, answering her question without having to say a word. She rested her hands on my biceps as I wrapped my arms around her tightly, not letting any space between us. I poured as much of myself into this kiss to ensure she understood how much she affected me. I didn't think I would want to be with someone so soon after getting my heart smashed—but this was different. It felt unlike anything I'd ever shared with anyone—not even Elise.

We continued to devour each other until her lips resisted. Then she pulled back. "Okay, you're right. We can't do this," she said breathlessly, pushing me away.

"Do you have any other questions?"

"No, no, none at all." She turned and walked towards the door, her face red from the heat between us.

I followed her, wearing a grin I couldn't suppress. When she reached for the doorknob, I drew her back to me by her waist until her chest rested against mine.

"I'll see you tomorrow," I whispered and leaned down for one last taste of her lips. I had thoroughly kissed the coffee away, but she was still the best thing I'd ever savored.

When we stopped, her eyes sparkled, and her smirk appeared. "Goodnight, Wil," she said and faced away from me. She opened the door to the apartment and peeked over her shoulder before leaving.

I couldn't move, feeling overwhelmed. Fear, confusion, elation, extremely liking this woman all passed through me at once. Then something occurred that made those feelings vanish. I grabbed my shoes and jacket.

"Wait, you don't have a car!" I called, rushing out the door to drive her home.

Norah

I walked into my apartment and saw Janet on the couch, with the remote in her hand, scrolling through channels.

"Hey, I didn't think you'd be here," I said while going to the fridge and grabbing some water.

"Byron flew to Florida to train with someone. He's gone for a month." She seemed less than thrilled.

I took a swig and watched her. "You okay?"

"I'm fine."

She was definitely *not* fine. I went to the couch and sat down next to her. "Why are you pissed?"

She put the remote down and exhaled. "I've been spending all this time with him..."

"Why do you say that like it's a bad thing?"

"I've made him a stand-in for Micah," she said, disappointed.

"What are you talking about?"

"I divorced my husband, then hooked up with some

guy I met at a bar. He's not the one, Norah. He's my rebound."

"You know that's not a factual term, right? Someone came up with that word so they could have sex with a stranger after they broke up with someone else and not feel guilty about it. It doesn't mean the next guy or girl you're with can't be important."

She glared at her fidgeting hands and sighed.

"I think you like him," I said with a smirk.

She looked at me.

"And I think you like him so much that you're trying to find an excuse not to like him."

Janet took an extended breath.

"How does he feel about you?" I questioned.

"We don't talk about that," she said with sadness.

I leaned towards her. "From what Wil says, Byron is the new girl every week kinda guy."

"Oh, great, thanks," she said sarcastically.

"But he's been spending a lot of time with you for weeks. Players rarely do that with someone they don't like."

She furrowed her brow. "When did you become the aforementioned player-whisperer?"

I gave her a knowing look.

She paused. "Sorry."

"It's fine. I know you hate it when someone proves you wrong. Go ahead, I can take it."

She laughed. "Shut up."

"Just ask him, Janet. You're both adults. If he's just messing around, and you're okay with that, no harm, no foul. But if you like him, he should know that too."

She twisted her mouth while she thought.

"Maybe he's just waiting for you to say it first. You

know how guys are," I said, rolling my eyes.

When she said nothing else, I knew not to push her into talking about it further.

I stood. "I know it's late, but let's order a pizza."

She grabbed my arm and pulled me back to the couch with force. "Oh no, you sit back down and tell me why you're so damn happy."

"Happy?" I asked, puzzled.

"You've been moping around here for weeks, now you're floating. Spill it."

I couldn't help the smile that crossed my face. "I think Wil and I are going to try…something."

"Oh, kinky. I like it." She raised an eyebrow. "Are you guys crossing over into BDSM?"

"What is wrong with you? No, I mean, I think we're trying to be a couple?" I didn't intend for it to come out like a question.

"You don't know?"

I stammered. "We… We haven't solidified it, but I think we're moving in that direction."

"Then why are you here?" There was obvious annoyance in her tone.

I paused and exhaled softly. "Because you were right. He slept with Amber on his birthday."

She looked at me, flabbergasted. "Wait, he told you?"

I nodded.

"Wow, he was honest about sleeping with another woman? What's that like?" she questioned scornfully.

I snickered. "I know it's noble that he told me at all, and trust me, I appreciate the transparency." I let my smile fade. "But shouldn't I be mad or disgusted about it?"

She shrugged. "You weren't together, and he obviously doesn't want to be with her, right?"

"That's what he says."

"Then you're fine. Just keep one eye open in case he's a scumbag and plays the both of you."

I looked away.

"But I highly doubt it," she amended. "Besides, the way he looks at you tells me all I need to know."

I smiled, thinking about the way Wil looked at me and knew exactly what she was talking about.

"Wil's a boy scout and loves relationships. You'll probably be married by Christmas." She unmuted the TV and sat back on the couch with her arms crossed.

I scoffed and shoved her leg, making her crack a small grin.

We ended the night when Byron called her. I snuck out of the room to give her privacy so they could have the conversation they needed to have. I was sure I would hear about it the next morning.

Around midnight, my phone vibrated beside me as I lay restless in the dark. Sleep was not coming. Both from the excitement of our breaking story and the absence of Wil. I lifted my phone to see my lock screen.

Wil: Why did I let you leave?

I smiled.

Norah: I wondered that myself.

Wil: I know it's the right thing to do and all, but you not being here is agony.

Norah: Now you're just being melodramatic.

Wil: I can't breathe without you. THAT'S melodramatic.

I laughed.

Norah: Haven't you ever felt that way about anyone?

Wil: I have. But that sort of bullshit line would never work on you.

Norah: You don't know that.

Wil: Norah?

Norah: Yes?

Wil: There has never been a woman more perfect for me than you. You own me.

Norah: (eye roll)

Wil: See.

Norah: LOL, okay, you win.

Wil: Hang on, let me try another one.

The little typing bubbles stayed for a good five minutes, then disappeared altogether. Nothing had come through.

Norah: Growing old over here.

Wil: Nah, never mind. I forgot what I was gonna say.

Norah: You know I know you're lying.

Wil: Doesn't matter.

I frowned at the screen, then hit call on my phone. He picked up on the first ring.

"Stalker," he answered.

"Tell me what you were going to say."

There was a pause.

"Tell me," I pushed.

"Another time," he answered softly.

I hesitated. "So this isn't some corny line you were going to lay on me. It was something you meant."

"I realize you're a fantastic journalist, but how do you know I'm not just messing with you?"

"'Cause you wouldn't be trying so hard to get out of it."

I heard him exhale with some frustration mixed in

with his decision to concede. "Just know that you're the first woman that I've wanted to get to know better in a long time."

I let that sink in. "Was that a line?"

"No," he whispered.

"Good." I smiled. "Because it worked."

THE FLIGHT TO Chicago was a fast two-hour jump from New York. I had kept my anxiety at bay due to my quick dip into my stash and the knowledge that Wil would be with me. I knew this codependency on him was not conducive to my wellbeing. I would eventually be without him for a flight, but I liked how his presence was soothing. It gave me hope I could eventually do this on my own. Something I hadn't felt since I was a kid.

The internet rocketed the article about John Thornton to the top story of the day on social media. It trended on Twitter and caused Thornton to release a statement calling us "fake news" and said we were "second-rate journalists." Didn't make the blowback any less costly for his business. It even caused a few women not on the lawsuit to speak out about how Thornton was sexually aggressive towards them too. He lost three major advertising deals in a matter of hours. I gave him five days to announce he was dropping out of the race to become president. Wil said three.

We met with a community leader on the Southside of Chicago the afternoon after we landed. We brought a photographer from the magazine with us to get stills and video footage of Terrance Ackerman and his organizer's program. We wanted to document their work in the community to stop gun violence that had skyrocketed in recent years. Ackerman was a former gang member turned activist who had dedicated his life to saving young people from falling into the same trap he did as a teenager. We visited a few places from Terrance's past, then met the kids he was working with.

I pitched the idea of making a mini-documentary to feature on the website to coincide with the piece for the anniversary issue. Jerry loved it and demanded the raw footage before we landed in New York.

"Once we get back, work with Tom. He's the audiovisual guy. He'll edit the video and record your voice-over," I said to Wil, typing on my computer.

We were in my room at a hotel on Michigan Avenue. Wil was on the love seat, his socked feet dangling over the armrest while he chewed on his thumb, focusing on the computer on his lap. I was sprawled out on the bed, lying on my stomach on a white-and-gray comforter, facing him.

"How are you comfortable?" he asked without looking at me. His screen lit his sexy smirk.

I tilted my head. "Did you hear what I said, or are you just being cute?"

He chuckled. "I heard you. Tom. I got it."

"I just shot him an email and cc'd you." I pushed myself up and sat cross-legged in the middle of the bed. I was doing what I could with the footage we got on my editing program. It wasn't perfect but enough to show Jerry what it should be.

"Norah?" Wil asked.

I didn't look up. "Yep."

"Will you go on a date with me?"

I met his ocean blue eyes with my mouth open. "What?"

"We don't have to leave until tomorrow. I don't want to be stuck in this room all night. Let me take you out on a date."

I smiled. "Let me get this straight. We are in a hotel room with a perfectly good bed." I patted the comforter under me. "And you want to go out?"

He smirked, laid his laptop on the ground, then stood and sauntered over to me, never breaking eye contact. Leaning his hands on both sides of me on the bed, he brought his lips inches away from mine. "We already know we're good at this," he said and nodded to the bed. "Let's see what else we can be good at."

"But I really like this," I said with a childlike whine.

"Oh, I do too," he whispered, running his nose along the side of my cheek, then brushing his mouth against mine. I exhaled loudly. "But there's a concert at Millennium Park I want to take you to."

"A concert," I replied, closing my eyes, wishing he would touch me. He continued to run his nose lightly against parts of my face, and I felt the heat of his breath along my neck and in my ear. I laid my hand on his shoulder, encouraging him forward so we could connect more. "But what if I wanted to stay in?" I asked, craving.

He pulled back and watched me. His smoldering eyes told me he was just as turned on as I was, but he didn't move. My breath was heavy, and my eyes pleaded with him to take me.

"Well, I do owe you one," he answered and stood, moving my computer off the bed.

He got on his knees and unwrapped my legs quickly, then pulled me to the edge of the bed, where he got to work on the button and zipper on my jeans. He got them off in seconds while I giggled at the swiftness of

M. Jane Early

his motions. I watched in shock as I hoped what he was planning was what I had ached for. His eyes were like diamonds and sparkled when he looked at me.

He kissed the inside of my thighs, nibbling and running his tongue against my skin. My hands found his soft hair, and the spontaneous moans emerged.

He leaned away, making me meet his eyes. "We're going to make this quick. The concert starts at eight." He smirked at me, and I furrowed my brows at him.

Without warning, he moved my panties to the side and ran his tongue against me. Every muscle in my abdomen flinched, and my fingers clutched the comforter instantly. Wil wasn't taking any time. He immediately went to my silky clit and stayed there, sucking and licking to make sure this orgasm was not only fast but satisfying. I threw my head back and focused on his talent. When he knew I was close, he slipped two fingers inside me, causing all the air to leave my lungs as the sweet sensation of his skills came to a head. I tried to lower my tone until he left me no choice but to give him the full-throated orgasm he obviously wanted.

Unable to hold myself up with my weakened arms, I fell back on the bed, drawing in the breath he had stolen with his oral attack. I watched him stand and smirk down at me.

"Be downstairs in twenty minutes, Matthews," he said, then gathered his things from the couch and left me on the bed.

I watched him walk out without looking at me again. "Son of a bitch," I whispered and laughed.

Chapter Twenty-One

Wil

I wasn't planning on anything sexual during this trip, but I couldn't help wanting to spend some time admiring Norah's beautiful body and listening to those angelic moans. Sex with her was top-shelf. There was no question she was quickly becoming the best intimate partner I had ever been with, but was it enough to fall in love with her? That physical act was important in any relationship, and since she and I started it straightaway, it was hard to separate what was real and what could just be lust.

We still had a big, blaring, pink dancing elephant in the room that wasn't leaving anytime soon. As much as I wanted to ignore the repercussions of the editor's job, it hung off my shoulders like an anvil and weighed me down the more I liked Norah. I wanted to believe it would be fine if we just stayed the course. If she got it, I'd be disappointed, but I wouldn't leave the magazine. I liked Jerry and the pieces assigned to me. Also, I enjoyed being back in New York. I'd forgotten how much I missed it. And no matter how much she'd fought against me, called me frat boy, and thought I was trying to take something near and dear to her, I liked her. I liked Norah.

We walked around Millennium Park, enjoying the weather and admiring the beautiful structures spread throughout the landscape. I took her to the Bean and the Crown Fountain before we went to the Jay Pritzker Pavilion and sat on the grass towards the back to enjoy the concert. Norah admired the building's architecture and the metal beams above the venue that stretched back to where we sat.

I laid down a blanket I stole from my hotel room and motioned for Norah to sit. She wore a sleeveless yellow sundress with sandals, showing off her firm legs and arms. I had a feeling she was making herself more enticing so we could finish what I started when we got back to the hotel. It was working.

"What are we listening to?" she asked, eyeing me.

"Debussy," I answered and smiled.

"Really?" She sounded surprised.

"You don't like classical?"

"It's not that, I just didn't know you did."

I chuckled. "I guess there's a lot we don't know about each other."

She rolled her eyes. "It's just a music preference, don't get dramatic. We *do* know a lot about each other." Her sweet tone made me smile.

"What's my brother's name?" I asked.

"Devin. What's my sister's name?"

"Myra. Who was the girl who broke my heart?"

"Amanda Klein." She stared at me. "And she was a

stupid girl."

I laughed and turned away. When I met her eyes again, she glowed from the light in front of us. The music began and floated above us like a bird flying through the sky, but I couldn't take my eyes off the woman beside me. I hated how complicated this was and how much I wanted everything to be normal. And if not for this petty part, it would be.

A vibration in my pocket drew me away from Norah. I hadn't noticed I was even leaning towards her until then. I pulled the phone out of my pocket and saw Amber's name scrolling across the top. I closed my eyes, then exhaled, silencing the ringer.

"Haven't told her yet?" she asked with her eyebrow raised.

"Haven't had the time," I said. The sounds of *Two Arabesques* played from the piano onstage.

"Are you avoiding her?" she asked curiously.

I nodded, watching the woman onstage deliver one of my favorite pieces beautifully. "I fucked up." I paused. "Now I have to be the asshole who has to tell someone they're not interested."

"And fuck up my free facial." She turned to me.

I looked at Norah and fell in love with the smirk on her face. I couldn't help but laugh.

"Just be honest with her," she said and faced forward again. "She might not like it, but at least she'll know."

I nodded solemnly. "Thanks."

She nodded too. The silence extended between us, filled by the melodies swirling around the park.

"Why *did* you sleep with her?" Norah asked suddenly.

I looked at her profile. "Truth?"

"No, lie to me. I like it," she answered sarcastically.

I laughed softly, then sighed. "Seeing you with Parker…" I paused and shook my head. "I've never wanted to throw someone out of my house just for being with someone I liked. And when you left, it bruised my ego. I thought, maybe, sleeping with Amber would help me move forward."

The smile I could stare at for the rest of my life retreated, and Norah looked down.

"I know that sounds like I used her… I guess I did. And, again, it was a galactically stupid decision. It wasn't fair to her. I'm a selfish prick."

Her eyes moved around the ground while she thought and played with her fingers in her lap. "I only brought Parker to your house because I wanted you to think *I* had moved on. That's why he left. He figured out I was essentially using him too." She shook her head and glanced at me. "So, we're both really awful people."

I exhaled and took her hand in mine. She watched me as I spoke, "Or we just really like each other."

"While being awful people," she said and laughed, leaning towards me.

I ran the back of my fingers across her cheek and pulled her towards me, meeting my lips with hers. The music in the background rose, and the warmth of her skin flowed through me. I treasured the feeling of her tongue against mine. She wrapped her arm around me and scooted closer until she was on my lap. We inadvertently gave the surrounding people a sideshow.

As much as I wanted to spend the night with her and finally wake up with her in my arms, I wouldn't do that. I had overstepped my imaginary boundary of waiting to touch her like that again. Whatever this was between us,

I needed to make sure it was more than sex. Norah was amazing, and someone I missed when she was gone and wanted to be with when she was near. But I had made the mistake of putting a woman over everything else in my life before, and it crushed me. I had to be sure this relationship would be worth whatever came. And with Norah, a lot was coming.

Norah

Wil and I sat in the deli for lunch the day before we were leaving for LA. Only Jerry would make anyone work over a holiday weekend. The Fourth of July wasn't a holiday I celebrated, but I still would have rather sat in my apartment and watched the New York skyline light up with fireworks than be on a work trip. However, since it was with Wil, I decided it was worth the sacrifice.

I got a text message and took out my phone.

Janet: I talked to Byron.

Norah: And? What did he say?

Janet: He wants me to fly out and see him for the Fourth.

Norah: See! That's great!

Janet: Should I?

Norah: Um, yeah. Why are you even questioning this?

Janet: I'm moving too fast with him.

Norah: No, you're not. Micah treated you like shit, Byron doesn't. Have a good time, but talk to him. Tell him how you feel.

Janet: Why is this sooooo hard!?

Norah: Because you're making it hard. Go! I'll see you when you get back.

Janet: Fine. Will you be okay?

Norah: I'll be in Cali with Wil. I'm perfectly fine.

Janet: Don't get pregnant.

Norah: Me? YOU don't get pregnant, slut…

Janet: Takes one to know one.

I laughed and put the phone down. "Janet's going to see Byron in Florida," I said and shook my head.

"Good." Wil took a sip of water. "He texted me yesterday. He's lonely."

"Is he?" I asked, then laughed.

"I don't think he's lonely for just anyone." He raised his eyebrows.

I chuckled. "You called it. Match made in heaven."

"They're good for each other." He paused, then looked at me. "Are you doing anything this weekend?"

I shrugged. "Probably hit a few parties, see if I can score some X and have sex with a bunch of strangers. Why?"

Wil's face was comical. He looked at me as if I were full of shit. Which I was.

I laughed and picked up my sandwich. "I wasn't planning on anything, Wilson. What's up?"

He made an irritated noise. "Please don't ever call me that. There's only one woman on this planet who calls me Wilson, and she gave birth to me." He put down his sandwich and wiped his hands on a paper napkin.

"How do you feel about staying in LA a little longer than a day?"

I looked at him, confused. "Why?"

"Every year, my parents have a barbeque for the Fourth. It's nothing big, just family. But I was gonna go since we'd be in town. Or rather, my mother would kill me if she knew I was in town and *didn't* come." He laughed. "I wanted to know if you wanted to come with me."

"Really?" I asked, surprised.

He smiled. "Yes, really."

"You… You want me to meet your parents?" I stumbled.

He laughed and said, "Is that so horrible?"

I furrowed my brows and stared at nothing in particular, gathering my thoughts.

"Out with it, Matthews. What are you thinking?" He put his elbows on the table, watching me.

I paused. "It's just, we haven't established what we are yet. Are you sure it's a good idea?"

"Okay, what are we?" His voice was soft.

"You tell me," I answered defensively.

He tried to get something out of the side of his mouth with his tongue while he thought. "I don't know if I'm ready to put a label on us at the moment, but I know I like you." He didn't look away from me.

My nervous smile emerged. "I like you too."

He watched me carefully. "Do you want to see anyone else?"

I shook my head. "Do you?"

He shook his head as well.

I looked down. "Okay."

"So, what do you say?" His tone was low and sexy.

I nodded and smiled at him. "Yeah. I'll go to the Lockwood family barbeque with you."

He laughed and nodded. His eyes bore into mine. "Good."

I couldn't keep the ridiculous grin off my face.

"By the way," he said and held his cup close to his mouth to take a drink, "don't take anything for the flight tomorrow. I have an idea."

AS NAUSEATING AS it was, I kept my promise to not medicate myself. I did, however, bring the bottle with me, just in case whatever Wil was planning didn't work. He picked me up to go to the airport early that morning. He didn't want to tell me what he was planning for fear if the element of surprise were absent, I would just talk myself into his efforts failing.

When we got to the gate, he held my hand and took me through some visualization exercises he had been studying online. Just the fact he had taken the time to do that made me smile through the nervousness.

When boarding began, my palms started sweating, and my heart raced. Wil stayed close, continuing to coach me through breathing techniques. When we sat, I tried to remain calm, but everything Wil had just said had flooded out of my brain, and panic quickly replaced it.

"I hope you have something else in the chamber besides breathing and visualization because I'm freaking out," I said while looking out the small oval window.

Wil came closer, and his hand landed on my neck, under my hair. When I turned to him, he was right in front of my face. His crystal blue eyes and shadowed beard gleamed in the sun coming from the window. He smelled delicious. That masculine fragrance of his sea-and-surf soap invaded my senses. I wanted to program it in my memory forever because of what it did to my insides. His minty breath covered me as I leaned forward to connect with his lips.

Wil and I were taking things painstakingly slow. We were spending time together, but we hadn't had any form of sex since Chicago, no matter how much I pleaded. When he presented an opportunity to break that pattern, I jumped at the chance.

His mouth stayed slow and methodical however long he continued to kiss me. He pulled me closer, and I happily let him. His hands traveled around my back, then in my hair, then down again. My concentration was solely on Wil and how my body reacted. I wanted so badly to cover us with a blanket and do more. The heightened sense of wanting Wil was more than I thought I could take.

When he finally eased his lips, he pulled back from me, staring intensely into my eyes. It was exciting and terrifying at the same time. No one had ever looked at me like that.

He leaned his forehead against mine, panting. "Should we put that on our list of acceptable distractions?"

I turned to look out the window. We were high above the clouds, the blues skies above us clear. I met his gaze again, shocked, and smiled. "I think that should be the *only* acceptable distraction," I answered, then kissed him again.

Chapter Twenty-Three

Wil

I was thankful the flight from New York to LA was five hours long. After kissing Norah for the first half of the trip, I wouldn't have been able to stand without getting amused and disgusted looks from the rest of the passengers. I honestly thought about taking her into the bathroom on the plane, but I didn't want to cheapen our next time. I hadn't touched Norah like that in weeks. A dirty airplane bathroom was no place to start our intimate relationship again.

We rented a car and drove to Santa Monica to prepare for our interview with David Powers. There had been a lot of buzz about the CEO of Imperium Communications because of what he did with his father's dying company, and how he created a nonprofit to explore new treatments for dementia patients—something his father had suffered from. He was newly engaged with a baby on the way and had an interesting and sobering backstory.

"So this guy talks openly about his dad cheating on his mom?" Norah asked as we drove to the interview.

I glanced at her. "Yeah."

"Wow," she whispered.

"And he doesn't hide how much he and his father didn't get along, even up to and until he died. He says it gave him a new outlook on life and how not to take anything for granted."

Norah turned quiet for a moment and looked out the window. "It'll be interesting to see how he feels about him now," she mumbled.

"What do you mean?"

"I mean, now that he's gone, does Powers still hate his dad for putting him through what he did?" she wondered with a sadness in her voice.

I glanced her way again, unable to see her expression. "I think you should ask him."

She turned to me.

"But very gently," I said and smiled.

She smiled back, but it didn't meet her eyes.

She took the lead when talking to Powers. The questions she asked were personal, but it didn't seem like she was asking for the piece. I'd never seen her more direct with her follow-up questions. I wanted to believe she had taken my advice, but this felt different. Like she was searching for an answer to a question she hadn't shared with me yet.

An hour later, we left the Imperium building, and Norah remained quiet while I went over the interview in my head. When we reached the car, I stopped and took her hand.

"Hey," I said, and she turned to me. "Are you okay?"

She broke out of whatever trance she was in and

smiled. "I am. I'm sorry."

"There's nothing to be sorry for." I moved closer to her.

She paused. "You know I've never been this close to the beach on the West Coast?"

"Really?"

She nodded. "Think you can show me the Pacific Ocean?"

I smiled. "Your wish, my command. C'mon."

We were a half a mile from the Santa Monica Pier. She didn't want to be around a crowd, so we walked along the beach beside it. The weather was warm, with a slight breeze coming off the ocean. The water in California differed from New York. I missed the clean smell of the salt water in the air.

"This reminds me of my childhood," I said breaking the silence between us. "My mother hated taking us to the beach, but we'd beg to go at least once a month when we were kids."

Norah glanced at me. "Why did she hate it?"

"Three kids getting sand everywhere and in everything was not Mom's idea of a good time." I peered at her. "It would take her days to get the car clean." I chuckled at the memory.

She laughed and nodded. "I didn't even see an ocean in real life until I moved to New York." She stared straight ahead. "My mother wasn't fond of doing many things with my sister and me. The only time we really got to go anywhere was for school trips. Even then, we'd have to pay sometimes, and I couldn't get the money." Her voice lowered, and I heard the anger.

I understood Norah's resentment towards me when we first met. My home life was something I had taken for granted, thinking everyone shared the same experiences. I had a mom and dad in the house, both of whom loved my siblings and me more than themselves. There was never a question about having what I considered normal things. House, cars, vacations. Norah had none of that. She barely had a mother that cared. Maybe not even that.

"What happened to your dad?" I asked.

"He left after I was born. I'm sure my mother drove him away. But Jerry and my aunt Lydia would send us gifts and cards for Christmas and birthdays to keep in touch. After I moved to New York, they told me my father was in Montana. He had started a new life with a new family." She paused. "He never really wanted anything to do with us."

I remained quiet. Norah was on the verge of opening up, and I needed to give her space to do so.

"My mom got married to Roy Baker when I was five." I watched the narrowing of her eyes and the clench of her jaw when she spoke his name. "We moved into his trailer, and Myra and I had to share a room, which is to say we shared the front room and had to sleep on a pullout couch." She shook her head. "He was worthless. He collected unemployment and reminded us daily how financially inconvenient we were. He hated his life, and he made damn sure we knew it."

Norah kept her focus forward as we continued to walk in the warm sand. The seagulls above us merged with the sounds of the waves crashing.

She continued, "Myra left when she was sixteen to go stay with her friend. She and Roy… They would fight a lot. And when she left, there was no one else there to take the brunt of his anger."

I stopped and moved in front of her. "He hurt you?"

She took a breath. "Occasionally, but the mental abuse was harder to take. The physical bruises healed, the mental ones..." She looked down and shook her head.

"Where was your mom?" I asked incredulously.

"Drunk and indifferent."

The anger rose in my body. I had the sudden urge to fly to Texas and find wherever these heartless bastards were to show them what it was like to be beaten because of rage.

"What happened to them?" I asked with disdain.

She looked at me. "He died of a heart attack when I was fifteen."

"Son of a bitch got off easy," I mumbled.

"Yes, he did. But she's the one I blame." Her eyes softened and tears pooled as she continued. "She let it all happen. She was too weak to leave or stand up for us. You're supposed to protect your kids against people like Roy. She didn't. She gave us up as lambs for the slaughter so he wouldn't come after her." Her voice broke at the end.

I pulled her to me and wrapped my arms around her protectively. There was nothing I wanted more than to erase what Norah had been through. Turn it into a terrible nightmare rather than her reality. I didn't know what it was like to be uncared-for by your parents. How hopeless and lonely it must have felt. I wished I'd known her then. I would have begged my parents to take her in so she could know what a family was supposed to look like. She would've known she was loved.

She pulled back from me with tears falling down her cheeks. "That was a lot. I'm sorry."

"Don't you ever apologize for telling me about your

past." I wiped away her visual pain with my thumb. "You had no control over any of that."

She sniffed and exhaled. "I need to clean myself up before I meet your parents," she said with nervous laughter.

I smiled and nodded. "C'mon." I took her hand and led her back to the car.

I LEARNED MORE about Norah in the two-hour car ride to Irvine. She stayed to herself in school and didn't have a lot of friends. With friends, you had to explain why they couldn't come over. Why she had to wear the same clothes and couldn't get what was in style. She got a job when she turned fifteen to earn money, but more importantly, so she could stay away from the dysfunction in her home.

She didn't mention her mother again, and I didn't bring her up. From what I could tell, the last time Norah talked to her was when she left Texas, and that wasn't even a conversation. She merely packed the things she wanted to take and left. She had only told Myra where she had gone.

We rode in silence until I glanced at her a few times. She turned to me and asked, "What?" when she read my expression.

"Do you know how amazing you are?" I said and watched her hair flutter around her face from our cracked windows.

She looked away. "I don't feel amazing."

"You should. Few people can rebound like that. You took what you went through and turned it into motivation. Look at you. You left Texas and went to New York,

Norah. *New York*. That city will eat you alive if you let it, but you didn't. My level of admiration and infatuation just went up to one hundred." I shook my head.

A smile inched across her stunning face. She leaned over and grabbed my hand from the steering wheel and interlaced our fingers. I watched her for a moment, then rubbed her thumb with mine.

We pulled up to my parents' house by midafternoon. Norah peered out the window at the two-story beige stucco house with black trim. My parents moved here when I was a freshman in high school and vowed to update it so they could sell it and use the equity for retirement.

"What do your parents do again?" Norah asked while getting out of the car.

"My dad's a lawyer with a habit of talking about baseball more than anything else, and my mom works for the transportation department but secretly wants to be Martha Stewart." I walked around to the back of the car and pulled our bags from the trunk.

"So that's how you afforded your Cornell schooling." She eyed me playfully.

"I thought we'd gotten past that?" I joked.

"The bear was a truce, not a statement saying I would never bring it up again," she said as we walked towards the front door.

"Don't let the big house fool you. I worked my ass off for scholarships and grants. I didn't want to have twenty-five years' worth of student loan debt or expect my parents to pay for everything." I knocked on the door and looked at her.

She got closer. "You know I know how hard it is to get into an Ivy League school, right? I just give you shit because I wish I could have gone to one too."

I stared at her. "You could've."

She smiled and bit her lip.

My mother swung the door open with a dish towel over her shoulder and her medium, brown hair falling in her face. Her jeans were covered in flour, and she'd folded her white shirt sleeves up to her elbows.

"What exploded?" I asked, smirking and scanning her from head to toe.

"You know what?" She came forward and hugged me. "You can keep the smart-ass remarks to yourself until you're all the way in the door." She squeezed me tightly and got the remnants of flour all over me too.

She pulled back and looked at the woman by my side. "And you must be Norah." My mother held out her powdered hand. "I'd hug you, but you seem sweet. I won't do to you what I just did to him."

Norah laughed and shook it. "It's nice to meet you, Mrs. Lockwood. Thank you for letting me crash your weekend."

"Alyssa, please. Come on in." She moved to the side. "Your father is in the den watching the Dodgers."

"Where are the others?" I asked, setting our bags by the stairs.

She led us into the newly renovated kitchen. "Melanie, Joseph, and the baby will be here tonight. Devin's out back pulling the picnic table out of the garage."

She walked around the granite countertop island, also new, and started mixing whatever concoction she was working on.

"How's he doing?" I remained at the entrance of the kitchen, and Norah stood close by my side, looking around.

"Good. He's going to a few meetings a day and works at Costco during the overnight shift." She shrugged. "It's progress."

I nodded and peered out the window, looking for my little brother.

"Hey!" I heard from behind me. I turned to see my dad approaching. His hair had gotten more salt than pepper since I'd last seen him, and he was moving a little slower than usual. His knee must have been acting up. He needed surgery, but damn if the man wouldn't budge on seeing the doctor.

"Dad, hey." I leaned in and hugged him. I pulled back and kept my hand on his shoulder. "What's the score?"

"Five, zip. The Padres are good this year." He shook his head, then turned to Norah. "Hi, I'm Bill." He extended his hand.

She took it. "Norah. Hi."

"I'm going to go make sure Devin found all the chairs in the garage." Dad walked past us to get to the back door.

"I'll help you, Dad." I walked with him.

"No, it's fine." He shooed me away with his hand. "Show Norah your room. Get comfortable." He walked out before I could answer.

I looked at Mom. "I saw the limp."

She shook her head and stirred more vigorously. "Don't even get me started. Go." She nodded towards us. "You two get settled in. Dinner's at six-thirty."

I turned to Norah and put my hand on the small of her back as we walked out of the room. I leaned to grab our bags and caught her eye. She looked overwhelmed.

"Are you okay?" I asked, walking towards her.

She nodded and laughed. "Yeah, it's just a lot."

I chuckled and turned towards the stairs. "That's just my parents. Wait until you meet the rest of them," I said, climbing with Norah behind me. We went down the long hallway, passing Devin's room, then stopped at my door. Ahead of us was the main bedroom where my parents slept.

I opened the white door and went inside. Norah came in behind me as I set our bags on the floor. She looked around, then immediately went to where my trophies sat. Her head angled to the top shelf as she crept to her left.

She peered at me over her shoulder, amused. "The debate team?" she asked with a smirk.

I nodded and smiled shyly back. "Yeah."

She turned back to my awards. "Chess club, Latin club. Math club?" Her voice rose an octave.

I joined her side. "Yep."

She turned to me. "These are all academic clubs."

I nodded again.

"No sports?"

"You seem surprised."

"No offense, but you're more the sexy, wide receiver–type rather than the brainiac."

I came beside her. "While I can tell you how to make a football and where the leather comes from, my hand-eye coordination is shit."

"Really?" She giggled.

"Don't sound so shocked," I answered.

She moved to her left again and stopped at my dresser. Going over the photographs I'd decided not to take with me when I moved. She picked one up and stared at it. Her smile widened.

"Is this you?" She traced the picture with her finger. "Prom."

She gasped. "Is this the infamous Amanda?"

I laughed. "No, she broke up with me in the middle of my freshman year. That's Katie Paulson."

She looked at me. "Girlfriend?"

I smiled. "No, just a good friend."

"You were cute," she said playfully, staring at the picture again.

"Was I?" I came closer to her. My chest touched her upper arm.

Her eyes traveled in my direction. "You're sexy as hell now. So yeah, you were cute."

I laughed as she set the frame down and walked away without looking at me, continuing to inspect my room. My wooden desk was to the right of my bed. She ran her fingers along the twin bed comforter and made her way to my prized possession. She lingered by it, her shoulders rising slowly, then lowering instantaneously. All the air rushed out of her nose.

"Exactly how long did this take you?" she asked.

I sat on the bed, facing away from her, and put my elbows on my knees. "About a month."

I turned and watched her tilt her head, still gauging the model. She walked over to where I sat and stood above me. "The Death Star?" Her left eyebrow rose along with the side of her mouth.

"Yeah, I was a nerd. What'd you want me to say?"

She laughed loudly, throwing her head back. She moved between my legs and put her hands on my shoulders. "I would have gone out with you in high school."

I gazed into her eyes and chuckled. "You would

have, huh?"

She nodded and ran her thumb over my neck. I pulled her closer by her hips and stared at the button on her jeans, then unbuttoned it.

"What are you doing?" she asked, hushed.

"I've been dying to try something." I pulled her zipper down.

"Wil," she whispered loudly and backed up.

"Come here," I said in a low tone, pulling her back to me.

My fingers traced the tops of her jeans as I tried to slide them down. She backed away again.

"No!" she exclaimed, laughing. "No," she repeated quietly.

"Why?" I whispered back. Her smile was intoxicating. It just made me want her more.

"We are in your *parents'* house," she answered, wide-eyed.

"So?"

She chuckled. "So, you know I can't be quiet and especially if you're planning on doing what I think you're about to do."

"Oh, I'm definitely doing that." I returned my hands to complete the task.

She pushed them away. "Wil, no." She undid the little progress I had made by pulling up her jeans, zipping the zipper, and buttoning the button.

I sighed, looked up at her, and stuck out my bottom lip.

She scoffed. "Don't look at me like that. We've been…whatever we are for a few weeks, and you chose *now* to want to start this again?"

"Trust me, this is the most action this room has ever

seen."

She laughed as she spoke. "Oh, so you're doing this for the benefit of the room?"

"Partly." I met her eyes. "But mainly because I've missed you."

Her smile faded, and she looked at me with confusion. "But I've been right here."

"That's not what I meant." I shook my head, then stood, laying my hands on her hips. "I've missed feeling your skin on mine. Making you moan in my ear. I've missed tasting every single part of you. Slowly."

Her breath became shaky as I brushed her lips with mine, then rested my head against hers. "I've been counting the hours until I can feel you under me. On top of me. Waiting to hear you tell me you're coming so I can too." I met her full lips with mine.

In a flash, she moved out of my hold, then said breathlessly, "You gotta go."

"What?"

She shook her head and pulled me by my arm. "I'm going to go splash some cold water…everywhere, then meet you downstairs when dinner's ready." She dragged me to the door, then turned to me.

"Are you sure?" I asked softly, moving against her again.

She pushed me back. "If you don't leave, I'm sure your mother will think I'm the most disrespectful houseguest ever with the amount of sex I want to have with her son right now."

I smirked, then ran my tongue against my molars. I tried the best smolder I could produce and lifted my hand to her neck. She slapped it away.

"Go, Wilson," she commanded.

My erection retreated directly. I threw my head back in irritation, then looked at her again. She softened from her hardened edge and came closer. She placed her arms around my neck, reaching to kiss me, careful not to give me any lingering hope I could do all those things I wanted to her.

She drew back, then moved to my ear and whispered, "I want you too."

I made a frustrated noise as she let me go, opened the door, and pushed me into the hallway, laughing.

Chapter Twenty-Four

Norah

My plan was to relax and push the sexual frustration away, but I was too tired to keep my eyes open. The bed was cozy and somehow held Wil's smell, proving comfy enough to lull me to sleep.

I woke up later and pushed myself up as the sun was setting. My phone read it was just after six. I blew out a sigh of relief that I hadn't missed dinner.

I couldn't quite pin it down, but something in me wanted Wil's family to like me. Normally, I didn't care what people thought of me. I had wasted a lot of time and energy growing up, wanting to be accepted by my mother, but rarely did I care what other people thought. This feeling wasn't the same as wanting my mother to think I was important enough to take care of. This was a feeling of wanting to be accepted. Wil's family was normal. They loved and took care of each other. To witness that was amazing, but to feel a part of it would be magical.

I gently climbed down the stairs, listening to the chatter going on in the dining room near the kitchen. The sounds of a baby happily making noises rose above everyone else's voices, and the delicious smells heavy in the air made my stomach growl.

I peeked my head around the corner and observed everyone sitting around the set table, talking. It was such a natural scene that I didn't want to intrude.

Wil caught my eye from across the room and stood. The brunette he was sitting with turned to look in my direction too. She had darker eyes than Wil but was overall just as beautiful as he was. The cherub-faced baby bouncing on her lap continued to make sounds gleefully while trying to shove a plastic toy in her mouth.

He approached me with that smile that unsteadied me. "Hey," he said with his hands in his jeans pockets.

"Hey," I answered, smiling.

"How was your nap?" he asked.

"Needed. You knew I was sleeping?" I tilted my head.

"I checked on you to see if you were okay...or had changed your mind." He smirked at me.

"Very cute," I whispered.

He chuckled, and his blue eyes danced with excitement. "Are you ready to meet everyone?"

"Do I have a choice?" I couldn't hide my nerves.

"No." He shook his head and smiled. He leaned over and kissed my forehead. "They don't bite."

He turned and moved to the side. I wanted to hide behind him. "Everyone, this is Norah."

All eyes hit me.

"Hi," I breathed and gave a small wave.

Random greetings filled the room. The baby made a loud, joyful sound, and everyone laughed, including me.

Wil took me by the hand and led me to the front of the table. "That's Melanie and Zoe," he said, pointing to the brunette and the baby. "Joseph, her husband." He paused and turned to me. "Melanie's, not Zoe's," he clarified.

"You're funny," I mumbled and eyed him.

"That's Devin." He pointed at his younger brother, who was just as handsome as Wil, but he looked exhausted. "The two old people you met before."

"Watch it," Bill said with a playful warning.

Wil walked past me, pulled out an empty wooden chair, and motioned for me to sit, then sat next to me.

There was an empty chair to my left, which I assumed was for Alyssa. She was still in the kitchen.

I leaned over to Wil. "Does your mom need help?"

"Oh god, no," Wil said with urgency. "This is her putting the final touches on the food. If you go in there, she'd just tell you to turn around and go right back out."

I smiled at Mrs. Lockwood's independence. It reminded me of my own.

Wil turned his attention back to his sister. They were discussing a case Melanie had just finished in DC. She practiced political law and was recently asked to speak in front of Congress about voting rights. I followed along but didn't interfere with their conversation.

I watched Zoe hold on to her mother's fingers as she diligently tried to put one of them in her mouth. Her beautiful, medium brown skin and dark, curly hair were nothing compared to her light hazel eyes. She was so delicate and round that even someone who didn't like babies would want to squeeze and kiss her cheeks. One bare chubby foot hung while the other showcased a sock that dangled from her toes.

I scanned around the table and did what journalists do. I observed. Devin was talking to his dad about the Dodgers' loss to the Padres. Joseph dug through Zoe's diaper bag, looking for something, then pulled out a teething ring and handed it to Melanie, replacing the other toy that had fallen onto the floor. She took it without breaking her conversation with Wil and helped Zoe grab it in her plump hand.

In the meantime, Alyssa sporadically showed from behind the counter with a new dish, setting them on the table, then disappearing again. She had cooked a four-course meal for the eight of us. I was in awe of her culinary talent.

When the last piece was laid, a beautiful spiral ham covered in pineapple and cherries, she sat down and leaned towards me. "Are you Jewish?"

"No," I answered.

"Vegetarian?"

"Nope."

"Okay, good. I forgot to ask Wil, so I made a vegetarian lasagna too, just in case." She set her napkin on her lap.

I smiled at her. "That's incredibly thoughtful. Thank you."

She winked at me.

Bill stood and called everyone's attention. "It amazes me to see all the people I love in one room. To see our family grow has brought joy to my heart I couldn't have imagined. So, I welcome Norah into our home and our hearts. Thank you for dealing with my crazy children, and I pray you love them as much as I do."

He nodded at me, and I smiled as a happiness spread in my chest. Wil reached over and took my hand in my lap. I turned to him, and he asked if I was okay. I nodded as we stared at each other. Wanting to lean over and kiss him, I looked away, finding his mom watching us, a sly smile creeping on her face. My cheeks lit up with embarrassment.

Dinner with the Lockwood's was definitely entertaining. Collectively, they hadn't seen each other since Christmas, so there was a lot to share within the last seven months. Alyssa's meal was delicious, and I was amazed to find she even baked two pies for dessert. She really was trying to be Martha Stewart.

I watched Wil more than the others. I loved how he interacted with his family. He grabbed Zoe when she got fussy, just to give Melanie and Joseph a break. I made her giggle with goofy faces and tickled her round feet. Soon after, Wil laid her on his shoulder and rocked her gently. It wasn't long before her beautiful eyes closed, and she had fallen fast asleep, drooling all over his T-shirt. I'd never thought about having kids until that moment.

"Devin, what's going on with you, man?" Wil shoveled Alyssa's cherry pie in his mouth while still rocking Zoe.

Devin was on the other side of the table, leaning his arms on top. "Same old. I got a new sponsor. Retired football player for the Rams. Wide receiver." He smiled.

"No shit?" Wil asked.

Devin nodded.

"At least you have a lot in common." Wil patted his niece's bottom when she stirred.

"Oh man, we talk for hours," Devin answered.

Wil turned to me. "Devin was all city in high school." He looked back at his brother. "All-star wide receiver." He beamed.

Devin looked at the table and tilted his head. "Yeah, until I got tackled and bent my knee ninety degrees the wrong way in college."

I winced and glanced at Wil.

"That was the beginning of the end for me." Devin gave me a smirk. I watched him while the rest of the table fell eerily quiet. "Eighteen months of surgery. More pills than I knew what to do with." He shook his head. "When I missed my window to go pro, I just felt worthless. I kept taking the pills to feel something other than the depression."

"How long have you been clean?" I couldn't stop myself from asking. My reporter hat accidentally came on, but it didn't seem to bother anyone in the room.

He smiled at me. "Two years, four months, nine days."

"That's a hell of an accomplishment," Wil replied.

Devin shrugged and looked away, embarrassed. "I've almost saved up enough money to move out of their way." He nodded at his parents.

"You know you can stay with us as long as you need to, Devin," Bill answered.

"Yeah, but I can't walk around naked."

"No, you definitely cannot do that," Alyssa said and laughed, then we all laughed with her.

It was well after eleven o'clock when we'd had our fill of Alyssa's feast. Even with my nap, I was stuffed and exhausted. Wil deposited Zoe back to her mother, her body twitching in the transfer, then took me upstairs to his room.

He closed the door and walked over to the window and cracked it lightly. "I'll be in the den. If you need anything, just text me."

"You can sleep up here." I looked at him as he froze at the window. "I don't mean with me, but I'll take the den."

"Do you know what my mother would do if she saw you downstairs on the pullout? I'd be drawn and quartered, banned from the house for life."

I rolled my eyes. "I highly doubt that."

"Besides, I haven't been able to sleep comfortably on that thing since I moved out. I don't mind, really." He drew me to him and kissed me softly. My insides burst into flames. I was tempted to ignore manners altogether while letting Wil do what he wanted, but it wasn't right. It certainly wouldn't win me any points with his family. I allowed myself to fantasize about him while we continued to kiss. We stopped when we heard the floor creak, and the muffled sounds of his mom and dad as they moved into their bedroom.

Wil sighed and looked towards the door. "They certainly know how to ruin a moment," he whispered.

I laughed, then let my face fall. "What is this?"

"What?" he answered, confused.

"Us. What are we doing?"

"Stop." He focused on me and exhaled. "Right now, we're enjoying a mini-vacation with my insane family. We'll get back to reality soon enough, and I promise we'll address this."

I exhaled as well and nodded. I didn't mean to ask such a serious question right before bed and not in his parents' house, but with everything around us, I needed clarity. He had brought me here, introduced me to his entire family, but I had no idea where we stood. Were we a couple? Were we just messing around? What would we do going forward, and what about the editor's job? There were so many puzzles floating around my head concerning Wil and me, I didn't know where to start.

Wil backed away and reached for the knob. When he opened it, he looked in my direction. "Tomorrow morning, six o'clock," he said.

I scrunched up my face. "Why so early?"

His gorgeous smile lit up the room. "Donut run." He raised his eyebrows, then ducked out the door before I could protest.

"YOU SERIOUSLY DROVE an hour for donuts?" I asked as Wil opened the door to Randy's Donuts in Downey. I walked ahead of him and looked over my shoulder. "We couldn't have gone anywhere closer?"

He smiled. "Nope. Once you've had these, you'll never be able to eat any other donut again."

There was a line ahead of us. All the patron's heads were down, looking at their phones while waiting. I stepped a few feet behind the last person.

"I used to live pretty close and would grab a few of these for my ride to work." Will rubbed his palms together with excitement. The gleam in his eye was utterly adorable.

"*Tsk, tsk, tsk.* What would Byron say?" I eyed him.

"Whatever. He's across the country. He'll never find out."

I laughed. "You're crazy."

"I'm telling you—"

"Wil?"

We both looked up and saw a tall and slender woman in line ahead of us staring at Wil. Her long brown hair was curled, and her bright blue eyes were wide and beautiful but stunned. Her full pink lips were ajar.

"Elise?" Wil responded in a low tone, and I gasped quietly.

I looked between the two of them, then noticed Wil's shoulders and jaw tense. Elise came towards us, adjusting her purse strap on her shoulder. .

"What are you doing here?" Wil asked with immediate anger.

She gave a small smile. "Donuts on Saturday. It used to be our tradition." Her voice was high and dejected.

The tension was suffocating. This moment between them felt private, and I didn't want nor need to witness it. The line had lessened, and we were falling behind.

I turned to Wil. "I'm going to order so you two can talk." I didn't wait for his response as I moved closer to the counter. Unfortunately, it wasn't far enough away to where I couldn't hear their conversation.

"How are you?" Elise asked.

"I'm good," Wil answered, his tone indicating he was anything but.

"Are you moving back or…?" Even I could read the hope in her question.

"Just visiting for the holiday," he clipped.

She paused. "Wil, can we talk?"

"There's nothing to talk about, Elise."

"Yes, there is," she said desperately. "You never gave me a chance to explain—"

"Explain what?" Wil's voice carried. I turned and looked at him over my shoulder. He met my eyes, then returned to face Elise. I looked forward as I moved farther away from them.

"Explain what?" he said lower. "That you cheated on me with that asshole because you thought I wasn't giving you enough attention? We were planning on spending the rest of our lives together. What else did you want?"

I briefly turned my head towards them, startled at what I'd just heard, when the cashier called me to attention. "Ma'am? Are you ready?"

I reluctantly pulled myself away from their exchange to place my order. Flustered, I looked at the menu above the teenager's head and started randomly naming donuts I hoped the Lockwood's would like.

I turned briefly over my shoulder to look for Wil and Elise again, finding they had moved to the corner of the room next to the hard plastic booths. He was talking to her with intensity while she was crying and begging. She took his hand in hers while saying please repeatedly. One hand was still with her, the other wiped down his face in frustration. When he turned to me, I turned away and pretended to watch the kid pack the donuts with interest.

The two boxes filled with my order sat in front of me by the register. I was told the total and reached into my pocket for my cash.

Wil came next to me. "I got it," he said in a low tone that was both exhausted and bothered. I glanced at him as he handed the cashier a fifty and waited for his change. I slid the boxes forward and turned to see Elise was gone. I peered at Wil again. He collected his change and took the boxes from me, meeting my eyes. He didn't smile, only looked away uncomfortably.

The ride home was loud with our unspoken words. I could feel and see the tension in Wil's entire body. He had clenched every muscle. I hadn't realized the hold

Elise still had on him. We'd talked about his relationship and why he left, but under that pain she'd caused, it was clear there were still feelings there.

We parked in front of his parents' home. "What did she say?" I asked when I couldn't take the quiet anymore.

He exhaled and unclenched his jaw. "She wants to talk to me." I could barely hear him.

"Is that something you want to do?"

He didn't look at me. "I don't know."

Wil's reluctance to say no confirmed everything I had assumed about them—he wasn't over her. While he thought escaping her would solve his problem, he didn't consider how it would only create a physical distance. He'd still have to deal with his bitterness.

I knew a lot about that.

"Wil," I said, but he wouldn't look in my direction. "I think you should talk to her."

His brows furrowed as his eyes went wild with confusion. He finally angled towards me. "What?"

"You obviously still have feelings for her, or you wouldn't be this angry." I kept my tone even and without hurt or annoyance. Internally, my chest felt hollow. "You said it yourself. You left without saying a word to her. You changed your number, and you never got closure."

He leaned forward. "Leaving *was* my closure."

"Was it? Because the way you're handling seeing her again tells me it solved nothing. You just moved."

He looked past me out the side window and chewed the inside of his cheek.

I exhaled. "Listen, it's up to you, but maybe you need to go talk things out with her. See where your head…and your heart's at."

His blue eyes met mine until his stare became

218

uncomfortable. I looked down and opened the door.

"Norah," he whispered.

Hesitant, I turned back to him.

"Are you sure?"

"Wil, we're not together. And even if we were, I couldn't share your heart with someone else." I got out and closed the door behind me, willing the tears not to fall.

Chapter Twenty-Five

Norah

I lingered at the double doors at the front of the house until I could keep my poker face steady. The two boxes of donuts were heavy in my hands. I cleared my throat as I rang the doorbell. When footsteps approached, I straightened and smiled as naturally as I could.

Bill opened the door with his glasses on the tip of his nose and a newspaper in his hand. "Norah, you don't have to ring the bell. Just come on in." He smiled. "Here, let me take those from you," he said, reaching for the boxes.

"Thank you," I responded and let them go.

We walked through the living room towards the kitchen. "Wil dragged you to Randy's, huh?" Bill verified with a chuckle. Besides Joseph and the baby, the rest of the family were already around the kitchen table again.

"Oh, hell yeah." Devin sat up, surprised when he saw his dad. He reached for a box before Bill even sat them down.

"Devin, damn, you act like you've never eaten one before." Melanie slapped the back of his head as she walked by.

Alyssa laughed and turned to me. "Coffee, Norah?"

"Yes, please." I went behind the counter as she handed me the mug.

"The sugar's right there, and there's cream in the fridge," she pointed behind her. "Is Wil parking the car?"

I spooned sugar into my white mug that read *World's Greatest Mom* in pink and gold glittered script but kept my head down. "Uh, no. He, uh…" All eyes fell on me. "Elise was at the donut shop."

A congregated groan echoed through the kitchen, and I peered at everyone with surprise.

"What did she want?" Alyssa questioned.

"For Wil to pay her rent, I imagine," Melanie mumbled and tore a piece of donut off to eat.

"I don't know what she wanted specifically. Just that she wanted to talk to him," I answered, still stirring the already dissolved sugar.

"And you let him?" Devin asked with annoyance. My head snapped up to him.

"Devin," Alyssa warned.

"I'm sorry, Mom, but why would she let Wil go with her? Aren't you supposed to be his girlfriend?" He stared at me.

"That's none of our business, D," Melanie replied, eyeing me.

"Wil left because of Elise." Devin's voice raised. "He flew across the country to get away from her. Why would you let him be around her?"

"Devin, maybe Norah doesn't know everything."

Bill leaned against the chair by the table.

"I'm sure she knows she cheated. Smashed my brother's heart with a fucking hammer."

"Hey!" Bill slapped the paper on the table.

The room fell quiet.

I took a breath and moved around the counter to stand where everyone could see me. "Wil and I aren't together," I revealed. "And I know that's weird with me being here, meeting all of you. But the truth is we had an assignment, and Wil was sweet enough to invite me to tag along for the weekend." I took an uneven breath. "I don't have the title of girlfriend to throw around to keep him away from Elise, Devin." Even I heard the sadness in my voice. "I'm actually the one that encouraged him to talk to her. So you're right." I nodded at Devin. "If you're going to be mad at someone, be mad at me." I certainly was.

Everyone's eyes dropped or looked away at the truth I'd just spoken. The guilt about telling Wil to talk to his ex hurt; telling his family about it made it real. I didn't *want* him to reconcile or even talk to her. I just wanted him to be okay. Better than he was in the car after he saw her.

When my sudden surge of courage dissipated, I wanted to remove myself from their gazes, which were choking me by the second.

"Excuse me," I whispered and left the kitchen.

As I climbed the stairs, I heard Melanie, "Why are you such an asshole, Devin?"

I blocked the rest of the chatter out as I went to Wil's old room.

I sat on Wil's bed and looked at all the memories of who he was as a child. The photos of his family, his various high school friends and girlfriends. The stacks of CDs in the corner with artists who ranged from Bob Dylan to Snoop Dogg. The posters on his wall of Einstein and Bobby Fischer. And the Death Star Lego set that sat on his desk. All of it was authentically Wil. My heart ached when I thought of him with Elise.

A soft knock brought me out of my thoughts, and I called for them to come in. Alyssa peeked her dark brown–haired head around the door. She had on reading glasses and looked more like a hot soccer mom than a grandmother. I smiled widely at her and how beautiful she was.

"Hi," I said, trying to keep the sorrow out of my voice.

"Is it alright if I come in?" she asked softly.

"Of course, yes." I moved closer to the head of the bed in case she wanted to sit down. She did just that. I could smell her clean, light perfume.

"Have you heard from him?" she asked.

I took a breath and shook my head. There was a pregnant pause between us.

She suddenly looked at me. "Do you like my son?"

I looked at her, unsure of what to say.

"And I don't mean, like as a friend. Do you care about him?" she clarified.

I stared ahead of me and smiled, thinking of Wil. "I do."

"Good, then I can tell you this." She turned to me. "Wil doesn't bring people around us who aren't important. You might not be his girlfriend, but there's something special about you he wanted us to see."

I watched her talk about her son with love and gratitude.

"My son lives inside his own heart, and I've seen the way he looks at you. You're not *just* his co-worker."

I exhaled. "This is so complicated," I whispered and rested my elbows on my legs, my head in my hands.

"Most things are," Alyssa said, then crossed her legs and leaned back on Wil's bed. We sat with that truth for a moment.

I didn't know how much Wil had told his mom about us. If she knew the circumstances concerning a job we both wanted, or if he told her how he felt about me. Then, a realization hit me like a ton of bricks. I wished I had someone like Alyssa to talk to about Wil.

I missed having a mom.

Not the mother I grew up with. A mom I could call when these situations came up. Someone to bounce my irrational thoughts off of, just so she could bring me back down to earth. But it all boiled down to just wanting someone to tell me it was going to be okay.

I took a long breath, and right on cue, Alyssa put her hand on my back. "You'll work it out," she said with assurance.

I tried to pull the tears back and kept my focus forward until I got a hold of myself. Then, I turned, looking at her, and said, "Thank you."

She smiled and nodded once. "Now," she stood and looked down at me, "there is a Scrabble tournament about to take place in the den. We are missing one of our most valuable players on my team, so you've been summoned to take his place."

I stared at her and flickered my eyes to the side. "Summoned by...?"

She shrugged. "Me."

"I see," I whispered, then laughed.

She walked towards the door and opened it. "Be ready to kick some ass in fifteen minutes."

"Yes, ma'am." I nodded.

She winked at me as she left the room.

AS MUCH AS I wanted time to fly by as we played Scrabble for the better part of the afternoon. It didn't. Wil's absence caused me to check the clock more often than I would have liked. Everyone figured I would be good at the game, considering I was a writer and would presumably know a lot of complex words, like Wil did. I beat Joseph first, then got creamed by Bill. He played a word worth over one hundred points, and I conceded. Melanie and I went back-and-forth with the lead in points. She was a worthy opponent, but one lawyer in the family had beaten the snot out of me. I didn't want the other one to too.

Everyone was gathered around us at the card table. Devin sat behind me on the arm of the couch. Bill, Alyssa, and Joseph stood far enough to let us concentrate but made sounds when someone had a good play.

I had four cream-colored tiles left and studied the board as if it were a chess match, and I was almost at checkmate. The word was there; I just needed to find it. A smile spread across my face as I laid my letters down. The Z landed on the triple-point square.

"Yowza," I said with a smirk.

Melanie stared at the word for a moment. "No way, that's not a word?" I loved that she even questioned herself. "Someone look it up."

Joseph pulled his phone from his pocket and searched. "Yikes." He met his wife's eyes, holding his screen so she could see. "She got you, babe."

"Nice," I heard Devin behind me.

"Shut up, D." Melanie looked at him and flipped him off.

I laughed.

"Good job, you two," Bill said and laid his hands on our shoulders.

When Melanie realized she was beaten, she exhaled. "Good game."

"Good game," I replied and smiled back at her.

"At least I had a fighting chance with you. Wil would have taken me out in ten minutes." She laughed as she put the tiles away.

Mentioning Wil made me look at the clock on the wall again. It was close to three and still no word. I furrowed my brow and helped her collect the letters.

The family split apart once we had cleaned up the den. Joseph went to get Zoe from her nap, and Melanie joined her mom in the kitchen to help prepare for the barbeque. Devin was in the backyard by the pool, smoking, and Bill had found a baseball game to watch. Before I went into the kitchen to see if I could help, I quietly snuck out the front door for some privacy. I took out my phone and texted Wil.

I wandered around the front yard, hoping he would answer me. I stared at the screen, waiting to see if the little bubbles would show but was disappointed. My imagination went crazy and in different directions, thinking about what could have happened. He could be hurt or in a car accident, or he could have not gone to see her at all and just needed time to figure out what he wanted to do. Or... I tried to stop thinking about the alternative I wanted so much not to be true. Maybe he did still love Elise and wanted to be with her. It had only been a few months since they'd been apart. Maybe I was the rebound he needed to find his way back to her. I took a long breath, keeping that thought at bay, and stuck my phone in my pocket, returning inside.

"Mom, I know. I called him. He won't answer," I heard Melanie say in the kitchen. I stopped at the mouth of the entrance. Both she and her mom had their backs to me.

Alyssa shook her head as she stirred macaroni in a glass bowl. "If that woman gets her claws into him again…"

"Wil's a grown man, Mom. It's not up to us to decide. If he's still in love with her, there's not a lot we can do," Melanie answered, peeling potatoes. The frustration in their voices was evident, and my stomach was in knots.

The pause in conversation allowed me to enter as if I hadn't been eavesdropping. "Hi," I said with a false cheerfulness.

Melanie turned around. "Hey."

Alyssa smiled warmly at me.

"Need any help?" I asked and approached the counter.

They both looked at each other. "Do you know how to make a fruit salad?" Melanie asked.

I nodded. "I think I can handle that."

"Awesome, c'mon." She moved over to make room for me. Alyssa searched for a cutting board and a knife in the cupboards below her.

An hour into preparing dinner, there was still no word from Wil. My alternative thought about how he missed Elise and wanted to be with her was looking more and more reasonable. I kept my composure through dinner, then through the fireworks. The Lockwood's backyard was a perfect place to watch the display in Irvine and across LA. Perched on a hill with no neighbors to their rear, the skyline was unobstructed, and we could see the splendid shows across the city.

Sitting in the dark on the grass, I glanced at Wil's parents holding hands, sitting next to each other on a blanket they'd retrieved from the pool house. Joseph and Melanie were behind me on a wooden bench. Little Zoe bounced on her daddy's knee as she fluttered her doe eyes at the sounds far away but otherwise paid them no mind. I exhaled at how amazing all of Wil's family was. How accepting they had been towards me, even when Wil wasn't around.

I directed my attention to the fireworks again when Devin sat next to me. I looked at him, and he handed me a bottle. "Water?" he asked.

"Thanks," I said and took it.

He sat his red plastic cup in front of him on the grass and wrapped his arms around his propped-up knees. "Sorry about earlier," he said, then smirked.

I glanced at him. "Don't worry about it."

He exhaled. "Did Wil tell you he was the one that took me to rehab? And when I say took, I mean beat my ass and dragged me into the building."

I laughed and shook my head.

"He's never let me down. Not once. Always there when I needed him." I could hear the pride in Devin's voice.

I let the sounds in the distance settle between us. "He's a good man."

"Best one I know." He took a drink. "When Elise cheated. I was the one who told him to leave. To get some distance between them. Don't even tell her, just go, I told him. And he did. I saw what she did to him, and I wasn't going to allow her to control him like that."

I nodded. "I'm sorry, Devin. Honestly, I know what Elise did to him was cowardice and broke his heart. But seeing him after seeing her... That pain he felt in that moment was all over him. I just wanted to take it away. I thought maybe if he got closure with her, he could... move on." My eyes brimmed with tears. I meant well and hoped my encouragement was a stepping-stone for Wil. I didn't think it would cause me to lose him.

"My mom always says, sometimes what we think is right isn't always best." Devin gave me a half smile.

I scoffed softly. "It's a hard lesson to learn."

"Yeah, it is," he whispered.

"I think that's it, folks," Bill called from behind us. The loud sounds in the distance had ceased.

Everyone got up and stretched, moving into the house while I stayed on the grass, staring at the city lights ahead of me.

"Norah?" Alyssa tried to get my attention.

I turned to her.

"Are you alright?"

I attempted to give her my most genuine smile. "Yes, I'm fine. I think I'm gonna stay out here a little longer."

"Of course," she said and put her arm around her husband's back. "The pool house is open if you want to relax in there. There's a TV and a couch."

"Thank you," I replied and watched them walk into the house.

I stood, wiping the grass off my jeans, and walked to the edge of their beautiful pool. The hollow feeling in my chest grew. Wil had been gone all day. Without a text, a phone call, nothing telling me he was alright. I wondered if he had gotten ahold of his sister and she just didn't tell me.

The chlorine smell coming from the water invaded my nose when I inhaled sharply. I watched the water ripple against the lights at each end. I folded my arms over my chest and put my hand over my heart, begging it to relax.

"Hi."

I turned and saw him standing near the double doors. The lights behind him on the main floor were off, and I could barely see his face.

"Hi," I breathed.

Wil walked closer with confusion in his hypnotic eyes. "What are you doing out here?" He had his hands in his pockets.

My shoulders barely lifted as I shook my head. "Thinking."

He came closer. His face wasn't bothered anymore, and he looked more relaxed. "About what?"

"You," I whispered.

He exhaled and stared at me. "I'm so sorry."

I looked down and put my hair behind my ear.

"I shouldn't have left you here for so long by yourself."

I gave him a small smile. "I wasn't here by myself." I looked towards the house. "You have an amazing family."

He glanced down and smiled too.

"We won at Scrabble," I said, then chuckled nervously.

He nodded, his smile growing. "I know. My mom sent me pictures of you playing."

"She did?"

"I think her precise words were, 'we may replace you next year,'" he joked and walked closer.

I wanted to laugh but couldn't get my body to let it, not with the fear and suspense choking me.

"Have you been with her this whole time?" I asked.

He avoided my questioning eyes. "No, I left a while ago. I drove down to San Diego to see Chase."

"Is that far?" I furrowed my brow.

He shook his head. "About an hour and a half." He scratched his forehead with his thumbnail. "I needed to think and drive. And I needed my uber-logical friend to intervene to bring me back to earth."

"Did it work?" My body shivered.

He smiled. "It always does."

My breathing became labored. "Are you going to tell me what happened?"

He nodded.

I watched as his face contorted, and he swallowed hard. "She wants to try again."

I looked down and nodded, not knowing what else to do.

He continued, "She wants to start over. She's even willing to move to New York to be with me."

It was like Elise punched me in the gut with Wil's words. Of course she wanted him back. She was a fool to let him go in the first place.

His brows furrowed. "There's something I didn't tell you about us." He crossed his arms over his chest. "I proposed to her in February."

"You were engaged?" I could barely get the words out.

He nodded. "A week after I gave her the ring, the guy

she cheated on me with paid me a visit at our apartment and told me everything. He said she was planning on breaking up with me so they could be together." He shrugged. "I didn't really consider us engaged given the short time." He squeezed his eyes shut and shook his head. "I thought leaving would help to forget. But seeing her again…everything came flooding back to me."

A tiny, painful hole in my chest grew.

"I know I had something to do with her cheating. It's never just one person's fault."

The hole stretched farther the more he talked. I backed away from him, and my hands went into my hair. I mentally prepared for him to break my heart completely.

"I can't deny what we had together."

The pain from the stretching hurt in my chest.

"Tonight, I realized—"

"Stop," I demanded and turned away from him. "You don't have to say anything else, Wil. I understand."

"What do you understand?"

I turned back to him. "You want to be with Elise. I understand that's what you want. We never established what we were, and I can't expect to be something more than her to you in a few months."

He reached me before I could get away from him. I begged him not to touch me with my eyes. I couldn't take feeling those hands on me again when I knew this was over.

I stared at him and tried to hold it together. "Just tell me what you want—"

His hand went around the back of my neck, and his lips were on mine instantly. He moved with intensity and pulled me into him, wrapping his arms around my waist. Feeling his entire body against me caused a tear to fall.

The connection between us was heartbreaking. I hated he was doing this when he wanted his ex-fiancée again, but I couldn't stop it either. I needed to feel him close again, especially if it was for the last time.

He slowed and broke away, staring at me. I didn't know if it was because I was losing him, or because these foreign emotions were getting the best of me, but the kiss felt different from anything I had ever experienced with Wil or anyone else. It was equally powerful and devastating.

"Are you crazy?" he asked breathlessly. His forehead against mine.

I paused. "What?"

"I told Elise no, Norah."

"What?" I asked again in disbelief.

He kissed me again. Not like the first time. It was slower, more tender. He stopped and ran his fingers down my cheek. "I don't want that anymore. I moved across the country to get away from her. I want this. I want you."

"But you said—"

"You didn't let me finish." His thumb caressed my bottom lip, sending tingles down my spine. "I realized being with her felt wrong. Because I don't belong to her anymore. I belong to you."

I stared at him, dumbfounded, then I exhaled. "Jesus, you *are* a good writer."

We both chuckled. His warm hands remained on my neck.

"How do we do this?" I asked, laying my hands over his.

He shook his head. "I don't know. I just know I want to."

"I do, too, but…the job—"

"I know it's important to you. It's important to me too. But there's a way. There's always a way." He paused and looked down. "Can we not think about that right now? I just want to be with you." He gently pushed his body against mine.

I looked up at him with confusion and an immense amount of fear in my eyes.

"I promise we'll figure it out," he answered.

He kissed me again, and I allowed my fear to retreat at that moment. This was complicated and confusing, but right there, standing in his parents' backyard, kissing him with all the want and need I had for him—I didn't care.

Wil

I realized as I watched Elise plead with me to take her back, she and I were mismatched. Being with Norah helped me see we were on two separate paths and made no sense anymore. Maybe we never did. My family continually tried to tell me she wasn't the one. I ignored them and thought I knew better than they did. I sunk every ounce of energy into making sure our relationship fit together. I even proposed because I thought that's what I was supposed to do. It was the next logical step. But today, with her tears and begging to give us another chance, telling me cheating was the biggest mistake of her life, I suddenly felt indifferent. While she sat in our old apartment, making her case for us to be together again, I kept comparing her to Norah. Norah's smile, her laugh, her sarcasm, her friendship. A yearning I hadn't felt before slowly grew within me. I couldn't pinpoint it until Norah's face floated to the surface of my memory.

I missed her.

I missed every ounce of her entire being but especially this. Feeling the warmth of her wrapped around me. My want for her growing every time her tongue collided with mine. Elise wasn't a factor in my life anymore. Even though the shock of seeing her sent me back to that moment when she hurt me, I no longer wanted or needed her. We were over.

I pulled back from our kiss by the pool, took Norah's hand, and led her into the pool house. I didn't recognize the new gray sectional and stone gas fireplace, but it was cozy and perfect for what I had planned. The floor-to-ceiling windows displayed the beautiful LA skyline clearly. The wooden beams above us were new, and I could smell the fresh coat of white paint on the walls.

Norah wandered around the room and stopped at the window, looking at the lights in the distance. I walked behind her and wrapped my arms around her front. She turned her head slightly and smiled. I squeezed and put my nose in her hair, inhaling the scent of her shampoo, always light and calming. She turned to me and ran her hands up my arms to the back of my neck. The look on her face was false. There was a question in her eyes that threw the façade of her smile out of whack.

"What are you thinking about, Matthews?" I whispered.

Her hesitation worried me. "This is going to mean something different, isn't it?" she asked.

I nodded. "I hope so."

"I don't know how to do this."

I furrowed my brow. "Do what?"

"Be a *girlfriend*," she said, then made a face that made us both laugh.

"It's no different from what you're doing now. Just more sex." I winked.

"Is that right?" Her genuine smile lit up the room.

"And I always want to wake up with you after."

She gazed at me with her mouth open, then rolled her eyes. "I hate when you're this fucking adorable. It makes it hard to say no to you."

I chuckled, then stared at her. "Good, because I don't want you to say no for the rest of the night."

THE FEELING OF being inside Norah was almost metaphysical. While I could feel her against me, in my hands, with my mouth—she didn't seem real. Every moan she gave, every shiver she produced, felt otherworldly. I had never experienced such a connection with someone in my life as I did when I made love to her. I wasn't a religious man and didn't care whether there was a higher power. But feeling her climb that mountain between us. Watching her eyes sparkle with tears due to the sheer magnitude of pleasure we created, and her body tensing right before her orgasm, was as close to God as I could feasibly get. It was overwhelming, and I would never tire of it. Ever.

She laid her forehead against mine, breathless, as I leaned against the sofa behind me.

"We didn't make it to the couch," she whispered, trying to regain her composure. The soft faux fur rug under us took the brunt of our coming together so quickly.

"Probably best," I responded, panting too. "It would be rather uncomfortable watching my parents snuggle next to each other in the same spot their son came really, really hard."

She nodded. "Same," she agreed and pulled back to look at me. "Was I loud?" Her face turned panicked.

I smiled and shook my head. "Unfortunately, no, you controlled yourself pretty well."

"Unfortunately?" she asked, confused.

"Are you kidding? That's one of the best parts of being with you. Your orgasmic yawps are what I live for."

She laughed louder and laid her head against my shoulder. Her body vibrated, trying to hold in her giggles. I rested my head on hers and felt her soft hair beneath my fingers until she could face me again. A beam of warmth spread from her.

I stared into those magnificent eyes and shook my head slightly. "You're so fucking incredible, and I want to hurt whoever told you you weren't."

Her smile faded with an understanding of what I'd just said. She wrinkled her eyebrows with a look of puzzlement, but her stare never left mine.

"The only reason they said you weren't good enough was because of the light they saw in you. They couldn't have it themselves, so they wanted to extinguish yours. And fuck them for not letting you shine. You're worth everything, Norah. Everything."

Her tears spilled over, and she no longer shook from laughter. She shook from years and years of pent-up anger and disappointment. I pulled her into me and let her cry, hating those monsters who should have never been parents to anyone, let alone the woman in my arms. I realized with her naked body sitting on top of me, her head buried in the crook of my shoulder, I wasn't the only one broken because of someone I loved. She was broken too. For a moment, I worried we wouldn't be able to overcome the fracturing we both shared, that the baggage we carried together would be too overwhelming. She needed to heal from her past, and I did too.

But I couldn't let her go.

It was selfish, and something I would probably come to regret, but the thought of being away from her was unbearable.

When her breathing returned to normal, she drew back and sniffed. Her eyes, usually bright, were red and irritated—but still stunning. I wiped her face with my fingers and stared at her while she ran her hand through her hair, then blew out a breath.

"Are you okay?" I asked.

She nodded. "Not really used to being this uncomfortable."

I started to transfer her off me.

She placed her hand on the side of my face. "No." I stopped moving and watched her. "I'm not usually this vulnerable with people. Especially men I've slept with."

I tilted my head and watched her grapple with something internally, giving her the space she needed until she was ready to tell me.

She took a shaky breath. "Just…promise me something."

I nodded. "Anything."

She paused. "That light you see. Don't let *me* put it out either."

Her eyes fell to my chest, and she swallowed hard.

I lifted her face with my finger under her chin to meet my eyes. "I won't. I promise," I whispered.

She nodded, then leaned in and kissed me. When her lips connected with mine, she told me it scared her to not only lose this but herself as well. I held her tighter, letting her know I wouldn't let that happen. Not a fucking chance.

We snuck into the house early the next morning while it was still dark, agreeing that getting caught in the pool house was a dead giveaway to what had taken place, multiple times, for most of the night. I shared a lot with my family, but this night was strictly for Norah and me.

I took Norah's hand and tiptoed through the first floor. She broke away from me when we reached the stairs.

"What are you doing?" I whispered.

She pointed towards the second floor, confused. "I'm going to bed."

I shook my head and pulled her by her hand into the den. I switched on the light and removed the pillows from my hideaway bed.

Norah caught my eye. "Why am I down here for this?" Her smile spread.

"What did I tell you earlier?" I hoisted the bed out of the couch.

She looked as if I'd lost her.

I took the sheet and spread it over the mattress. "I said I would always wake up with you if we spent the night together." I glanced at her face, which was still perplexed, and I chuckled. "I had to go three nights without you being there in the morning, and I refuse to let there be a fourth."

She gave me a quiet laugh and looked down. "But I thought you didn't want to give your family the impression we slept together. Isn't that why we left the pool house?"

I pulled the sheet to fit the mattress. "It's cold in the

pool house, and there's no bed."

"Won't this be the same thing?"

I stopped all movement and met her eyes. "Norah," I said, lowering my voice.

She watched me and waited.

I leaned on the bed with my hands. "I want to wake up with you next to me today. Is that okay?"

The shine from her smile lit up my world, and she nodded while biting her bottom lip. I smiled back at her and took off my shirt and jeans but kept on my boxer briefs. She took off her pants, leaving just her underwear and T-shirt.

"Should we be this naked?" she asked, giving me a shy smile.

I laughed. "I'll admit this could test our limits a bit, but after everything that just happened outside, I think I can behave myself. You?"

She gave me a doubtful look. "I, unfortunately, was not born with that kind of impulse control, but we'll give it a try." She got under the sheets and faced me.

I went to turn off the light, then joined her. I held my arm out so she could sneak next to my chest. Her arm draped over my abdomen, and she entangled our legs together. I wrapped my arms around her and squeezed, kissing the top of her head. I exhaled with a sense of fulfillment for the first time in a long time. Norah was here in my arms, right where I needed her to be. We both drifted off into a deep sleep as I tried to push away the worry of what was to come.

Chapter Twenty-Seven

Norah

It was the first time I had spent the night with anyone on purpose. I had fallen asleep at Parker's once because I was exhausted. The rest of the short list of men I had been with physically were one, maybe two-night stands max. I never spent the night, and I never made a commitment. This was all new. Having these feelings for Wil, knowing we were on a slippery slope and unsure about what our future held, was more frightening than any plane ride I could imagine. He was the first person to know about my past besides Janet. The first man I wanted to spend time with outside the bedroom. Which made whatever came next between us so much more complicated.

The smell of breakfast woke me. I inhaled deeply, letting the mouthwatering scent of hash browns and sausage fill my nose. I didn't realize how much I was starving until my belly rumbled.

Wil was spooning me and rubbing his nose against the back of my neck, telling me he was awake too. He wrapped his arms around me, drawing me into him. I immediately felt his erection against my ass.

"Someone's up," I said and giggled.

"Sorry. Not much I can do about it. Unless…you'd like to help him go down." He suggestively rubbed his early riser against me.

I turned my head over my shoulder. "We're in the house, and at the very least, your mother is up and in the kitchen."

"There's a bathroom over there. I'm sure we won't take long." His hand cupped my breast and played with my nipple.

I took a sharp inhale, maneuvered out of his grip, and moved away.

He laughed and said, "I'm kidding. Come here." Then pulled me to him again.

He took in a long breath and exhaled with a sigh. I smiled at the sound of Wil's contentment.

"I feel like an idiot," I mumbled.

He lifted his head to look at me. "Why?"

I rolled on my back. "I told your family we weren't together yesterday."

He paused. "How did that come up?"

"They asked where you were. When I told them, Devin was not pleased. He asked how I could let you go with Elise if we were together. I told them we weren't. So, there might be questions."

The side of his mouth curled up, and he nodded slightly. "I can handle questions."

I inhaled and blew out my breath with puffed-out cheeks. My nerves had surfaced thinking about going back to New York.

"Out with it, Matthews." Wil pulled me closer and rested his hand on my abdomen.

I looked into his beautiful eyes, then ran my fingers against his two-day-old beard. "I'm a little nervous to leave," I whispered.

"Why?"

"Going back to real life as…us. It's a little terrifying," I answered.

"We could move into my parents' pool house. I'm sure that would thrill my mother." He smiled, making me smile too.

When Wil saw the fear I held was not only real but also bothered me, he moved over me and gently rested his body on mine. "Nothing will change if we don't want it to." He ran the backs of his fingers on both sides of my cheeks while watching me.

I couldn't answer him and gave what I hoped was a convincing smile, but the worry didn't change in his features.

"Wilson! I don't know what you're doing, but I'm not coming in there to find out. Breakfast is on the table!" Alyssa shouted from the kitchen.

I laughed through my nose, and Wil's abdomen jiggled with his own amusement.

"I guess we have answered the questions," he surmised.

"Guess so," I responded with widened eyes.

Wil exhaled and got out of bed, then gathered his clothes. He nodded towards the door down the hall. "The bathroom is yours. There're new toothbrushes in there."

I nodded and got up too, picking up my jeans, then sprinting out of sight just in case someone was nearby.

I brushed my teeth and combed out my hair with my fingers after I got dressed. I came out to Wil with his cute, dark blond curls in disarray. He looked absolutely perfect.

He walked by me and dragged his hand across my stomach, causing my muscles to tense. "I'll be out in a sec," he said.

I took the sheets off the mattress and put away the hideaway bed just as Wil walked out. He smiled and took me into his arms. He leaned in to kiss me, causing my insides to stir.

I pulled away. "You're gonna get us in trouble," I whispered.

He kissed me again, but when he leaned back, his face was serious. "Last night was amazing. But I'm not nearly satisfied. I need more of them with you."

I nodded. "I do too."

His smirk appeared quickly, then fell. His eyes searched mine as if he were trying to ask me something. I waited to see if he would verbally include me in his thoughts.

His normal demeanor returned. "Come on, before she drags us up there by our ears," he stated, taking my hand and leading me out of the room.

WE STOOD OUTSIDE Wil's parents' house to say our goodbyes to the family. Melanie, Joseph, and the baby would be there for another day, but Wil and I had to head back to New York. Jerry wasn't altogether thrilled about our detour. Either because we weren't working or because Wil and I were spending time together—I couldn't tell. Nevertheless, we had work to do and couldn't delay it any longer.

Bill gave me a quick hug and told me not to be a stranger. I smiled at his warmth and thanked him. Devin didn't seem like a hugger, so I simply waved at him. He gave me a smile and a nod back. Melanie held Zoe face-first in her arms, and she reached for me when I came near.

"Oh, well, look who wants to say goodbye?" Melanie said to Joseph, standing next to her. She put both of her hands under Zoe's little, exposed arms and held her out to me.

Flustered, I took Zoe and cuddled her against my shoulder, like Wil had done at dinner that first night. Zoe squealed and made wet noises in delight, causing me to laugh nervously. The smell of pureed strawberries and baby powder filled my nose. I turned to Wil with widened eyes. He watched me as he placed our luggage in the car. His smile grew and made my breath retreat. I turned back to Melanie and carefully passed Zoe to her. I tickled her bare feet and told them all goodbye.

Alyssa went over to Wil and gave him a full-bodied hug, holding him tight. I envied the relationship they had, and how much she adored and supported her children.

When she was done, she came over to me and pulled me into a hug, just as close as she did him. "I'm so happy we got to meet you, Norah," she said warmly.

"You too. Thank you for welcoming me into your home."

"You're always welcome." She squeezed me tighter.

I couldn't help the singular tear that had escaped my eye. I wiped it away quickly before she drew back.

"Remember, next year, Scrabble tournament. You against Mr. Smarty-Pants over there." She pointed at

Wil.

"I'll try my best," I answered, laughing.

She gave me a wink and turned to join the rest of her family.

Wil opened the passenger side door for me, and I got in. I looked at his family one last time and gave a wave, wondering if I *would* join them next year or if I would see them ever again.

We landed at JFK five hours later. I needed no pills or distractions during the flight—I was dog-tired. I fell asleep on Wil's shoulder before we left the tarmac.

Wil had left his car at the airport, so we drove straight to Brooklyn. I rested my head against the seat with my eyes closed.

"So, your place or mine?" Wil asked.

I raised my head and smiled. "I need a bath and my bed tonight."

He kept his eyes forward. "Your place it is, then."

"Wil, we just spent all weekend together. You have my permission to go home," I said lightly.

He glanced at me. "You don't want to spend another night with me?" He tried to keep his tone playful, but there was disappointment in his eyes.

"It's not that. I'm just not going to be any fun. I'm going to eat, take a warm bubble bath, then go to bed."

"It's not always about sex, Norah." He shrugged. "I just want to be around you."

I smiled. "Good, because I enjoy being around you too."

His grin spread.

"But tonight, I want uninterrupted sleep, and if you're there, I guarantee it will *not* be."

He started to defend himself.

"And I'm not talking about you. It's me with the self-control problem, remember?" I leaned over and rested my chin on his shoulder, staring at his perfect profile. "Is that okay?"

He glanced at me, then kissed my forehead. "Of course it is."

Chapter Twenty-Eight

Norah

Monday morning, Wil and I walked into work together. I did just as I said I would and went to bed early the night before. Janet hadn't returned but texted me, saying she was going to stay in Florida for another few days. Apparently, the talk had gone well.

The red light on my office phone was blinking when I reached my desk. I picked up the receiver and pressed my voicemail button. The call was only a few minutes old.

"Ms. Matthews, this is Elliot Pressley, lawyer to John Thornton." The bored voice on the other end held a long drawl to his cadence that made me uncomfortable. He sounded squirmy. "Mr. John Thornton would like a meeting with you about the so-called story you wrote. He'd like to give his side so the article can be balanced."

Mr. Pressley droned on for another few minutes

about how Mr. Thornton was a fan and wanted to give me the exclusive for the *Chronicle*. I noticed how he didn't say anything about Wil being invited. The more he spoke, the deeper my confusion became.

Wil walked towards my cubicle as I set down the receiver. "Hey," he called above me.

I looked up at him, still thinking about the phone call.

He stopped and studied me. "Are you okay?"

I shook my head quickly. "Yeah...yeah, I'm fine."

His brow furrowed. "You sure?"

I smiled and nodded. "I'm fine. What's up?"

There was a pause before he spoke; he could tell something wasn't right but didn't press me further. "Jerry wants to talk to us."

"Okay." I kept my voice upbeat. "I'll be there in a second."

He stared and nodded, then walked away.

I got up and went towards Jerry's office, thinking about what to do about this phone call from the lawyer. Thornton was obviously trying to intimidate me, but he piqued my curiosity. He wanted to meet with me specifically and not Wil, even though his name was on the byline too. I needed to talk to Jerry about it, but I would wait until Wil wasn't around. I couldn't pinpoint why I didn't want Wil to know, probably because if he did, he wouldn't want me to go.

"How was LA?" Jerry asked, his eyes bouncing between us as we sat in front of his desk.

Wil and I glanced at each other. "Good," I answered as Wil nodded.

"We'll have the interview with Powers for you later today," Wil said.

Jerry stared at me. "And the rest of your weekend?" There was an edge to his voice.

"It was fun," I said and glanced at Wil again. "Wil's family is really nice."

Jerry twisted his lips into a pensive scowl. I made a sound in my throat and turned to Wil. "Can you give us a moment?"

He looked between Jerry and me. "Sure," he said, then walked out the door. He took out his phone and leaned on a metal file cabinet nearby, with his back to us.

I faced Jerry again. "What's the matter?"

"Where did you sleep?" he probed.

"What?"

"When you were with 'Wil's family,' where did you sleep?" He made air quotes, as if he didn't believe me.

I laughed. "Okay, first, I really was at Wil's parents' house. With his mother, his father, his brother, his sister, her husband, and their baby. Do you want pictures?" I'd never seen him like this. All fatherly and protective. It amused me.

He scowled.

"I slept in his room, and he slept in the den," I answered.

"And nothing happened?" he questioned with disbelief.

"Jerry!"

"What? I'm trying to make sure…"

"You're trying to make sure what exactly?"

He exhaled. "Listen, I get it. He's an attractive guy, and you're a beautiful girl."

"Woman," I corrected. "A grown woman, Jerry. One who can make her own choices."

He looked away uncomfortably.

I slumped in my chair. "If you're worried about the magazine—"

"I'm not worried about the magazine," he interrupted and took a minute. "Before your aunt died, I promised I would take care of you."

My defenses lowered. "And you have. But you're not my warden, Jerry. You're my uncle." I paused. "I know what I'm doing."

"What happens once I decide?" he challenged.

I straightened. "Have you?"

He shook his head. "Not yet."

I exhaled and dragged as much confidence to the surface as I could. "We'll handle it."

He looked at me.

I kept my tone even. "Decide who's going to be best for the job, and don't do it worrying about Wil or me. It'll be between us at that point."

He continued to stare at me as if I would give something more away. When he realized this wasn't within his control, he nodded once while closing his eyes, surrendering to his defeat.

I nodded towards Wil. "Should I call him back in here?"

He exhaled loudly. "Sure."

I stood and walked towards the door. "I love you too, by the way." Jerry looked up at me, and I smirked back at him.

I opened the door, called Wil back in, and we both sat.

"Okay," Jerry said as he put on his glasses, telling me he was no longer Uncle Jerry but Editor-in-Chief. "Norah, Marcus called and had to change the date for Tylesha Morris's interview to Monday. It was the only date he had available."

I nodded.

"Wil, there's a mother in SoHo who owns a nonprofit to help women get back on their feet after leaving abusive relationships. I want you to interview her and take Joey to get some good photographs."

"You got it," Wil answered.

Jerry's phone rang, and he didn't hesitate to answer it. I looked to my right, meeting Wil's eyes. He leaned his elbow against the armrest and ran his finger along his bottom lip. His eyes blazed. I bit the inside of my cheek and fantasized about what I would let him do to me later, hoping that same look would still be there.

"I'm not sure I'm comfortable with that," Jerry said, making me turn away from Wil's and our sexual tension. Jerry was already staring at me.

"I understand he wants to tell his story, but—" Jerry was interrupted. "Can I offer someone else?" He glanced at Wil, then looked down at the desk in front of him. "I see," was all he said. "I'm sorry, I don't know if our magazine wants this story that bad…I understand. Thank you." He hung up the phone, louder than I expected.

I waited to see if he would talk first. He didn't. "Who was that?" I asked.

Jerry peered at me for a moment, then went back to his computer. "Nobody."

I sighed. "Are we really going to play this game? It's going to be a lot easier and less time-consuming if you just tell me now."

He gave me an exacerbated look, and I cocked my head to the side. He leaned back in his chair and threw down his pen. "It seems Thornton is looking to tell his side of the story."

I felt Wil's eyes on me as he leaned forward.

"He wants to do an exclusive interview with you." Jerry raised his hands, ran them through his thinning hair, then placed them on the back of his head.

"Mr. Pressley?" I exhaled.

"How do you know that?" Jerry asked flatly.

"Because he left me a message too."

There was a private showdown going on between Jerry and me. I knew what he wanted to direct me to do, and he knew that wasn't going to happen.

"No," he answered my thoughts.

"Why?" My shoulders slumped.

"Because he only wants to meet with you."

"So?" I didn't see the problem. "Jerry, he wants to do an exclusive interview with our magazine, the same magazine that broke the story, and you said no?" I asked, confused.

He remained calm, but his face reddened a small percentage, telling me he was about to get angry. "I will not put you in harm's way for a piece where all he's going to do is say he can't tell you anything anyway. He's doing it for intimidation."

"The story's out and has been picked up a thousand times over. There's nothing he can do about that. But why not take advantage of his ego and see if he digs himself deeper into this hole?" I questioned.

"Norah, no," Jerry said, then came forward in his chair. It bounced at the shifting of his weight.

Wil leaned towards me. "Norah, he's right. It's not a good idea." Wil's tone was serious. "He's got seven sexual harassment lawsuits against him, and he wants to be alone with you."

I scoffed. "Okay, well, I'll make sure it's in a public

place then."

"Absolutely not," Jerry answered.

"No," Wil scolded.

I scooted forward in my chair until my ass was on the edge, holding up my pointer fingers to both men. "Okay, both of you, listen. I'm an adult. And neither one of you is my daddy nor husband. That means neither of you get input on what I do or do not do." I took a breath while both men calmed down. "Now, while I agree meeting with Thornton alone is a bad idea, I'm also not going to let the opportunity of getting his story on the record go. He still hasn't dropped out of the primary, and if he's going to allow me to question him about these women, I think, as a woman, I should be able to do so." I lowered my hands. "You should know by now that I can handle myself. But…I will have my phone on me the whole time and will record everything. Both of you will be on speed dial after I call the police if need be."

Jerry and Wil looked away from me, frustrated.

"Jerry?" I said.

He met my eyes.

"Call Mr. Pressley and tell him I will meet with Mr. Thornton if, and only if, it's in a public place during the day." I looked between the two men. "Is that acceptable to both of you?"

Neither spoke.

"I will take your silence as a yes." I stood and walked out of the office.

While I appreciated the protection of the two most important men in my life, I wasn't a fucking child. I didn't need guarding like I was weak or helpless.

Wil caught up and stopped in front of me. "No."

I exhaled. "Wil—"

"No. I won't let you be with this man alone. Call me whatever names you want, but I will not risk your safety because you want to prove something." There was fear in Wil's eyes, and I read the tension in his body.

I closed my eyes and took a deep breath to calm down. When I had control over my temper, I opened them again. "I love you want to protect me, I really do. But this isn't your decision, it's mine."

His eyes begged me to change my mind, and the anxiety continued to dominate his entire demeanor.

"Okay," I said, grabbing his warm hands. "I'll make you a deal. You can drive me there and wait outside. That way, if there's a problem, you can be close, and I'll throw whatever bat signal you want me to if I need your help."

He looked at me and thought about the offer.

"Take it or leave it," I said, raising my eyebrows at him.

He exhaled. "Why do you have to be so goddamned sexy and pigheaded all at once?" He looked away.

I smiled and shrugged. "Luck of the draw, I guess."

We locked eyes.

"Okay," Wil said, accepting his loss. "I'll drive you and wait outside. But if that bastard tries to lay a finger on you, I want to know before it connects. Do you understand?"

I couldn't help but chuckle. "Yes, Kevin Costner, I understand." I bit my lip at how cute he was.

He stared at me and shook his head once, then grabbed my hand. "Come here."

I looked behind me to make sure Jerry wasn't watching as Wil led me to the stairwell door.

He opened it and pulled me to him, immediately kissing me, then forced my back against the wall. His hands went down my body, and his tongue invaded my mouth. I pulled him closer, turned on by the want in his touch and frantic movements of his lips. His hand went into my hair while his other grabbed my ass. I moaned in his mouth, ready for him to take me against the wall. I hitched my leg behind him and squeezed, pushing his arousal into me.

His fingers jerked the button to my slacks open, and his hand went over my panties and found the wetness he'd caused with ease. My breathing went ragged as he inserted two fingers. He broke away from the kiss and watched me as he increased his speed, rubbing against my clit with his palm. I couldn't let go like I wanted and had to suppress the full-throated orgasm rising to the surface.

Wil's ocean eyes bore into mine, and when he mouthed, "Come," I did. Vehemently. The tension that had been there a few minutes before was gone, and my entire body relaxed.

I tried to pull as much air into my lungs as I could, but it wasn't enough. Wil held me up so I wouldn't collapse in the stairwell. Because of the heightened sensitivity he'd created in my body, I giggled, not sure what else to do with the emotion. Wil tucked in my shirt and buttoned my pants, all while wearing the most ridiculous smile I had ever seen.

"What?" I asked, still breathless.

"Nothing," he answered, then stared at me with that same grin.

"Not nothing. What?" I pressed.

He leaned his hands against the wall on both sides of my head. His eyes shined. "I've never been with someone who exasperates and tempts me as much as you do."

"Yeah?" I asked in a low, seductive voice, then leaned towards him. "Same." My back settled against the wall again. "Was that what this was about? You needed to take out your frustration on me?"

"And then some," he responded, glancing at the floor. When he looked at me again, his smile had disappeared. "I still don't want you to do this."

"I know." I laid my arms around his neck. "But you have to trust me."

His eyes went to the door, and he nodded, still obviously annoyed.

I put my finger on the side of his chin and turned him back to me to kiss him before returning to work. I appreciated how much this interview bothered him, but I had to be my own person. The risk I was taking was to show I had the balls to face men like Thornton without a man to protect me. That's what a managing editor does, and regardless of what I felt for Wil, I still wanted this job more than anything. Maybe even him.

Chapter Twenty-Nine

Norah

Jerry set up a meeting with Thornton for later in the week. Thornton insisted we meet at a posh restaurant in lower Manhattan called Coasters. He didn't seem bothered by my demands, which made me relax. Wil, however, was still on edge as he drove me to the bistro.

"A man like Thornton doesn't let people tell him what to do," Wil said and glanced at me. "I'm telling you, something's not right."

I pulled down the visor mirror to put on my nude lipstick. "Wil, relax. Maybe he just wants to tell his side of the story." I took off the cap.

His voice rose. "For Christ's sake, Norah, you know what he's going to say."

"Do I have an idea? Yes. Do I think he's guilty? Absolutely. But the man has yet to remove his name from the primaries, and I may get more information out of him. Men like Thornton have a tendency to incriminate themselves the longer they talk. And if there's one thing I can do, it's get men to talk."

Wil glanced at me again. "Don't you dare," he commanded.

"What?" I stopped putting on my makeup and stared at him.

"Don't you dare flirt with him," he said, watching me.

"Why not?"

He continued to glance between the road and me in disbelief before he hastily pulled into a parking spot on the street.

"What are you doing?" I asked.

He turned to me, his gorgeous face more than bothered—I had pissed him off. "This man is dangerous, and if you're going to act and behave as though he's not, I'm driving you home right now."

I understood Thornton was dangerous, as most powerful men were. I didn't need to hear it from Jerry or from Wil. I was smart enough to know what I was dealing with. I didn't need to be reprimanded like a child or a naïve girl with no life skills or wherewithal. This interview was part of my dedication to my job and clenching this promotion. Had Thornton requested Wil instead of me, there wouldn't have been a question about his ability to do so. But because it was me, and because my boyfriend and uncle were standing roadblocks between me and conducting what could be a game-changing interview, they forced me to think about whether I was ready or able.

Fuck that.

"Fine." I turned away from him. "I'll walk." I got out of the car and slammed the door.

My heels stomped against the sidewalk as I got away from Wil as fast as I could. He called my name behind me, but I didn't stop. He caught up to me and spun me around by my elbow. We glared at each other. The aggravation in his features told me he was at the end of his rope. He placed his hands on his hips as he paced back and forth in front of me. His anger was not only clear but deafening without saying a word. I didn't speak, knowing I had said everything I needed to in the car. After what felt like hours of silence between us, when I knew neither of us would back down from this muted battle we were locked in, I walked backwards and away from Wil. His face contorted with fury, but he didn't move. When I knew he wouldn't follow, I turned and walked towards the restaurant a few blocks away.

The walk helped my rage retreat. I stood in front of Coasters, taking deep breaths to calm down. Wil hadn't followed me, and I didn't see him waiting by the restaurant. I was alone in this, which was fine by me.

I took out my phone and adjusted the settings to silent as to not be interrupted, then walked through the black double doors. The moment I entered, the typical noises from a busy restaurant on a weekday afternoon were missing. There were no clinking of glasses or dishes, no mumblings of the waitstaff, or soft music playing in the background. But more obvious, no chatter of patrons.

I turned the corner and entered the main dining area. Dozens of black chairs were upside down on top of the empty tables. The black bar that stretched over the back wall was lit but vacant. Complex crystal chandeliers hung above us with lowlights, and the giant black-and-white checkered tiles beneath me were spotless. There were no chefs in sight or smells of food coming from the kitchen. My heart rate increased as I noticed an occupant at a singular table in the middle of the room. The slicked-back, black-haired man sat at one end, facing me, cutting up something on his plate with a knife and fork, while the other chair was empty across from him.

A burly bald man in a maroon suit stood with his hands crossed in front of him to my right. He was so still I barely noticed him. I didn't make eye contact with the bodyguard but moved forward to meet my host. There were only three of us in the room, maybe in the building.

When the man at the table looked up, he put his knife and fork down, picking up his napkin from his lap and wiping his mouth. He was in his late forties, thin and athletic. More attractive than his photos let on. The dark blue tailored suit matched his eyes. His facial features were sharp and narrowed. He looked like a businessperson. There was no humor in his demeanor. He read no-nonsense from his Allen Edmonds shoes to his two-hundred-fifty-dollar haircut.

He stood. "Norah Matthews." His tall frame moved towards me as he buttoned his jacket.

I tried to keep my nerves to a minimum and outstretched my hand. "Mr. Thornton." I kept eye contact. "A little odd that a restaurant in Manhattan would be empty this time of day during the week," I inquired.

He returned to his chair and sat. "It's my place. I thought we could have some privacy." He motioned for me to sit with his hand.

My insides shuttered, and my appendages turned cold.

"This wasn't our deal," I said, not moving. "My editor told you that this needed to be in a public setting."

Thornton put his hands out on both sides of him.

"It's a public restaurant, and it's daytime, Ms. Matthews. I kept my end of the deal."

"Not quite." I turned on my heel. "Call me when you're ready to talk, Mr. Thornton."

The burly man stepped in front of me with an unamused look.

I stopped and exhaled. "Really? We're gonna do this?"

"Mr. Thornton wasn't done speaking with you." The bodyguard's voice was deep and menacing.

I looked over my shoulder to Thornton. "You wanna call off your giant before I call the police and let them know you're holding me hostage in your restaurant?"

He sat back in his chair and scoffed. "Ms. Matthews, no one is holding you hostage, but I think it would be best if you sat and heard me out."

I turned around to face him. "Why is that?"

"You only told one side of these ridiculous claims. I'm an innocent man. Don't you want to save your journalistic integrity?"

I chuckled as I stepped forward. "I beg your pardon?"

"I could make things very good or very bad for you." His smile faded, and he stared at me with malice. "You're gaining notoriety in this city, I'll give you that. But you're a nobody from Texas who only got where she is because of nepotism." A disturbing smirk appeared.

My lips parted for a moment in surprise.

"Oh, yes, Ms. Matthews, I know exactly who you are. Probably more than the average person. And because I'm going to be the Republican nominee for president, you might want to tread carefully from now on."

I couldn't help the laugh that escaped.

His left eye twitched. "You don't believe me?"

I tilted my head. "I suppose you have as good a shot as anyone. But it's pretty presumptuous to say you're going to be the nominee in a field of thirteen."

He chuckled and looked away. "Semantics, Ms. Matthews." He held out his hand to the open chair again. "Please. I promise George won't get in your way if you want to leave. Just hear me out."

I debated on what to do. While I was uncomfortable in these surroundings, I also wasn't ready to run just yet. I had just told Wil I was going to do this with or without him. My ego wouldn't allow me to back down now. I took a breath and sat in the chair at the table.

"Would you like something to drink or eat?" He turned over his shoulder. "Armand!"

A gentleman in a white chef's outfit pushed open a pair of swinging doors by the bar and waited for instructions. Mr. Thornton looked at me.

"No, thank you. I'm fine," I answered.

Thornton raised two fingers in the air, dismissing the chef, and Armand retreated to the kitchen. It relieved me that at least one other person was within earshot. Although if it came down to it, I was quite sure he wouldn't turn on his billionaire employer.

I pulled my phone out of my pocket and sent a text. I pressed a few buttons, put the device to sleep, and set it facedown on the white linen table.

"Full disclosure. You're being recorded," I said, resting my back on the chair, and looked at him expectantly.

A smile that wasn't unkind but definitely not friendly appeared. "Fine," he answered.

A small shiver crawled up my spine. "The floor is all yours, Mr. Thornton. Tell me your side of the story."

I hoped my poker face was that of boredom and not the panic coursing through me.

"It's really very simple, Ms. Matthews. I would never cheat on my wife with any of these women. Every single one of them wanted more from me than just friendship, and I wouldn't oblige. Unfortunately, that led to their obsessive behavior and in turn, my having to dismiss them." He spoke matter-of-factly.

"And what about your former secretary, Lucy Cunningham?" I asked.

"What about her?" he replied with slight annoyance.

I smiled. "I have her on record about the night she walked in on you and one plaintiff in a very compromising position."

Thornton laughed. "She was mistaken."

I crossed my arms. "So, you weren't penetrating this woman against your desk doggy-style while pulling her hair by the roots? Ms. Cunningham can even describe the tie you were wearing." I nodded at his chest. "Kind of like the one you have on now."

He glared at me. "Like I said. She was mistaken."

"I see." I nodded slowly. "Did you also know that she kept a very detailed appointment book about your other meetings with women? And I'm not just talking about New York. All over the world actually."

"I meet with many people, Ms. Matthews. It doesn't mean I'm sleeping with all of them." He didn't notice his slip.

"So, you were sleeping with *some* of them then?"

His jaw tightened as he exhaled through his nose. "No," he answered.

I looked away and took a breath. When I gathered enough courage, I leaned towards the table. "Mr.

Thornton. You and I both know you've been cheating on your wife for years. There are dozens of women going on record against you, saying you were sexually active with all of them. Some say it was consensual. Others, not so much. You're not fooling anyone with your lame attempt at a defense. If you wanted to make this bullshit claim, you could have just told Jerry over the phone. You didn't need to waste my time with this." I stared at him. "So, why don't you tell me why you really wanted to see me."

He straightened in his chair and turned his head slightly as he watched me. That smirk appeared again, and he laughed once. The corners of his mouth evened out, and he leaned forward, folding his hands on the table. "I want a retraction."

I smirked at his ridiculous request. "I'm sorry?"

"Retract the story, and I'll let you follow my campaign around the country as my personal biographer. And when I win, I'll make sure you're part of the White House press corps."

I laughed. "Why don't you just promise me a unicorn of my very own, that seems more feasible."

"Ms. Matthews, it's not a good idea to make enemies in such high places. I have enough money to fund my campaign and the backing of very prominent people that want me in the Oval Office. I will be the next president." Thornton's kindness was all but gone. "Retract the story."

"Absolutely not." I annunciated each syllable as I glowered at him.

He pulled up the corner of his mouth. "You obviously don't understand who you're dealing with."

"Enlighten me." I tapped my phone with my fingernail.

He shook his head, lowered his eyes, and gave me a terrifying smile. "Do you honestly think that a nobody—less than nobody—from a second-rate magazine who probably fucked her uncle to get this job is going to bring me down? I'm about to be the most powerful man in the world and could have you wiped out in a second," he raged quietly.

I stayed still and narrowed my eyes at Thornton. "Is that right?"

"That *is* right. All of you bitches trying to take me down don't stand a chance in hell. You'll regret the day you ever crossed me, just like those whores who worked for me." He scowled at me.

I smirked and stood. "Thank you for your quote, Mr. Thornton. Good luck on the campaign trail." I went to grab my phone, but Thornton stood and grabbed it first, throwing it against the wall behind him. It shattered everywhere, triggering me to jump slightly at the noise.

My breathing sped up as I stared at him. Fear kept me from moving, but I didn't let him see.

"Prove it now, bitch," he said and got in my face.

"I'd back up if I were you." A voice from the other side of the room startled us both.

I looked over Thornton's shoulder and saw Wil coming towards us. I stepped back and walked through the tables to him. We both turned and looked at Thornton. Wil held up his phone, recording everything on video.

Will looked at me with concern. "Are you okay?"

I nodded, not taking my eyes off the billionaire or his bodyguard, who had now started walking towards us. Thornton held up his hand, causing the massive man to stop in his tracks.

Wil moved me behind him and walked backwards.

"And in case you're wondering," he called to Thornton, "she had me on the phone the whole time, and I recorded the entire conversation. You'll be getting a bill for her phone."

Thornton's jaw tensed and his chest rose and fell.

"Anything else you want quoted for tomorrow's story, Mr. Thornton?" Wil asked.

"This isn't fucking over," Thornton said and scowled.

Once we got through the doors to the kitchen, Wil turned me around and pulled me past a confused Armand to the back alley entrance. We rushed to Wil's car at the end of the opening. When I got in, I tried to regulate my breathing. My adrenaline was fading, and absolute panic had set in. I was hyperventilating.

Wil pulled me to him. "Holy shit, come here. Shh. I got you," he said breathlessly. "I got you."

Chapter Thirty

Wil

I took Norah back to my apartment and made her some tea. We were still reeling from what had just happened with Thornton. She had regained her bearings but was still scared about what could happen next with the mogul.

I handed her a mug of chamomile. "We have enough on him, he'll have to drop out now. The lawsuits will go forward, and God willing, he'll go to jail for what he did to those women. He won't have time to think about you."

She leaned her head back against the couch and let out a breath. "Did you send the voice files to Jerry?"

I nodded. "Yep, he's got them. He wants you to call him."

She rolled her eyes. "Why? So he can tell me I was wrong, and he was right?"

"He just wants to make sure you're okay."

"I can't believe that fucker broke my phone," she

said, irritated.

I mimicked her head against the couch and chuckled. "I'll buy you a new one."

She took a sip, then stared at my ceiling. "Where were you when I texted you?"

"In the back alley." I didn't look at her, but I felt her stare.

"You didn't leave?"

I met her eyes. "Of course I didn't leave," I whispered.

There was no way I was going to abandon Norah. As pissed off as I was, I cared more about keeping her safe than leaving her alone with that deviant. When she texted me to answer my phone and start recording immediately, I didn't hesitate. It took everything I had not to bust into the building right after I got her text, but I refrained. I wanted her to know I trusted her, but I needed to be nearby. I stood in the back alley until the chef left to take out the trash, forgetting to lock the door behind him. I snuck in, preparing to make up some ridiculous story about why I was there, but then I heard the phone shatter and rushed into the dining room.

Norah turned to me and tucked her feet under her legs. She took my hand in hers. Her eyes were misty as she stared back at me. "I'm sorry," she whispered. "I should have listened. I just wanted to prove to you, and Jerry, and myself that I could do it."

I watched her and exhaled. I took her mug from her and set it on the end table, then pulled her into me. Her hand traveled across my abdomen and squeezed.

I put my nose in her hair. "You scared the shit out of me today," I said, then kissed the top of her head. "But I know why you did it."

She sniffed.

I exhaled. "I just need you to understand how important you are to me."

She said nothing but nodded against my chest. We sat like that for a while until we got hungry. I wanted to have a normal night with her. We were going to be buried in Thornton's story soon, Norah was leaving for Atlanta that following Monday to interview Tylesha Morris, and we still had the looming decision hanging over us. For a few hours, I wanted to be still, watch TV, and be close enough to touch her whenever I wanted.

There was a knock on the door while we ate. I glanced at Norah, then set my plate down. She widened her eyes at me as I got up.

I looked through the peephole, and my heart dropped. "Fuck," I whispered.

Norah had lowered the sound on the TV. I looked over my shoulder and gave her a tentative smile as she watched me. I opened the door and saw my temporary distraction standing in the hallway.

"Hey, Amber," I said.

She was casual, in tight, light jeans and a white crop top with long sleeves. Her arms crossed tightly in front of her chest, and she looked less than pleased.

"You ghosted me," she said, irritated.

"I know. I'm sorry. I was going to call you—"

Her eyes darted over my shoulder. "Who's that?"

I turned and saw Norah walking towards us.

"Hi, Amber," Norah said. She pointed at herself. "Norah. We met at Wil's party."

Amber eyed her from head to toe. "Oh, yeah. You were with that other guy, right?"

"Yeah, um," Norah looked at me, "I'm gonna let

271

you two talk." She backed up and collected her things behind me.

I held up a finger to Amber and walked back to Norah in the living room. I touched her arm. "Stay."

She turned to me. "Wil, you need to talk to her."

I took her hand in mine and interlaced our fingers. She looked at me and stopped moving. "I'm going to talk to her. Don't go anywhere."

I moved away from Norah and went back to my waiting guest. Having to tell Amber the truth would be hard, but I wasn't willing to let Norah leave after everything she had been through earlier. I needed to rip off the Band-Aid with Amber. Whatever came, I would handle it.

Walking out into the hallway, I closed the door behind me. Amber backed up as her anger grew.

I took a breath and rested my hands on my hips. "I'm really sorry. I shouldn't have spent the night with you."

She gasped.

"And that's not anything against you," I defended. "I just wasn't in a good place. I took advantage of you, and I shouldn't have. I'm with Norah." I gestured towards my door. "I'm so sorry," I repeated, then exhaled.

I watched Amber carefully. At first, her chin trembled, causing me to walk towards her to comfort her. I was the dick that used her. She had every right to hate me. When I got closer, her sorrow turned to rage in seconds. She cocked her fist back and hit me full force in the stomach, knocking all the air from my lungs. My arm immediately crossed over my abdomen, and the pain radiated to my groin. I doubled over.

"Fuck you, Wil!" Amber yelled over me. Her manicured toes and flip-flops walked in the other direction as spews of profanities left her mouth. "I can't believe I ever slept with you. You think you can just treat me like trash! That bitch in *there* is trash!" The insults finally faded when the stairwell door closed.

I coughed and put my hands on my knees, hoping the pain would subside. My door opened behind me.

"Oh my god," Norah said and rushed towards me. "Are you alright?"

I took a breath and groaned as I straightened. "Yeah. She's a lot stronger than she looks."

Norah laughed. "Oh, poor thing." There was both sympathy and mocking in her tone.

I looked at her gigantic grin and laughed too. "Why is this funny?"

She pulled my arm over her shoulder and moved me back into the apartment. "It's not. I'm sorry," she said and tried to suppress her lingering chuckles.

I leaned against the counter, arching my back to stretch out my stomach muscles. Norah came next to me and tenderly touched that area.

"I guess I deserved that," I mumbled.

She fit herself under my arm. "That's it, right? There's no other women you have to resolve anything with?" She eyed me with a smirk.

I wrapped my arm around her. "Nope. Just you."

I meant it as a tease, but it turned into a sobering moment between us. Norah's body tensed.

I sighed. "Maybe we should—"

"No," she interrupted, looking at me. "I've been through enough today. Let's just be us tonight." Her eyes pleaded to not bring up anything that could throw us into an argument or decision that would pull us apart.

"We're going to have to talk about this—"

"I know, Wil." She hugged herself to me. "But not tonight."

My tensed shoulders fell. I pulled her closer and nodded. We both felt the impending decision that hung over us. It was pressing down on me, as I imagined it was heavy on her too. The lack of communication about the editor's job was going to come to a head before we knew it.

THE NEXT MORNING, I took Norah home to change. The space in her apartment was small, she was right about that, but it was newly updated and cozy.

I sat on her couch, going through my phone, when the door to a bedroom opened and heavy footsteps came towards the living room. Janet's black head of hair was the first thing I saw over the lamp to my right. She was in a white, large, familiar T-shirt and boy shorts. She scratched her scalp and yawned. She hadn't noticed me yet. There was a long sigh when she coughed the morning air out of her lungs and opened a cabinet door to grab a mug.

"Awe, yes," she said enthusiastically in a hushed tone. "She made coffee."

I smiled, then spoke, "I made the—"

"Oh my god!" she yelled and turned around violently. Her wide onyx eyes stared at me.

I waved. "Morning," I said, smiling.

She exhaled, pissed. Her hand landed on her chest. The T-shirt she wore showed the name of Byron's gym. "You scared the shit outta me." She turned around and continued the task in front of her.

"Sorry," I said, chuckling.

274

She turned over her shoulder and glared in my direction. It just made me laugh more.

When she finished making her coffee, she sat at the small white dining table that separated the living room from the kitchen.

"How was Florida?" I asked, uncomfortable with the silence.

She glanced at me. "You haven't talked to him?"

I shook my head. "No."

A smile lit up her face as she brought the cup to her lips. "It was fun," she mumbled.

I nodded and smiled too.

"So, that Thornton guy almost killed her?" she asked but didn't look at me.

I tilted my head for a beat. "That's a bit of an exaggeration, but it was scary nonetheless. How did you know?"

"Norah sent me a message through her computer. She told me that asshole shattered her phone. She didn't want me to worry if I couldn't reach her." Janet rose out of her chair and walked towards me. She sat on the floor in front of me with her legs crossed. A worried expression covered her face. "She's okay, right? He won't come after her?"

I leaned forward with my elbows on my knees. "No. He won't. John Thornton has bigger issues than Norah right now. She'll be fine. I'll make sure of it."

She watched me. "You really like her, don't you?"

I looked down, then met her eyes. "Yeah, I do."

She nodded. "She told you about what happened to her growing up?"

I took a deep breath, still angered by her guardians. "Not everything, but a good part of it."

She looked away, then back to her coffee cup in her hand. "Just…don't hurt her, okay?" she implored softly.

I paused. "I would never."

She smirked. "Good." Her voice rose. "So I won't have to kill you." Janet took a drink from her mug.

I gave her a smile in agreement.

She set her coffee down, and a different apprehension crossed her features. I watched her as she debated something.

"Has Byron ever been serious with anyone?" she asked with hesitation.

I nodded. "Yeah. Yeah, he's been in relationships before."

She didn't look at me. "He just seems like he's too busy to be tied down."

I smiled and leaned back against the couch. "I know Chase and B call me the serial monogamist—"

"They had a bet going about how long it would take you to get with Norah." She drank and smirked at me.

I scoffed. "Assholes," I whispered.

She laughed.

"Nevertheless, Chase married the woman of his dreams right after college, and Byron likes relationships too. Don't let him fool you."

She stared at me, then nodded.

The sounds of Norah coming down the hall made me turn in that direction. She peeked into the living room when she came around the corner.

"You guys okay?" she asked, fastening her earring. Her skin glowed against her white blouse. I'd never tire of her entering a room and taking my breath away.

I smiled and stood. "Yeah, we're good." I walked to her and took her hands. "You look amazing."

"Gross," Janet said over my shoulder. She stood and went back into the kitchen, pouring her second cup.

Norah ignored her and smiled at me.

I looked at my watch. "We'd better go. Jerry awaits."

Norah rolled her eyes in resignation, then nodded. She kept my hand in hers as we walked towards the door.

Chapter Thirty-One

Norah

We printed the story about my meeting with Thornton at the restaurant, causing his lawyers to phone our legal department within the hour. It featured some of the audio Wil recorded on the website, then was picked up and distributed across the globe via major news sites. Congress and other presidential nominees publicly demanded John Thornton remove himself from the presidential race. By the end of the weekend, he had.

The tongue-lashing from Jerry wasn't as bad as I thought it would be. When Wil relayed that my actions equally annoyed him, it calmed Jerry down. While I worried about Thornton coming after me personally and through the courts, Jerry made it very apparent that he had handled it through the paper's lawyers. We had Thornton on tape, so there was no way to claim defamation or libel. Jerry mentioned there were already phone calls between the two sets of lawyers about a restraining order and hinted we still had information we kept out of the piece, so we'd have leverage. Just in case Mr. Thornton had any other ideas about getting to me. Jerry was minimal on any further details but said it had been resolved.

"Are you sure you don't want me to come with you to Atlanta?" Wil asked.

We were in my bed. It was warm in the city, so we kept our clothing to a minimum. His head rested on my bare stomach, and his half-naked body lay sideways.

I propped up my pillow so I could see his face. "Yes, I'm sure," I said, playing with the curls in his hair.

He watched me for a moment, then looked at the ceiling. His face turned pensive.

"Are you worried about me flying alone or me screwing up the interview?" I asked with my eyebrow raised.

He turned to me with a smirk. "I'm not worried about the interview."

I tilted my head. "What's that? Does the great Wilson Lockwood think my skills have reached his acceptable level of satisfaction?" I teased.

He rolled his eyes. "Funny," he replied, then looked at the ceiling again. "Did you set up your phone?"

"Yeah, it's done." I looked at the side table where my new phone sat. "Thank you, by the way."

"I wasn't going to let you leave the city without one," he answered indifferently.

I smiled. "I do have a question."

He turned his face to me.

"Would you come with me to Myra's wedding?"

"You mean, be your date?" he asked with fake confusion.

"Yes, smart-ass, my date."

He inhaled. "I don't know." He turned away from me. "That's pretty serious. What will she think?"

"All you have to say is no," I said, laughing.

He smiled at me and lifted himself. He moved to where I could feel his breath against my nose. "Of course I'll go with you," he whispered, then leaned over and kissed me.

He returned to lying on my abdomen, and I continued to run my fingers through his soft hair. His eyes became heavy as I gently scratched his scalp with my nails. Soft moans that escaped him filled me with contentment.

Watching Wil with his eyes closed in this peaceful state between us was what I never knew I wanted. I was fine going through life alone. The household I was raised in caused a lot of doubt about whether I would ever consider a relationship or even marriage. I always thought having a man around would just be a burden. I didn't want to subject myself to someone sweeping me off my feet, then turning into a completely different person. I was always trying to identify another Roy Baker entering my life. But Wil wasn't Roy, and I was cognitive enough to understand my circumstances growing up weren't necessarily extraordinary, but they didn't have to be a pattern if I didn't want them to be.

The vibration of Wil's phone against my side table startled us both. He exhaled and looked at me. I raised my eyebrows at him as he turned and reached over to grab the device.

"Hey, Jerry," he said, then moved to sit on the edge of the bed.

I watched him in bewilderment as he had a minimal conversation with my uncle. Answering only with yeses and noes. He glanced at me and told Jerry "okay" in a solemn tone, then ended the call. He laid the phone down again and ran his hands over his face.

"What's wrong?" I asked, eyeing him.

He looked down and shook his head slightly. He finally turned to me and scooted closer. When his eyes met mine, he tried to relax and smiled.

"This doesn't mean anything," he began.

I rested my back against the bed and waited.

"Jerry gave me the Joshua Benton assignment."

I looked away and exhaled.

"I'm leaving for Wyoming tomorrow," he said in a low voice.

The Democratic presidential nominee story was going to Wil. The one thing that gave me a hint about where Jerry's head was at when picking the managing editor's job, and he chose Wil for it. Disappointment filled my body, and I pulled my legs into me.

Wil came closer, leaning his warm, bare chest against me. His soft hands wrapped around the sides of my neck and his thumbs caressed my face. "You have your interview with Morris tomorrow, and this was the only time Benton was available." He paused. "It doesn't mean anything," he repeated.

I looked into his clear blue eyes and nodded. "Yes, it does," I whispered. "Jerry would never give his number-two this piece. He's going to pick you for the job."

He drew back and removed all contact with me. We sat in silence. The temperature in the room changed, and the tension between us grew.

"So, what does this mean?" he asked, staring at me.

"What does what mean?" I replied, irritated.

"What if I get the job? What does that mean with

us?" He asked with frustration.

"I don't know." I moved away from him.

"What?" he clipped.

I got out of bed and stood. "I don't know, Wil." My defenses rose.

"Why don't you know?"

I put on a T-shirt and placed my hands on my hips. "What does it change for you?"

"Nothing," he answered directly.

"Really? So, if I'm your editor, you'll be perfectly happy you moved across the country and didn't get what you moved for?" I put on my shorts.

He stood and faced me. "I moved to New York for several reasons. The job was just one of them. But it wouldn't change how I feel about you."

I watched the sincerity in his eyes change to disturbed when I didn't answer.

"Can you say the same?" he demanded.

I liked Wil, and I liked who we were together. A lot. But I didn't know if I could handle him having the one thing that truly mattered to me and still be with him. There would be too much animosity, too many hurt feelings on my part.

When I said nothing, he scoffed and shook his head, then got dressed. My pride wouldn't let me tell him to stay. My heart, however, screamed at me to stop him and figure out a way to work this out.

When he'd finished, he looked at me. "I hope your interview goes well in Atlanta," he said curtly, then left out the door.

MY XANAX WAS almost gone. Even though I took two

before my flight, I was still anxious on the plane. Not having Wil to hold my hand or kiss me as a distraction during takeoff made the nervousness horrible.

I hadn't heard from Wil since our argument in my bedroom. Of course, I hadn't tried to call or text him either. I was giving him space to calm down. Or maybe I was too afraid to face what we knew was coming.

When Wil came into my life, he wasn't supposed to stay there. He wasn't supposed to be someone I would be with more than once or twice, and it definitely would not be more than just sex. But something unexpected happened. We connected in a way I didn't think was possible for someone like me. Now I had to choose between something I desperately wanted and someone I didn't know I needed.

I landed at Hartsfield-Jackson Atlanta International Airport Monday afternoon and made my way to Senator Morris's office at the Coverdell Legislative Office Building. Marcus met me after I went through security.

His dark facial hair complemented his brown skin. He'd pulled his long braids back into a ponytail at the nape of his neck. He stood with his hands in his pockets and wore a gray suit that fit his bulky frame perfectly. His red tie and pocket square matched his cognac-colored leather shoes. Anyone with eyes could see Marcus was handsome as hell.

"So, you're the one who's been bothering me all this time," he said as I approached. His southern accent just made his overall attractiveness more present.

"Oh, come on," I said as I stopped in front of him. "Tell me you didn't enjoy all of those early morning phone calls."

"Early morning, midafternoon, *and* late evening." He

rolled his eyes.

"Hey, nobody told you to pick up."

He turned and started walking away. "Yeah, I really enjoyed it when I went on vacation and came back to thirty-two voicemails and emails from you."

I made an oops face when I caught up to him. "You were in Houston, right?"

"Visiting my mother, yes." His tone was playfully irritated.

"She needs national attention, Marcus. Grassroots money from people all over the country to get rid of your opponent. This article will do it." We walked towards the elevators.

"If it gets you off my phone, I'll do anything." He continued to stride forward without looking at me.

I laughed. "How much time are you gonna give me?"

"She's got another meeting across town in two hours. Think that'll do?" he said and glanced at me.

"Perfect." I smiled at him. "I love you, Marcus."

"Yeah, whatever," he jokingly dismissed me.

Tylesha Morris's office walls were covered with dark wood paneling that matched everything from the bookcases to the enormous desk at the far end of the small room. The American and Georgia flags stood proudly in the corner, and her degrees from Spelman and Harvard hung on the wall.

I sat in a black leather chair in front of Senator Morris's desk and pulled out my phone while I waited. I opened my voice memo app and set it on my lap. Not wanting to be clicking away on a computer during the interview, I brought a notepad and pen to jot down my thoughts and questions that came to mind.

My thoughts traveled to Wil and how I wished he were here with me. He hadn't talked to me all day. I didn't know when his flight left or landed or where he was even staying. I pushed the hurt behind him getting the Benton interview to the side while my heart longed to talk to him. He was obviously still mad, and I didn't blame him—it was my fault. I couldn't overlook Wil becoming my superior. Especially for something I had worked my ass off for.

But at that moment, I missed him.

My phone buzzed in my lap. I grabbed it and looked at the lock screen.

Wil: Good luck today…

I exhaled and closed my eyes, waiting for the pain in my chest to subside.

The door behind me opened, and I grabbed everything in my lap to keep it from falling as I stood, then turned to see Senator Morris walking in. She was about my height and curvy. She held herself with perfect posture and a no-nonsense attitude. She was intimidating but had wisdom and kindness behind her chestnut eyes. Her long, black box braids were tight and sat on her head like a crown. The bright blueberry-colored suit was brilliant against her auburn skin.

"Ms. Matthews," she said in a rough voice as she reached her hand out to me.

I shook it. "Senator." I watched her walk around the desk to her high brown leather chair. I didn't sit until she did.

"Marcus tells me you've been bothering him for months about meeting with me," she said but was distracted with papers sitting on her desk.

"Persistence gets you pretty far." I smirked.

"Seeing as how you're sitting here, I guess you're right." She moved the papers around her desk to make room for her resting, intertwined hands. "Why do you want to talk to a Georgia state senator so bad?"

"Because I read a story about you, several stories actually, about how you're thinking about trying to make it to DC this year."

She tilted her head. "Is that so?"

"Yes, ma'am." I nodded.

She paused. "Where you from?"

"Texas."

"I thought I recognized a southerner," she said and smiled.

"I ain't no Yankee." I winked at her.

She laughed once and leaned back in her chair. "So what makes you so special that you think I would divulge that decision to you."

I shrugged. "I don't. But hope is an amazing thing when you got nothing to lose."

With her smile still in place, she narrowed her eyes. "I said that."

"Yes, you did."

She studied me, then nodded once. "Okay. Ask me your questions. Let's see how much you got to lose."

We discussed how she wanted to concentrate on the school system and to tamper down on the gerrymandering getting out of control in her district. Voter rights, police reform, healthcare for everyone were high on her list of priorities. When she dug deeper into the issues around Georgia, I remembered what Wil had said about not being a cookie-cutter journalist. I needed to go deeper and get more personal.

We talked about how she met her wife, Marianne,

286

of seven years and how she'd adopted Marianne's two twin boys after their wedding. One son was going to Morehouse in the fall, the other, Berkley. She talked about their boys lovingly and even teared up thinking about them leaving.

I asked about her childhood and how she handled growing up in the South, then coming out to her family. She said it wasn't easy, but her single mother loved her regardless. The rest of her Southern Baptist family was a little uncomfortable at first but then grew to adore Marianne and the boys. They were happy because she was happy.

There was a knock on the door ninety minutes later, and Marcus entered when it was time for the senator to leave for her next appointment. He stood next to me to announce her remaining schedule for the day.

"Get everything you needed?" he asked, looking down at me.

I nodded and glanced at the senator. "Yeah, I did."

He smirked at me. "You owe me," he said and walked to the door.

I laughed and turned back to Ms. Morris and tilted my head. "Does he like sports?"

"Baseball," she answered.

"Braves?"

"Phillies."

I scoffed. "That's sacrilegious."

She widened her eyes. "I know."

I twisted my mouth, thinking. "Think he'd be okay behind first base?"

"I think that would appease him for a spell," she answered, nodding.

I smiled and gathered my things to stand. I looked

Senator Morris in the eye as she stood too. "It was a pleasure." I reached out my hand. "Thank you so much for doing this."

She took it and covered my hand with hers. "You're welcome, Ms. Matthews."

I nodded at her and walked to the door.

"Ms. Matthews?"

I turned. "Ma'am?"

She stared at me for a moment, then nodded her head. "I'm announcing my candidacy for the US Senate on Wednesday."

My mouth fell open.

"You're more than welcome to post this interview, but only after I announce."

I choked up. "Senator Morris, thank you so much."

She straightened her jacket. "Anytime you need something, let me know."

My heart swelled. "Absolutely." I couldn't get my smile to lessen. "Thank you. And good luck."

She nodded once and smiled as I turned and walked out the door.

I MADE IT back to New York that night so I could continue writing without interruption. Senator Morris was going to announce her candidacy in two days, and I wanted to be ready so we could drop the article right after.

I locked myself in my room and finished by two in the morning. It was good, probably the best thing I had ever written. I was excited for Jerry to see it but more excited to show Wil.

I came in the next morning and found Wil's desk was

empty. I took a breath and walked around our partition to dump my things, then made a beeline to Jerry's office.

I knocked and heard, "Come in."

I stuck my head in. "It's done and in your inbox."

He glanced at me. "How'd you do?"

I stood there silently, deciding which tack to take. Either reply with my typical cocky attitude or change up my response. "I'll let you read it and let me know."

He tilted his head at me. "Wait, you're not bragging about how great it is and how much I'm gonna love it?"

I smiled. "I think it's good," I said simply.

He watched me, then nodded silently.

"Where's Wil?" I couldn't help but ask.

"He's still in Wyoming. Benton is taking him around his hometown today. He didn't want to miss the chance." Jerry smirked.

I gave a half-hearted smile. "Okay." I closed the door and walked back to my desk.

I hadn't responded to Wil's text the day before because I didn't know what to say. A thank you probably would have sufficed, but I didn't know if that would elicit a conversation or if we would return to being mad at each other.

The day crawled by. I had hoped Wil would have shown up regardless of what Jerry said but was disappointed. My brain told me this wasn't that complicated and to just pick up the phone and call the man. My fear told me that would only lead to more pain between us. The feeling of helplessness consumed me. I shook my head as I got up to leave for the day.

I walked from the subway to my block with my earphones in, feeling the warmth from the sun on my bare arms. My phone rang, and I picked it up without looking at it, hopeful.

"This is good, kiddo. Really, really good," Jerry said.

I took a deep breath, then smiled. I could hear the pride in his voice. "I'm glad," I answered.

He was typing in the background. "I'm going to run it once on Wednesday as an exclusive…"

I stopped moving in the middle of the sidewalk. My heart sank.

"You killed this one, Norah. You really did," he said, then prattled on about the parts he liked.

I leaned against the black iron fence in front of my apartment to gather my bearings. My eyes watered, and all I could do was nod at his praise.

Exclusive.

I had suspected Wil was going to get the editor's job, but this just solidified it. The exclusive was an apology from Jerry for choosing him over me. Everything I had worked for in the last decade was about to come crashing down around me. Wil, the man I cared about and wanted to be with, was about to take the only thing more important to me than anything, even him. He would be my boss and would help steer the magazine into the future, calling the shots, making all the decisions Jerry didn't want to make or thought Wil could make better.

My mother's words haunted me. *You're not good enough. You'll never be good enough.*

Chapter Thirty-Two

Wil

I landed at JFK late Tuesday night. I'd let Byron use my car while I was gone and had him come pick me up to drive me home. Nearly exhausted, my first thought was to find Norah. I hadn't talked to her, even by text, in days. Everything felt different, and Jerry hadn't even decided yet. Frustration lived inside my entire being. I hated what was happening between us, but I couldn't figure out a way to fix it. I just knew our separation was growing wider with each passing minute.

"How was tooling around with the next President of the United States, Lockwood? Did you get the rights to write his post-presidential biography?" Byron laughed, his hand draped over the steering wheel.

I would have rolled my eyes, but I was drained. "That man has the energy of a twenty-two-year-old. For two days, he was up at six in the morning and didn't stop until well after midnight." I shook my head. "He took me on walks, bike rides, to his favorite restaurants, where he grew up, where his wife grew up, his high school... He even remembered his old locker combination." I brought the back of my hand up to my mouth and yawned.

"Damn, that old man kicked your ass." Byron glanced at me. "Did you want me to take you to your girl's?"

I looked down and exhaled. "I haven't talked to her. I don't know if she even wants to see me."

"What happened?"

"This fucking job, man. She thinks because I got the interview with Benton that Jerry's going to give it to me. But I gotta be honest," I looked at his profile, "I want this."

"As you should. You've been working towards this for your entire career, Dub. There's nothing wrong with wanting it."

"Even if it means I lose her?"

He glanced at me, his brows furrowed. "Listen, I know you like her. But if she can't handle you getting this job, then maybe that's not the kind of partner you want."

"It'd be easy to say she's being unreasonable, but she's not. She's worked so hard for this, and if I hadn't come along, this job would be hers," I mumbled.

"That's bullshit. There's a reason your boss brought you in. He obviously wasn't sold on her. She can't fault you for that. If anything, she should be mad at him." He eyed me.

"So, if you and Janet were in the same situation, you'd tell her to just deal with it and expect her to be okay with that?" I looked at him doubtfully.

He shrugged a shoulder, trying to come up with a

good comeback.

"Exactly." I peered out the window. "If I get this, it's basically the end of us. And I'm not okay with that."

He glanced at me again. "So what then? Are you honestly going to give up this chance for her?"

I paused. "I don't know."

"There has to be a way to keep the job and the girl. You earned this, Wil." I could hear the frustration in his voice.

"Did I?" I questioned skeptically.

He looked at me with confusion.

I sat up straight. "I went to an Ivy League school and immediately got a good job out of college. I used every privilege to my advantage to make sure I got to where I am. Hell, B, even you struggled when we graduated, and we went to the same damn school." I shook my head. "Norah had nothing. She graduated from high school and moved to New York with the clothes on her back to get away from her asshole mother. She started in the mailroom and is now on a level playing field with me—the Cornell graduate." I paused. "Who deserves it more?"

He softened. "I get it, man. And I know she's been through some shit to get here. But it doesn't discount your worth. You're a hell of a writer and your boss knows that. Hell, Norah knows that. If you get this job, it's *your* opportunity. Maybe hers just hasn't come yet."

I exhaled. "Something tells me she won't see it that way."

The war inside me was making my already worn-out body heavy with guilt and remorse. If managing editor was mine, I couldn't see a way where everyone was happy. I needed to see Norah to talk this through before

Jerry decided. We had delayed it for far too long, and that was as much my fault as it was Norah's. But it needed to happen when I saw her so we could finally resolve this. Whatever the outcome was.

JERRY TEXTED ME the next morning, telling me to be in around nine for a meeting. By 7:30 a.m., I was already out the door. I was tired of playing the waiting game with Norah. We needed to work this out before it went any further. I understood her hesitancy and fear, but we were both adults. It was time to act like it.

I parked outside Norah's apartment just in time to see Janet coming out of the building. Her sports bra, leggings, and shoes matched perfectly, and her long black hair was in a high ponytail. Her back was towards me when she stretched her arms and legs on the steps.

I walked to her, calling her name, but she didn't hear me. I tapped her lightly on the shoulder. She turned around quickly and gasped loudly. I backed up and held my hands up in surrender.

"Jesus Christ, Wil. Stop doing that!" she said, annoyed, ripping out her earphones.

"I'm sorry. I called your name," I defended, chuckling.

She made an aggravated sound. Her chest rose and fell with the fright I had just given her. "What do you want?"

"Is Norah upstairs? I wanted to give her a ride to work."

"She left already. Jerry texted her this morning, telling her to be in early." She put her earphones back in and turned her back on me.

294

My face fell. I touched her elbow to regain her attention. "Did she say what for?"

"No, she just said she had to go meet with him." She analyzed me. "What's wrong?"

I looked around and thought. "He asked me to meet with him at nine."

"So? Maybe it's about a story."

"Or maybe he's decided." And you rarely tell the person who got it first. "Shit," I whispered, running back to my car.

My heart was pumping pure adrenaline, striding into the building of the magazine. A slew of conflicting emotions flowed through me. On one hand, I may have secured the one thing I've wanted in my career and moved my life from one coast to another for. I was finally a managing editor for one of the most prestigious magazines in the country. It also got me one step closer to editor-in-chief when Jerry retired.

And then there was Norah.

My elation ceased when I thought about her disappointment and how much this would hurt her. Panic set in as I realized what this probably meant for us. She would be angry and frustrated, and I wouldn't blame her for it. But was it worth ending our relationship over?

As I rushed out of the elevator, I walked towards Jerry's office and stopped in my tracks—my heart sank. Norah sat in front of his desk, her head down. There were no tears. Norah would never do that, but I could see the immense distress with the parting of her lips and the furrow of her brow. She nodded but didn't look up at Jerry as he spoke. He was animated with his hands, like he was giving the most in-depth explanation he could. He stood and came over to her and leaned back on his desk.

She glanced at him and nodded. Norah took an extended breath and rose. Rounding her chair, she moved to the door and looked back at Jerry as he said something else. She didn't respond, just opened the door and walked out.

She moved towards me without looking at where she was going. I said her name, but she continued to stride past me.

"Wil?" I heard from Jerry's open office door.

I looked at him as he motioned for me to join him. I turned my head over my shoulder and saw Norah open the door to the stairwell without a backwards glance.

I ignored Jerry's invitation and jogged to the stairwell. When I entered, the door to the roof closed above me. I climbed the stairs two at a time and opened the door with haste. Norah had gone to the ledge and stopped. She looked out over the city, her arms crossed over her chest, and the light breeze blew through her hair. I took a breath and walked towards her. She was still like a statue.

The busy noises from the city below were faint. There was a greater peacefulness this far from the usual chaotic metropolis than I was used to. It was opposite of the woman standing in front of me. She was a ball of resentment and sorrow.

When I reached Norah, I leaned on the raised ledge, facing her. She didn't acknowledge me with a glance or gesture. Her eyes were glued to the skyline before her, and her jaw was tense.

I stared at her, hoping to get some sign of what she was thinking. We were in each other's presence for what felt like hours in silence.

"Tell me what you want me to do," I whispered, unable to take the torture any longer.

She inhaled slowly and closed her eyes. When she opened them, she softened and looked at me.

"Do you want me to turn it down?" I asked.

A slight smile crossed her face for a moment, then disappeared. "I would never ask you to do that." She removed her eyes from me again. "Because I would never do that for you, even if you asked."

A slight pain released from my chest. That comment shouldn't have affected me. She was mad and had a tendency to speak out of anger. Still, it was a bitter response I didn't expect.

I watched her exhale and then shake her head. "I'm sorry." She glanced at me. "I need to be alone for a while."

I hesitated, not wanting to leave her, but then nodded and stood.

She raised her head and sniffed, and the tears pooled in her eyes. My shoulders dropped, and my heart broke for her. I wanted to hold and comfort her, tell her it was going to be okay. But that's not what *she* wanted right now. I wouldn't force Norah into accepting this truth until she was ready. She needed her space, and I was willing to give it, but I didn't know how long that space would last or if we'd come out on the other side of it alright or together.

I began to walk to the door when she called my name. I paused, then turned and watched her struggle with what she wanted to say.

"Congratulations," she said, low, then tried to smile. Her eyes were glossy from the tears about to spill over.

I took a step towards her when she turned away from me and watched the city again. Defeated, I faced the door, thinking about how this moment should have been one of the happiest of my life. Instead, it was crushing me by the second.

Chapter Thirty-Three

Norah

Pissed, livid, torn apart, hurt… Devastated.

Standing on that ledge, thinking of all the things I'd done, or should have done, to get this job threw me into a tailspin. While I had a hunch this position would be Wil's, Jerry sitting me down in his office and delivering the news face-to-face was worse than I ever thought it could be. He told me he needed someone to take the reins eventually, and that I still had growing to do while Wil could step in right away. As if I had been sitting back doing nothing for the last decade of my life, watching and learning as much as I could to be ready for this moment. Jerry jabbered about how Wil had better discernment for stories given his writing career. After that, I tuned out, too angry to continue to care what Jerry said.

Because reality was, Jerry didn't think I was good enough. Plain and simple.

I'd started to believe maybe I wasn't a viable option

for the job from the beginning. Jerry wouldn't have brought Wil in if I were. Maybe I would have never got promoted to managing editor and was being placated to spare my feelings, because I was his niece.

I went home that night and sat on the couch with Janet and a full bottle of sauvignon blanc, which emptied within a few hours. I ignored the calls and texts from both Jerry and Wil for the rest of the night and cried on Janet's shoulder. I needed a few hours to mourn what I had worked so hard for but regardless, hadn't come to fruition.

I was determined to go forward. I would not quit the magazine. No matter what I had just gone through, I still loved my job, and I loved the publication I worked for. Although my anger was very much present and unleashing my rage on someone was always within reach, I tried to keep it at bay as best as humanly possible.

A few days had passed, and Wil gave me the space I needed to deal with the loss. The day Jerry announced his new managing editor to the rest of the staff, I called in sick. I didn't want to be the pouty brat in the corner when they congratulated Wil and patted him on the back for his new accomplishment.

There was a soft knock on my door later that evening. Janet was at the bar, and I already knew who the sound belonged to. I opened the door without looking through the peephole. Every time he darkened my doorway, I couldn't get over how gorgeous he was, or how his smile blew me away. But it only took a second before my heart betrayed me and sunk to the floor. No matter how beautiful he was, my pride was still fragile. His attractive presence was a constant reminder of how much of a failure I was.

"Hi," he greeted in his deep voice.

I didn't respond, just watched him.

"Are you alright?" He wasn't concerned as much as he was troubled. He knew I wasn't sick, but he also knew I was breakable.

"Yeah, I'm fine," I answered softly. "Come in." I moved to the side and let him enter.

The awkwardness between us was palpable. We hadn't been alone together since the roof, and the distance created since then was broad.

I walked into the kitchen and opened the fridge. "Did you want something to drink?" I asked, grabbing a bottle of water.

"No, I'm good." He looked at me, standing uncomfortably, like he wasn't sure what to do next.

I walked past him into the living room and sat on the couch, giving him the signal to do the same. I searched for the remote and turned off the TV as he joined me, sitting far enough away to show he was not here for any physical contact.

I exhaled and turned towards him. His nerves were just as evident as mine. This felt like a first date or the end of a relationship. Neither of us not knowing what to say. If he started talking about the weather, I was going to scream.

"I don't really know what to do here," he admitted.

My resting bitch face broke, and I gave him a slight smile. "I don't either," I agreed.

"Are we through?" he asked abruptly.

"Do you want to be through?" I replied with my brow furrowed. I didn't know what my truth was just yet, but my feelings for Wil ran deep, and the pain of not being with him was real. At the same time, I couldn't decipher what was hurting me worse. Not being with him or losing the job *to* him.

"No, I don't." He looked at me. "But I feel like you do, and you just don't want to tell me."

I stared at the floor in front of me. "I don't want to hurt you, Wil…but I don't know if I can be away from you either."

He exhaled. "Norah, come here," he whispered, then pulled me back to him, wrapping his arms around me while my head rested against his shoulder.

I inhaled him and felt the tears form. Everything inside me was being thrown around like a cyclone. My heart was his, there was no denying that, but the rest of me was still reeling from my disappointment. My mind, rational or not, told me this wasn't his fault, but it also told me there was plenty of blame to throw at him for stunting my career. Had Wil not come to New York, I could have beaten out whoever else Jerry was considering with my piece on Senator Morris alone. But Jerry pitted me against the sensitive Cornell grad who wooed him with seductive tales that pulled at his heartstrings. The same man I idiotically slept with on the first night and continued to sleep with throughout this process, even after I knew who he was.

My mother's voice rang in my ears. *Weak.*

Wil kissed the top of my head as we came to a silent agreement. We would make no decision at that moment. Thoughts of letting him go continued to plague me, but I wasn't fond of the idea—I still liked him. Feeling his body against mine, and his strong arms holding me close to keep me comforted, was all I needed to keep the negativity temporarily quiet. I wished I could silence them forever and I could enjoy him. Enjoy us, like it was before.

I TRIED TO ignore all the commotion about Wil's new status over the next few days. Making sure my headphones were firmly in my ears, I needed to wrap up some pieces. The actual test would be later in the afternoon when Wil held his first assignments meeting that Jerry had pawned off on him. It was usually just a formality and done by email, but it seemed Wil wanted to introduce himself to his subordinates personally.

I walked into the conference room and sat a few chairs away from the new managing editor standing at the head of the table. I knew him personally, more than anyone else in that room, so I figured I could keep my distance. Even so, he suspiciously eyed me anyway.

"Good afternoon, everyone," he started. The group mumbled a response. "I had a meeting with Jerry this morning, and we need a few more pieces before we release the anniversary issue. I'm handing out assignments across the board. I don't know whose will make it, so, you're just gonna have to impress me."

I glanced at him, knowing there would be a sly smirk planted on his face. I was right. Wil told everyone in the room about the articles they were to contribute. Everything was fairly standard. Tom got an athlete, Tessa got a designer. I didn't pay anyone any mind until he said a name I recognized.

"Jamie," Wil called, making Jamie straighten in her chair. "Prisha Anand will be in New York next week."

"Who's that?" Jamie asked, confused.

Wil froze, watching her. "The Pulitzer Prize-winning author." When she merely stared back at him, he continued, "She won for *The Seven Maids of Casper* last year?"

Jamie shrugged.

Wil put down the piece of paper in his hand. "You *are* the book reviewer, right?"

"Yeah," she answered.

He scrunched up his face. "So, you don't know who that is?"

Her head joggled.

I inhaled, annoyed. "I'll take it. I know who she is. Who do I need to contact about sitting down with her?"

Wil continued to watch Jamie for some sort of flicker. I wanted to tell him it was a lost cause but held back. When he eventually looked at me, he spoke, "Norah, I have you with Kennedy Clemons."

I narrowed my eyes. "That Disney child star chick?" I clarified. "I thought she was in rehab."

Wil shook his head. "No, she…just got out."

"Okay." I hesitated. "I'd still rather take Anand."

"I appreciate that, but I'm assigning you to Clemons." His authoritative tone was both dismissive and pissing me off.

"Wil, Jamie doesn't know who Prisha Anand is. I don't think it's a good idea to put someone unfamiliar with her into that situation. No offense, Jamie."

Jamie glanced at me like a deer in headlights.

Wil looked at me. "I'll help her. We need to give everyone the opportunity to contribute. You can't be the only one with the big assignments."

I jutted my bottom jaw out in irritation. "I'm sure Jerry would want someone else to do this, Wil."

All of his patience left instantly. He flopped the remaining pages down on the table, then placed his hands over them, leaning towards me. "Norah, Jerry has entrusted me with this job and these assignments. As managing editor, I think I can make these decisions all by myself."

The rest of the group grew more uncomfortable, shifting in their seats and clearing their throats. We continued to glare at each other.

"You have Clemons," Wil finished and straightened.

My anger peaked as I tightened my jaw, gnashing my teeth. I faced away from him and scowled at the table in front of me until he dismissed us. I didn't give him the chance to catch me before walking out.

This idea that Jamie could become a good journalist overnight *with his help* gnawed at me. Jerry initially hired Wil to help me, but now he was helping Jamie too? As if he had become the savior of substandard writers. It could have been my anger and pride talking, but Wil's new pedestal was too high for me.

The irritation that was growing wasn't a shock. Not even close. I saw this coming, knew it was a foregone conclusion, and walked into it anyway. Now it was all changing. It was different. He was different, and so was I.

I went back to Brooklyn without a word to Wil. Riding home on the subway, I considered quitting. I could get a job at any other of the many publications in the tri-state area. Maybe even the *New York Times* or the *Post*. But by the time I had begun the walk to my apartment, my temporary fantasies of being the darling new journalist at a more prestigious newspaper flew away. I loved the *Chronicle*, and I loved what I did. I couldn't leave it any more than I could leave New York. It was my home.

I was still deep in thought when I got closer to

my building's door, but there was an interruption. His presence was both annoying and welcomed. I looked up to see Wil's perfect blue eyes staring at me, resting against his car in front of my address. I slowed my stroll before I reached him, and he pushed himself away from his vehicle to meet me.

He put his hands in his pockets. "You didn't let me drive you home," he mumbled, barely meeting my gaze.

"Sorry," I responded. "I needed some time alone."

He stepped closer. "Can we talk?"

I paused and watched him wrestle with this new definition of who we were together. I was glad I wasn't the only one who felt the transformation, but I was irritated that it was happening at all. I nodded as I made my way to the door.

We climbed the narrow stairs silently. It didn't matter how mad I was or how much I wanted to ignore Wil, my body wouldn't allow me to. From his warmth to his natural scent, every molecule that made up who I was knew he was there. He took my breath away by just being nearby. I cursed and rejoiced in my weakness for him simultaneously.

I opened the apartment door and waited for him to enter before closing it behind him. Setting my things on the kitchen table, I then turned to him and crossed my arms over my chest.

He stared at me for a split second before his sideways grin showed, and he laughed once through his nose, shaking his head, then looking away. "What happened today in the meeting…" He exhaled. "I understand you're disappointed about this whole situation, and I'm trying to give you the time you need, but you can't do what you did today."

"I can't speak up when I think something's wrong?" I asked defiantly.

"I'm not saying that—"

"So, what are you saying?"

He closed the gap between us but didn't touch me. "I don't want to fight with you." I looked away as he continued, "Jamie has some…shortcomings in her writing. But I believe she can do this interview."

"No, she can't." I unintentionally raised my voice. "And had you asked me or even Jerry, we would've told you that."

He backed up slightly. "Am I supposed to run every decision I make by you first?"

"I didn't say that. But you don't know these people like I do, Wil. I've been here for ten years. I know who is ready for that kind of work and who is not. Jamie is not."

"Alright, but you should have talked to me about it in private. Making a spectacle of us in the middle of a meeting was childish and disrespectful."

He walked away from me to stop his voice from rising. When he collected himself, he turned back to me but didn't come any closer. "We have to find a way for this to work, Norah. I know you don't like it, but I'm the managing editor, and your direct superior."

"I'm aware, Wil. I'm also aware of how little you actually know to have gotten this position." I couldn't stop the words from coming out.

He froze, stunned. "What the hell does that mean?" he spat.

I shut my eyes and blew out a breath to calm down. This was going too far.

"Norah?" he called after me to answer him.

I walked away and went into the living room. He

remained near my small dining room table, fuming at my slip.

"I have never lied to you about this job," I started, quieter than before. "How important it was to me and how much I wanted it."

He crept towards me with a hurt in his eyes I had never seen before. "Yes, Norah, but you didn't get it. I did. And like it or not, I'm the one who makes these decisions whether or not you agree with them." His voice shook with fury.

"Had you not come here, they would have been my decisions," I mumbled.

"Had I not..." He couldn't repeat my sentence. "I took nothing from you, Norah." The enunciation of each syllable masked the rage bubbling under his surface. "You might not want to believe it, but I earned this."

I scoffed quietly and looked away.

"Or maybe Jerry brought me here because he knew you weren't good enough," he retorted.

A sharp pain ran from my chest to my legs in a matter of seconds. I tried to comprehend the words Wil just tore me apart with. *Not good enough.*

I slowly turned to him, dazed. "What did you just say?"

His wrath retreated when he saw the look on my face. He moved closer. "Norah, I'm sorry. I-I didn't mean—"

I backed away. "Get out." My tears welled, and I trembled with hurt and anger.

We stared at each other for what felt like forever. Wil had become someone I didn't recognize in an instant. A stranger who'd used my mother's words to wound me. My heart shattered.

He came closer and reached for me. "Norah."

I stepped back. "Just go," I whispered, dodging his intense, pleading eyes.

He hesitated, then turned away, slowly meandering to the door. I turned my back on him so he couldn't see my tears fall. When the door closed, I slumped to the ground, sobbing, and wrapped my arms around my knees, like I did when I was a kid back in Texas.

Chapter Thirty-Four

Wil

I sat outside Norah's apartment for a half hour, belittling and tearing myself apart for saying what I'd said. She threw the first punch, but I had no right to knock the wind out of her with that lie about Jerry thinking she wasn't qualified to be editor. Saying exactly what her mother used to say to her when she couldn't accept how smart and capable her daughter was. It was a low blow, and I felt like shit.

My eagerness to see Norah and clear things up kept me from sleeping. I tried to text and call her, but she ignored me until she turned off her phone completely. Showing up at her door was rash, and she was already seething. I didn't want to make it worse. This had gone too far, and I was fearful we couldn't move past it. I counted the minutes until I could speak with her at work.

Norah walked from the elevator to her desk around nine, without so much as a glance in my direction. I took a deep breath and stood. I was going to need to do some serious apologizing to make this right, and I was ready to. As much as she frustrated me and pushed every button I had, even discovered some new ones, I wanted us to work. There was a way to do this. We just needed to figure it out together.

My anxiety grew the closer I got to her cubicle. I peeked over the top but didn't see her. I looked around the floor, trying to gauge where she had gone, when I heard my name.

I turned to see her standing by the door to the conference room. Her black dress was form-fitting, but she looked thinner. The stress in her eyes was covered by a façade of calm and cool. She intertwined her hands as she waited for me to join her.

I guardedly approached and stopped plenty of feet away. "Hi," I breathed. There was a hint of a smile around her beautiful, full lips, but it was miles away from her eyes.

She glanced at me. "We should talk," she said confidently and turned on her heel to open the door.

This isn't good.

I walked past her and turned in her direction as she closed the door. She took a long, shallow breath as I sat on the edge of the table, rolling out my shoulders to ease the heavy tension between us. My nerves continued to fray at the ends with every second she didn't speak.

"Norah," I whispered, and she looked at me. "I'm so sorry. What I said yesterday was completely out of line. I never wanted to hurt you, and I did, blatantly." I exhaled and observed her. "Look, you have every right to be angry, but I know we can work through this." I didn't realize I had walked towards her until she was

311

right in front of me. I reached out to touch her face, but she moved her head out of my reach.

"I'm leaving for San Antonio tomorrow instead of this weekend," she said.

I let my hand drop. "Did you still want me to come or…?" I asked, but I already knew the answer.

She didn't look at me. "I think I need some space," she whispered.

"From me?"

"From everything." Her voice was brittle.

I walked away from her with my hands on my hips while she stayed still by the door. I turned around and ran my hand down my face. What I had done the day before was fucked up. I could own that, but ending us because of a fight, I couldn't understand.

"So, we're over?" I questioned, defeated.

She exhaled. "I don't… I don't know." Her arms crossed over her chest. "There's a lot I need to figure out."

"You're running." My anger grew.

"I don't want to be mad at you, Wil. But I'm confused and hurt, and whether or not it's right, it's being directed your way."

"That's your excuse?"

Her hand flew to her sides. "What do you want me to do, Wil?" Her voice rose with frustration.

"I want you to want to be with me!"

Her head snapped up as I turned away and paced. The silence between us stretched around the room while I internally panicked. I didn't want to lose her, not like this.

I walked to her again. "I hate that you're unhappy, and I really hate that I'm the reason, but after everything, you're just going to throw this away?"

"You're not the reason," she whispered.

"Then what is?"

"I am." She met my eyes. "I banked on this job so hard, it didn't occur to me that I never had a chance."

"That's bullshit," I spat.

"Is it?" Her volume increased again. "Do you really think if I was a serious candidate, Jerry would have even brought you here in the first place?"

"You know that's not true."

Norah stilled. "No, I don't." She gave a shaky exhale. "What if she was right, Wil? My uncle didn't think I was good enough for a position he's basically groomed me for. My whole life, my mother's voice has been on repeat in my head, telling me this was a waste of time."

"She was wrong, Norah." I exhaled and tried to soften my tone. "I read your article about Senator Morris. It was amazing. You can't tell me you weren't born for this. Yeah, I got this editing job before you. It doesn't mean you're not talented or your poor excuse for a mother was right. It's a job, Norah. One job," I pleaded.

She swallowed hard and looked away. "I know you just want me to let this go. But I'm telling you I can't."

I leaned my head so she would have to look at me. "You're doing exactly what you told me not to let you do. You're trying to put out that light I see. Hell, that everyone sees. You're allowing someone who doesn't know you, who never knew you, to damage your self-worth."

I watched her deal with that truth. Norah was stronger than this, and she was allowing her mother to dictate who she believed herself to be. It was heartbreaking, but she also knew she could spend her entire life trying and would never please someone like that. Nothing would've ever been good enough for Norah's mother, because it had nothing to do with Norah and everything to do with her mother's own insecurities. Norah was smarter than this, and it pissed me off she was using it as a crutch.

"If you don't want to be with me anymore, fine," I said, my irritation returning.

She looked up at me, her beautiful pale lips parted.

"If you want to run off and bury your head in the sand, fine. But I won't encourage it or baby you. You belong here…with me. But you're an adult, not that kid that was abused and lied to. And you have to decide if any of this is worth it. If *we're* worth it."

My heart thudded in my chest as I walked past her. I laid my hand on the handle and turned my head to the side but didn't look at her. "Take all the time you need," I said, then walked out the door.

I didn't drive her to the airport or text her before she left the next day. She wanted her space, she would get it. I was angry and frustrated at our situation but not surprised. We had ignored the problem for too long, and now we were here. I could only hope she would come back with a new perspective about all of this but especially about us.

Chapter Thirty-Five

Norah

It had been a few days since I'd flown into San Antonio. The plane ride was rough, and I had to apologize to the guy next to me several times for hating to fly. It was hard without my security animal. I had told Myra I was coming early for a short vacation before the wedding. My usually unobservant sister asked what was wrong, and I told her nothing out of habit. Still, it was a shock when she showed up at my hotel room the next day.

"You don't have to be here until Friday," I said suspiciously. "Why did you come early?"

Myra's blue-green eyes were gorgeous, and I had always envied them, but they were troubled, staring at me. "Something's wrong with you, and I needed to find out what."

"A phone call would have sufficed," I mumbled, walking to the bed to sit.

The Opposite of Fiction

Her slight frame walked forward and stopped at the edge of the bed. I never could figure out how she only made it to 5'4" while I had grown to 5'8". Our hair was the same dull blonde, but both of us covered it with color. Right now, hers was a soft brown.

"Don't you have a million things to do? You don't have time to stop your planning to check on me," I said and eyed my sister.

Myra and I had progressed in our communication over the last few years, and I was grateful, but her being here because she thought something was wrong with me was out of character.

She exhaled through her nose and sat, crossing one leg over the other. "I realized something."

I looked at her.

"Jeremiah's family is enormous. I mean, I've been with him for three years, and I still don't know all the names of his aunties and cousins. It got me thinkin'." Her southern drawl was way more pronounced than mine. "You're really all the family I have. Which means I'm the only family you have too."

It should have been obvious, but that fact had never occurred until she said it. I was always good with being by myself. Jerry was there, and Janet was as close to a sister as I had. Those two were the only family I needed. Then I met Wil.

"So, seeing as how we are sisters and will be until we die, we need to be there for each other. Hell, I'm about to get married, and no one's going to understand how I do not want it to turn out like mom and Roy's more than you." She smiled.

I smiled back and tilted my head in agreement.

"You and I are it, and if you're hurting, I want to

know about it," she said with sincerity.

I furrowed my brow. "What brought all of this on?"

She straightened her back for a moment with the intake of a long breath. "Honestly, there's been a question I've wanted to ask you for a while."

"What is it?"

She twisted her mouth for a moment. "Do you feel like I abandoned you when we were growing up?" she asked, and I watched her eyes turn sad. She pushed her hair behind her ear, then played with the charm on her necklace.

"No," I answered quickly. "I was glad you left. Jealous but glad all the same."

She paused, then looked away. "I should have taken you with me," she admitted and shook her head.

"Hey." I leaned forward. "You were sixteen, and I wasn't your responsibility," I responded, and she turned to me. "I didn't have it half as bad as you did. Most of the time, they just ignored me." I rested my back on the headboard again. "Besides, Mrs. Donahue wasn't going to take the both of us in."

A smile broke across Myra's face. "She was so nice. I couldn't believe she let me live there."

"You and Tory were like sisters. Mrs. Donahue thought of you as another daughter." I stopped and laughed once through my nose. "Mom was so mad when you left."

Myra stared off into space. "Wouldn't know it on my end."

"She disowned you. Not that it made any difference." I played with my fingernails. "She was never very attentive even when you were around."

She glanced at me. "I guess we kind of raised

ourselves, huh?"

"Didn't have a choice," I said while chuckling without humor.

Looking back, it amazed me how we got by. Myra would steal money from Roy, then buy snacks for us at the convenience store down the street. We became very handy with a microwave and a hot plate. Myra and I wore the same size clothes for a lot of our lives, and when Myra's best friend Tory let her raid her overly full closet, we would have new clothes to wear to school. After a while, Myra would show up with trash bags filled with stuff she said Tory didn't wear anymore. At the time, the charity was not only welcomed, but it was also needed.

"Will the Donahues be attending the wedding?" I asked, pulling my head out of our fucked-up childhood.

"Mr. Donahue died a few years ago, but the missus will be there."

"How old is Tory's son?" I asked.

"Nine." She widened her eyes.

"Wow." I stared at the white-and-gray comforter that covered the bed. It was eerily similar to the one in Chicago. "Can I ask you a question?"

Myra nodded.

"Everything that we went through. How did you... How did you move on?" I wrinkled my eyes and forehead.

She shrugged one shoulder. "Alcohol at first."

I made a small sound. "Yeah, I remember that."

The corner of her mouth raised. "I was a bona fide alcoholic in college. The first year, I flunked every class because all I wanted to do was forget. I wanted to feel numb."

I nodded solemnly, understanding the feeling.

"When I came home that summer and Mrs. Donahue

saw me, she knew I was in trouble. When I say that woman locked me down…" Myra laughed and took off her shoes. She turned to me fully on the bed and crossed her legs. Her pink toenails glowed against her tan skin. "She took me to therapy and got me involved with AA. She saved my life. Again." Her smile got wider, then faded. "What about you?"

I exhaled. "I don't know. I…threw myself into the magazine the first chance I got. It was an obsession for a while." I stopped and chuckled. "I guess it still is." I paused. "But things about mom have been coming up more frequently lately. I mean, since I met…Wil."

"Where is he anyway?" Myra questioned.

I blew out a breath. "We're taking a break."

She hesitated. "He got the job then?"

I nodded.

"That's rough." She looked down at her hands. "How do you feel about him?"

His eyes flashed in my mind, and I smiled. "I've never met anyone like him. He's…so sweet and kind, and he cares about me," I said with disbelief. The sorrow in my chest made me miss him.

"So, what's the problem?" She tilted her head.

"I worked so hard for the editor's job. The magazine was my escape when I left Texas." I readjusted myself to sit up straight. "I remember Mom bought the *Chronicle* one time and just kept ranting about how Jerry had this big job in New York and how the least he could do was help support us." I looked at Myra with annoyance, thinking that our mother would have the audacity. "I knew right then that I had to make it to New York, to see if Jerry would give me a chance to make something of myself. To prove Mom wrong."

"Well, you did that."

"But I lost the job," I whispered. "It's made me question a lot about myself. I can still hear her. It's like, recently, she hangs out on my shoulder during every decision I make, and I don't know why." I looked at Myra for answers. Ones I couldn't create myself.

She blinked a few times. "I was lucky to have Mrs. Donahue to take me in. And I know Aunty was there for you too. But when she died, who did you turn to?"

"Jerry was there. He did what he could, but he was grieving. I didn't want to be a burden to him. Janet's been my main sounding board, but she's got her own problems." I looked down at my hands in my lap.

Myra watched me for a moment. "I'm going to turn big sister on you, and you're going to listen." She scooted closer. "You need to talk to someone about what happened to us as kids. You cannot work this out on your own. Trust me, I tried. It didn't hit you immediately like it did me, but it's hitting you now. If you don't deal with it, it's gonna tear you apart from the inside out."

The last few months and everything I had been through rolled over me with the weight of the world. Meeting Wil, having something I wanted snatched away from me, then losing Wil, was all too much. The tightness in my chest grew, and my emotions took over as the tears collected. I had pushed aside the things I went through as a kid, most likely as a coping mechanism, but I couldn't run from it anymore. It was sinking me farther and farther into a place I didn't know if I could get out of alone. My palms began to sweat, and my heart rate increased as the panic set in.

Myra pulled me to her and held me as my anxiety took over. Sobs escaped as my body trembled. This feeling was worse than any flight I had ever taken, and as much as I wished Wil was here with me, I was thankful it was my sister who was comforting me at that moment.

When my nerves unraveled and my breathing went back to normal, Myra pulled back and looked at me. Her eyes were glossy red, and her makeup was ruined. We both sniffed, then searched around the room for something to blow our noses into.

We sat back on the bed and laughed at the messes we had made of ourselves. I smiled at the small connection I'd never felt with her before. Myra and I had been apart for so long, I hoped this was a step towards us being closer moving forward.

"If I asked you to do something, would you trust me?" She crumpled the tissue in her hands as she waited for my answer.

I nodded with a questioning look.

She leaned forward and took my hand. "You need closure. I'm not saying this will fix everything, but it's a good way to start your healing."

"What is it?" I questioned cautiously.

She took a breath. "We need to go back to Lubbock."

THE DRIVE TO our hometown was long and quiet as we made our way into the city. There had been growth in businesses and housing, but it was still familiar and looked the same. There were churches and small mom-and-pop shops everywhere, and the population, now over two hundred thousand, still swam in a sea of red and black. People proudly wore the colors of the Texas Tech Raiders everywhere. I wished I had the warm, fuzzy feelings of being back home, but it was anything but.

We had made it to our destination by 6:30 p.m. The sun was still high, and the heat was near ninety-one degrees. Myra looked out her window towards the small hill in front of us and exhaled. She turned to me with hope in her wide eyes.

"You ready?" she asked.

I looked past her with a ridiculous feeling of fear. There was no danger up there, but it terrified me all the same. I nodded and got out of the car. I climbed the hill, passing by markers of people I didn't know that had been there for decades. There were American flags posted in the ground from the Fourth of July and flowers that desperately needed to be thrown away. I followed Myra and made sure I didn't step anywhere I shouldn't out of respect.

She stopped at a slate marker embedded in the ground. There were no flowers, no signs that anyone had been there recently, or even in years. The headstone was dirty from the last time it rained, and pieces of leaves were stuck in the N and T.

Anita Matthews
1974–2014

It wasn't her, but the representation of her. She was buried six feet below us, and I was still scared and angry to be anywhere near her. There was nothing under the date of birth and death. Nothing showing she was a wonderful mother or wife. I was thankful Myra didn't make our mom something she wasn't just because she was dead. Because she wasn't a good mother. She was a coward.

Jerry had gotten a call from Myra the night they had found Mom in her trailer, alone and dead, nearly three days before someone came looking for her. She'd had a heart attack in bed with a Jack Daniel's bottle next to her. Jerry sat me down and told me what had happened and asked if I wanted to come back for the funeral. The lack of feeling briefly disturbed me. There was no sadness, no empathy, no wishing I could have said goodbye. There was nothing. I told him no and went on about my day as if he had just told me a stranger I once met had passed on.

"So this was as close as you could get her to Buddy Holly, huh? I remember her being very specific about how she wanted to be near him after she died." I glanced at Myra.

"He's all the way across the cemetery," she said. I looked at her, and she smirked.

I laughed once through my nose, staring at my mother's name. A need in me I had never felt before grew, and I understood why Myra wanted me to come here. Not only to see that the woman who lived in my head and constantly made me doubt my self-worth was dead, but also to say things I'd wanted to say for at least a decade.

I turned to Myra. "Can you give me a minute?"

She gave me a knowing smile and nodded. "Sure."

I stepped onto my mother's grave and kneeled in front of the headstone to get comfortable. "I'm sure you're surprised I'm here," I started. "Trust me, I didn't think I would be anywhere close to you for the rest of my life. But I'm here. And there're some things I'm going to need to say to start the process of closing the door on you and what you did. I will not let you do this to me anymore… You were wrong. I am good at something. At a lot of things. And to be honest, being here, and seeing how you ended up, dying alone with no one beside you, makes me realize you got your payback."

I leaned forward, staring at the letters in front of me as if they were her eyes. "And I refuse to let you live in my head any longer. You were a shit mother, and that's how you'll be remembered. You're not worth any more of my time." I stood up and brushed off my jeans, ridding myself of anything related to Anita Matthews.

"Goodbye, Mom. Going forward, I will make sure I am nothing like you." I turned and walked away, taking my power with me.

Chapter Thirty-Six

Wil

It had been days since I'd talk to Norah. The weekend went by at a snail's pace while I did whatever I could to keep my mind occupied. I even stalked her social media to see pictures from the wedding. She looked beautiful in her clementine-colored dress, but there was still a sadness in her eyes. One I feared would never go away.

The fiftieth-anniversary issue was nearly done and set to go out in a month. While going through all the articles, I swelled with pride over the ones Norah and I had written together, along with the ones she did on her own. She had grown so much in so little time in her writing. I marveled at how amazing she was before it occurred to me how separated we were.

The option of leaving New York and returning to LA entered my mind. I hated seeing Norah like this. Together or not, she would always look at me as someone who took something precious from her. I vacillated with that choice for a while, not sure which would be the right decision for the both of us.

Jerry leaned against my open office doorway by midmorning. We were both exhausted. His was probably because of the long hours we had been working on the anniversary edition. Mine was the blonde woman I was losing day by day.

"Did you get a tux for tonight?" he asked, removing his glasses and rubbing the bridge of his nose with his thumb and middle finger.

"Yeah. It's ready to go," I answered. He had slated for me to go to a fundraiser for keeping music programs in the New York public school system.

"Thanks for stepping in. Norah didn't know if she was going to make it back in time." He cleaned his glasses with his tie.

I hesitated to ask the question I had been asking for the last couple of days, but Jerry saw right through me. "No." He eyed me as he put his glasses back on. "I haven't heard from her."

I smirked at him, then laughed with absolutely no humor. She hadn't called him or me since she'd left. Jerry had only gotten emails. He appeared more understanding at her silence and less worried than me. I was losing my mind trying to reason with Norah in my head. Maybe I needed a break too.

"Do you think after the anniversary issue comes out, I can take a few days off?" I asked, averting my eyes.

He shrugged. "That's fine." He glanced at me but then watched me when I didn't answer. "Something going on?" He moved into the office and closed the door.

I took a breath. "I think I'm going to go back home

for a few days. Make sure this is what I want."

Jerry's eyebrows pulled together. He put his hands in his pockets and walked forward. "Are you having second thoughts?"

"Not so much second thoughts as an attack of conscience." I rolled my eyes and looked away.

I felt his heavy stare. "It's Norah."

A rush of air left my lungs, and I shook my head. "Goddamn that woman," I whispered.

A hint of a smile crossed his face. "She can be unreasonable for sure. But I don't think you quitting is going to make her happy."

I looked at him. "It can't make it any worse."

He leaned against the back of the chair in front of my desk. "I didn't pick you over her because you're a better writer, Wil. I picked you because you want to be editor-in-chief one day. Norah doesn't. Plus, she's developed a new spark when writing, and she's getting better every day. I know she's going to come into her own and find her niche. I don't want to suppress that, I want to help her uncover it. Giving her managing editor now wasn't what was best for her. It was what was best for you."

I nodded slowly. I wished what Jerry said made me feel better or Norah more accessible.

He walked back to the door. "But it's your decision." He placed his hand on the knob and looked at me. "I was married for thirty-five years to the love of my life, and there was nothing I wouldn't do for her. But in the end, there were things she wouldn't let me do for her because it wasn't good for me." He opened the door and walked out. "Have fun tonight," he said over his shoulder.

I didn't want to leave the *Chronicle*, but more, I didn't want to leave Norah. Take away what we had romantically, she was still my friend, and I would miss her. But she was also hurting, and I could take her hurt away. I could find another editor job, and I probably wouldn't have to leave New York to do it.

I would give myself some time in a few weeks to decide what to do. Until then, I hoped something would get resolved between Norah and me, even if it was to say goodbye.

I WALKED INTO the fundraiser, already uncomfortable. Going to these things alone was not preferred. Having Norah here would have presented the opportunity to flirt in our black-tie fashion. Then watch her work the room, coming together later to spill the juicy gossip she had collected. I exhaled at the constant thought of her and willed myself to let it go.

There was a slew of entertainers there for the cause. I spotted a few as the night progressed and tried to interact to write a quick story for the magazine's website. I needed to get quotes from some of the more notable people about the reasons they supported the charity, then I could go home.

I stood from a table and turned, feeling the weight of someone's stare in front of me. I locked eyes with her standing six feet away.

My mouth fell open, and bewilderment hit me. The lights around the room shined off the delicate beading sewn on the strapless white dress she was wearing. It landed just right on all her curves and made her already gorgeous body more immaculate. Her hair was up, showcasing her glowing, soft skin. She was radiant, enticing, and elegant. The stars in the room didn't compare to the sight of this woman before me. She had descended from a different solar system, another galaxy.

I approached her carefully, never leaving her eyes. Hers traveled down and back up my body as her breathing increased. I stopped before I got too close, knowing I only needed the smallest reason to reach out and touch her. Given where we were, both mentally and physically, I didn't know if she wanted that.

"You're like a dream," I blurted, unable to stop myself. Because she was.

Norah smiled and looked down. "I borrowed it from Janet."

"I thought you weren't going to make it." I stepped closer to her.

She shrugged one shoulder. "I made a commitment to be here."

"When did you get in?"

"Early this afternoon."

I tilted my head to meet her eyes. "Why didn't you call me?"

"Because I didn't know if you wanted to talk to me." She hesitated. "I'm painfully aware of how I've treated you over these last few weeks and how unfair I've been. Turns out, I was chasing a ghost that couldn't be caught—I finally realize that now. Not getting this job, your job, hit me hard, but I had no right to take it out on you. I really am sorry, Wil." She inhaled. "You and I can't be together, and I guess that's okay. I just hope we can get back to a place where I'm not hurting you anymore. Then maybe we can be friends again."

My shoulders fell with disappointment. "Is that really what you want?"

She stared at me, her eyes misty with tears. "Of

course it is," she breathed.

I looked away, exhaling. It took a few moments for me to realize what she was saying. When it made more sense, I nodded and said, "Okay."

And that was it. I had wondered for days how we could go forward together. I just needed to know she wanted to do the same, but she didn't. We were over.

She nodded and scanned the room, wiping the corner of her eye, then turned back to me. "I'm going to see if I can get some face time with J.Lo." She rolled her glossy eyes and chuckled. "Are you staying?"

I shook my head, still watching her closely. "No, I'm going to go. Seems you've got everything under control."

At that moment, everything became distant. Her wall came up, and my armor to protect my heart was back in place. The warm feeling between us had turned colder in an instant.

"I'll see you tomorrow?" she asked, hopeful.

I nodded.

She turned slowly and walked away.

Chapter Thirty-Seven

Norah

The wedding was gorgeous, and everything had gone without a hitch, but I wasn't happy. You're never reminded of how alone you are until you go to a wedding. I didn't know anyone there, but everyone had been kind, especially when I told them I was Myra's little sister. All of her friends and Jeremiah's family gushed about how amazing Myra was and how excited they were to have her in the family. It thrilled me to know she'd be surrounded by people who loved her, hopefully for the rest of her life. It had come thirty years later, but she finally got the family she deserved.

I thought about Wil continuously. I wanted to call or text, but that wasn't what we needed. We had to talk about us. More than that, I had to apologize. My actions in these last few weeks were unforgivable. I had acted like a child. Not even a child, a toddler throwing a tantrum because she didn't get what she wanted. There was no way he could forgive me, but I needed to get it out. He deserved at least that much.

The conversation at the fundraiser was expected but no less painful. After everything I had put Wil through, how could I expect anything other than what I got? He was done, and I couldn't blame him.

I walked into the apartment around midnight, exhausted. The dress was cute, but it was cutting off circulation, and I was emotionally depleted. I just wanted to take a shower and crawl into bed.

Pieces of black and pink luggage were in the living room, with a jacket lying over the handle. I walked around the corner to see Janet's door cracked and her light on. I walked to it and knocked lightly, pushing open the door.

"Hey," I said, watching her pack a box.

Her black eyes met mine. "Hi! Welcome back!" She came around her twin bed and gave me a hug. She was obnoxiously happy.

She pulled back, and I furrowed my brow, then spoke. "What's wrong with you?"

"Well," she said and pulled me by the hand to sit me on the bed while she remained standing. "Byron asked me to move in with him." She beamed.

"Wait, what?" I asked, shocked.

She nodded. "He's picking me up in the morning."

I twisted my mouth. "Janet."

"I know, I know. It's too soon. I just got a divorce…" She sat and bit her lip. "But he told me he loved me."

I smiled. "And I take it you—"

"Love him too, yeah."

I laughed. "You know this is completely insane… But I've never seen you so happy. I'm on board."

She squealed and hugged me but then stopped and pulled back, suddenly serious. "What happened with Wil? Did you see him?"

My smile faded. "He was at the fundraiser."

She searched my eyes. "What happened?"

I looked away. "It's over."

"Oh, honey." She grabbed my hand.

"It's my fault," I acknowledged and sniffed. "I couldn't expect to treat him like I did and have him still want to be with me."

She made a sound. "Now I feel guilty for leaving."

I shook my head. "Don't. This is huge for you. I'm glad you're moving on."

"Should I have Byron talk to him?"

"Janet, no. I need to take responsibility for my actions. I've been avoiding that for too long… I'll be okay." I looked at her and smiled. "Since this is our last night together, I say we find a good bottle of wine and have a *Hamilton* sing-along all night."

We both laughed and stood.

I had watched enough movies to know this feeling was only temporary. As thrilled as I was for Janet, it just reminded me how far Wil and I had disconnected. At least one of us got our happily ever after.

I WENT TO work the next day with a hangover. Everything was bright in the office, and I could feel the looming headache beginning to jackhammer in my brain. I glanced toward Jerry's and Wil's offices. Both men were occupied with their work as I made my way back to my lonely cubicle. I sighed as I set my things down and jiggled my computer awake.

Once I popped two ibuprofens, I went to Jerry's office. I had barely spoken to him since he had decided about managing editor, and it was time I made amends with him too.

I knocked on his door. He looked at me through the glass window. "Hey," I said, peeking my head in.

He leaned back in his chair. "I didn't expect you in today."

I moved inside, leaving the door open. "Why not?"

"I figured you'd be too tired from the wedding and the flight." He watched me.

I nodded, then looked around the office.

"How was it?" Jerry asked.

I turned to him. "Good. Myra thanks you for the wineglass set. She said she'll call you when they get back from Maui."

The side of his mouth raised as I sat in the chair in front of his desk and blew out a breath. "I just have one question."

He didn't move.

"Was I seriously being considered, or did you make your mind up when you hired Wil?"

He stared at me for a moment before he spoke. "Yes, you were seriously being considered."

My shoulders relaxed.

He leaned forward. "It has nothing to do with lack of talent."

"I know," I answered softly. "I'm sorry I took it personally."

"You're an amazing writer," Jerry said with pride.

I smiled. "Thank you. I know I still have some growing to do."

"And you will. I'll make sure of that."

I took a deep, cleansing breath. "Whenever the next managing editor position comes around…"

He smirked. "You do know there are other management positions here. Ones that may need to be filled quicker than you waiting another ten years."

"Yes, please." I eyed him and stood.

"There's an assignment in your inbox," he said as I left.

I nodded and closed his door behind me. Wil was in his office on his phone when he caught my eye and stopped moving. There was concern on his face as he watched me. He had a tremendous responsibility now, and him worrying about how I was going to react every time he saw me was not what I wanted.

I exhaled and walked over to his office, then opened the door. "Morning," I said and smiled.

He still had his phone in his hand. He moved it away from his face. "Morning," he answered, surprised.

I looked down so I wouldn't cry. I gave him one last grin, letting him know I was okay, and what happened between us was done. We needed to go forward. We had a job to do.

WIL AND I were cordial over the next month. We treated each other with kid gloves for a while until the friendly teasing began again. We seemed to hit a pleasant rhythm where we were more comfortable with each other. There would always be some awkwardness between us, but for now, it was tolerable.

There would be things he did as an editor I would question, but I listened to what he had to say and saved my comments for when we were alone, which I made sure wasn't too often. I still missed him when I was away from the *Chronicle*. It was only a matter of time before he would date again. Maybe he already was, but I tried not to think about my replacement. I would deal with them when the time came, and not a moment sooner.

Janet and Byron planned a housewarming party after she finally settled in. It was her way of redecorating to give Byron's apartment some Janet flair. I arrived early to help set up, happy to find they seemed to still be in the honeymoon stage.

Byron's flat was huge and had an open design. The walls separating the rooms didn't reach the high ceilings, and the brick walls and contemporary decor were impressive. Byron knew his color schemes well, or at least his decorator did.

As the night progressed, more people showed, including Wil. I smiled when he noticed me and was thankful he was alone.

After greeting the happy couple, he walked towards me with his casual sexiness I still thought about too often. We said our hellos, and I asked if I could get him a drink. After he agreed, he followed me into the kitchen. Oddly, my nerves emerged. We hadn't been in a social situation for a while. I wasn't sure how I was supposed to act.

"Are you making sure I don't spike your drink, or…?" I opened the fridge and grabbed a bottle.

"I don't know. Just force of habit," he said behind me.

I glanced at him over my shoulder. "Following me into the kitchen?"

"Following you anywhere," he answered.

I smiled and popped the cap off his beer. When I handed it to him, he thanked me, and I leaned against the counter.

"So, how have you been?" he asked.

"I just saw you yesterday. You know how I've been." I laughed, taking a sip of wine.

He rolled his eyes. "I mean outside in the real world, not at the *Chronicle*."

"And how am I at the *Chronicle*?" I asked teasingly.

"You're amazing."

I met his eyes and quietly laughed once, then let my smile fall. "I'm okay."

He put his hands on the counter and leaned forward. "Why just okay?"

"I have a lot of free time on my hands." I hoped he understood the connotation.

He said nothing and let me take a moment before I continued.

I cleared my throat. "I've been talking about my past with a therapist. I'm hoping I can learn from the memory of my mother instead of trying to please it."

He smiled and nodded. "I'm happy for you."

I nodded too. "What about you?"

He straightened. "I've been so busy at work, I haven't had a lot of time for anything else."

"Is that by design?"

The corner of his mouth raised. "Probably."

I walked closer to the counter in the middle of the room. "So, you're not seeing Amber again?" I joked.

He laughed. "Oh, no, she hates me."

"I mean, can you blame her?" I drank from my glass, watching him.

"Don't act like you didn't have something to do with that." He pointed at me with his beer in his hand.

I shrugged. "Girl's gotta do what she's gotta do."

The smile on his face faded and made me pull back from the cute banter we were having. He furrowed his brow. "Listen—"

"Hey!" Janet called from the living room. We both turned towards the booming sound. "The two of you better get out here where I can see you!"

I shut my eyes, laughing.

"There better not be any ass prints on my table!"

"Wow," Will breathed and then laughed, looking at me. "Now I kind of wanna do it."

I walked around the counter. "Oh no, you don't want that smoke. C'mon." I walked out of the room with Wil at my heels.

Once all the guests had arrived, we sat in their gray, black, and white living room, watching Janet open their gifts. Just with her facial expression and fake compliments, I could tell what she liked and what we would return that next weekend. I quietly laughed every time she glanced at me with a knowing look.

Wil sat on the other side of the room. A friend of Janet's from the bar made her way to him as the night progressed. I tried not to watch with any interest but couldn't help glancing at them.

I was in the corner, talking to a client of Byron's, when Wil broke away to come talk to me. He joined me when the gentlemen, I couldn't remember his name, had started talking about how much he could bench press, to which I quickly lost interest.

Wil touched my arm and glanced at the gym rat. "Excuse me." He turned to me. "Can I borrow you for a second?" He raised his eyebrows.

"Yes," I said enthusiastically. When we walked away, I leaned into him. "Thank you."

"You looked like you needed help." He led me away from the crowd towards the front hallway. He leaned against the black metal banister that led to the second floor, and I stood by the wall next to the front door. The feeling of awkwardness returned once we were alone again.

"Looks like you have a fan." I motioned my head toward the living room.

He shook his head. "Not interested."

I gave him a small smile. "How much trouble do you think I'm in since I gave them a Cookie Monster cookie jar?"

"A lot. You think B's gonna let that thing sit in his kitchen?" he asked, then chuckled.

"She loved it. Bet you it's still there in six months."

He twisted his mouth. "I may just take that bet."

We watched each other with sadness between us. I genuinely missed Wil. He was someone I could relate to and have fun with. I never thought when we had that one-night stand it would turn into something so much more. Not only was he my lover, but he was also my friend. I'd missed both.

I joggled my head. "I should go. I still have to pack for my flight to North Carolina on Monday."

"What time is your flight?"

I made an irritated sound. "Seven." I rolled my eyes.

"Are you... Will you be okay?" He stepped towards me.

"Oh, yeah. It's another thing I'm working on. All the flying I've done since March has helped. It's not nearly as dramatic as it used to be." I smiled. "I guess I have you to thank for that."

Wil's stare was intense.

I turned from him and grabbed my jacket. Slipping my arms in the sleeves, I faced him again. He was closer than he was a few seconds ago. I inhaled. "Can you tell them goodnight for me?" I asked, but he remained still. "I'll see you in a couple days," I said, then opened the door and headed down the stairwell.

I hated this. All of it.

I hated that I was leaving without him.

I hated that he let me.

I hated that I didn't need him to take flights with me anymore, but I still wanted him there.

Everything I had experienced with Wil was vacant from my life, and again, I hated it. With time, the hate would fade into acceptance, and just like flying, this wouldn't be so bad.

Until then, I would try as best as I could to make tonight be the new normal between us. Lighthearted and fun, like friends should be. If this was all I could get, I would keep my torment to myself.

Norah

I sat at the airport gate, reading the fiftieth-anniversary issue of the *Chronicle* I picked up at the newsstand. I skimmed all the articles Wil and I had done together and smiled. We were an amazing team. His sensitivity and my facts melded with such synchronicity and beauty, it reminded me of Debussy. It brought me back to that night we sat in the park, getting lost in each other while the music floated all around us.

Wilson Taylor Lockwood.

I exhaled and closed my eyes, thinking of him and how I wished he were sitting by me in this uncomfortable black plastic chair, waiting to get on a plane, bantering back-and-forth about whatever we wanted to tease each other about that day. Staring into his perfect blue eyes and wishing we could be alone while surrounded by a sea of people. Even if we couldn't be together, just having him here at this airport, talking me through my nerves, comforting me like no one else could, would have been plenty. More than anything, I wanted to know if he thought about me half as much as I thought about him. If he blamed me for everything I put him through. If he could truly ever forgive me. I wondered if he thought of that night in Chicago or any night we were together.

Before I could chicken out, I took out my phone and opened my messages.

Norah: *I bought a copy of the anniversary issue and was just thinking of Chicago. I know this is probably breaking the rules of our agreement, and I'm sorry. But I think of that night a lot. I think of you a lot. The work you and Jerry did was brilliant. Congratulations on this issue and thank you.*

I put my phone down, not wanting to obsess over if he was going to answer me or not. I just wanted him to know and left it at that.

I kept thumbing through the pages until my phone buzzed on the hard seat next to me. I picked it up and looked at the screen.

Wil.

I hesitated, wondering if I should answer it or just let it go to voicemail. I didn't know if I was ready to speak to him after the ridiculous declaration I had just made, over text message no less.

I took a breath and answered. "Hello?" Even I could hear the fear in my voice.

"I think of that night all the time," he said in his sexy, gravelly morning voice.

I smiled, unsure of what to say next. "Sorry if I woke you."

"You didn't."

The silence between us was far and wide, and I

wanted to confess more to him. Even if he didn't feel the same, I had to get it out.

"Wil," I whispered, then hesitated. "I miss you," I confessed, closing my eyes.

He didn't answer me, and I immediately regretted my admission. Of course he didn't feel the same. I had caused too much damage between us, and he had moved on.

I cleared my throat and started to tell him goodbye.

"What took you so long?" he asked. I thought I heard relief in his voice.

"What?" I uttered.

"I've been waiting for you to get here for weeks." He chuckled. I heard noises around him, like he was in a crowd of people.

I thought maybe he was speaking to someone else. "Wait, are you talking to me?"

He laughed. "Yes, Norah, I'm talking to you."

My heart rate spiked. "What are you saying?"

"You know how much you've missed me?" he answered.

"Yeah."

"Times that by about a million, and you'll have a small idea of how much I've missed you."

I exhaled, and my eyes filled with tears. "Why didn't you say something?"

He sounded rushed. "I knew you were going through a lot. I didn't know if you would ever get to this point, and it terrified me to think you were over us, over me."

I took a shaky breath. "I'm not over you, Wil. I've never been over you." I sniffed, wiping my tears away. "Fuck! I have to get on this plane, and all I want to do is see you."

"Your wish, my command," he said, then the line went dead.

I took the phone away from my ear and looked at the darkened screen. Realizing what he'd said, I jerked my head up, stood, and looked around. Standing in front of me, with flashes of people crossing between us, his crystal blue eyes stared at me. His phone in his hand, and his carry-on on his shoulder.

He dodged the crowd, never taking his eyes off me until he dropped his bag at his side and crashed against my body, his lips immediately meeting mine. It had felt like years from the last time I was in his arms. I pulled him closer to me as I treasured this moment and silently promised I would never take it for granted ever again.

We filled each other with all the time spent apart. Then he pulled back and looked at me. "Hi," he said and smiled.

"Hi," I breathed. "You're here," I replied, shocked.

He took my hands in his, and his beautiful eyes bore into mine. "I've hated this. Trying to pretend that working back up to being *friends* was enough—it's not. I woke up this morning and needed to see you. I needed to be here with you on this flight and to tell you I can't just be your friend. I need more... I need you."

I exhaled and laid my forehead against his lips. "Same," I whispered. We lingered in each other's arms, and a sense of peace came over me. I drew back. "You're really coming with me to North Carolina?"

He nodded, and his cute smirk appeared. "Support animal."

"You're more than that," I said, my voice thick. "So much more than that."

He kissed me again, and for the first time, when they

announced the plane was boarding, it didn't terrify me.

I never thought I was worthy of a fairy-tale ending. Never thought the man I wanted to be with for as long as possible would begin with a one-night stand. Being in Wil's arms, hearing him say I was his, telling him he was mine, was something I thought I would never get or deserve. Our romance wasn't a made-up story that could be removed with a delete button or eraser. It wasn't fiction...because the opposite of fiction is facts.

Epilogue

Wil

Norah sat at her desk, typing away for the new story she broke the night before. A source told her one of the new senators from Georgia got caught with an underage girl in a hotel room in Atlanta. His career was all but over, and Norah wanted to give the other newly sworn-in Senator Morris a chance to provide a quote and perspective. It was damage control, not only for the state but for the sake of the government itself. Norah hadn't spoken to the senator since she was elected. They talked for about an hour, and Norah had a lot to get down before she could publish it online.

I walked over to her cubicle and stuck my head past the partition. "How's it coming, Mrs. Lockwood?"

She held up the finger with the engagement ring I had proposed with two weeks ago. "It's still Matthews until we decide on a date."

"I say June." I shrugged and waited for her reaction.

She glanced up at me. "Wil," she warned.

"Alright, alright," I conceded. "When you're done with your latest masterpiece, Jerry wants to see you in his office."

She stopped and stared at me. "Am I in trouble?"

"Why? Have you done something you weren't supposed to?" I mused.

Her eyes darted side to side. "No." Her answer was suspect.

"Liar." I grinned at her and walked away.

She took a long breath and went back to typing on her keyboard. Norah stayed at her desk for another hour before she joined us in Jerry's office. When she looked through the glass, she looked surprised to see me in the room with him. I casually leaned against the heavy black cabinet next to Jerry's desk, my arms crossed over my chest.

She didn't bother knocking and opened the door. "What are you two plotting?" She eyed us.

I laughed once. "We'll leave the plotting to you." I pushed off the cabinet, then sat in the chair farthest away from her, motioning for her to join me.

Norah furrowed her brow as she sat. Likely leery about this ambush.

Jerry came forward in his chair. "Wil and I have been talking—"

"I gathered that," she interrupted and glanced at me as I tried to hold back my laughter.

"And we're looking at branching the political section into its own magazine. I'm sorry, its own digital magazine."

"No print?" she asked.

"No print," Jerry answered.

Norah's mouth parted in shock. "But you hate politics."

"True," he said and nodded.

"So, what does this mean?" she asked.

I leaned forward. "Jerry will remain editor-in-chief, but we want you to run it."

She turned to me sharply. "What?"

"This is your wheelhouse, Norah. Politics are where you shine." I smiled at her, loving her reaction. The glimmer in her eye, and her slowly rising smile, made me fall in love with her all over again. This happened at least once a day, and I enjoyed it every time.

The realization hit her as she blinked rapidly. "You're really going to let me run it?" She looked at Jerry.

He nodded at her. "It's all yours."

This was as speechless as I had ever seen her. Jerry and I glanced at each other and then back to her.

"What do you say?" I asked, taking her ringed hand in mine.

"I say yes." She looked at me and laughed. I reached over and hugged her. She clung to me for a moment, then drew back and kissed me lovingly.

"Hey, no, not in here. Do that on your own time," Jerry interrupted.

Norah and I laughed against each other's lips and stopped our PDA to appease our boss.

Norah stood with my hand still in hers. "Will you excuse us for a moment?" She didn't wait for an answer, just dragged me with her.

We went past everyone's staring eyes and headed to the stairwell. I laughed when I realized where we were going and what we were about to do. When she opened the door, she pushed me against the wall and kissed me fiercely, making it known the few encounters we had there were all about to be outdone.

She stopped and looked at me, and I looked back at her with as much love as I'd ever felt in my life. Norah was in love with me, and I couldn't imagine life without her.

The End

Acknowledgments

To my family, I love you more than anything. Thank you for being there and putting up with me when I'm writing. You all push me to keep going when I'm crying in the corner, thinking this is never going to work.

J.R., you sacrifice so much, and you'll never understand how much that means to me. I love you more and more every day.

To my beta readers, Christy, Hayley, and my mommy-in-law, Debbie. Thank you for continually believing in me and reading my smut! Love you!

Thank you to my editor, Michelle Rascon, and graphic designer, Clarissa Kenzen of CK Book Cover Designs. I adore you both and couldn't imagine doing this without you. You two complete me.

To my friends and fellow authors on Instagram, Katrina Lewis and Charlie Murphy. Thank you for being my book besties. I will never forgive you for 365 Days. LOL!

To you, the reader. Whether this is your first or fourth time reading my work, thank you for all the love and support. I hope I've given you something to look forward to.

Until next time,

M.J.

Other Titles:
Before We Get Carried Away
Delicately
The One of Many